Jemez

A Matt Bertram Crime Novel

Mark David Albertson

Irish Viking Publishing

Jemez

Paperback ISBN: 979-8-218-18878-8

Hardcover ISBN: 9798390139752

Library of Congress Control Number: 2023903427

Other Books by Mark David Albertson

Steaming: A Sea Story

Spying: A Sea Story

Stalking: A Sea Story

Acknowledgements

There are very few creative works that are solo endeavors. Writing a book is no exception. Yes, the author has an important role, but there is a supporting cast that is critical to the book. I want to thank my family, who are so supportive, and most especially my wife and fellow author, K.E. Meuir, without whom this or any other book I have written would be forever locked in my brain. I appreciate the honest dialog, ideas, and conversations over wine as this book was written. I am also grateful to Matt Henderson-Ellis, my developmental editor extraordinaire. His hard work, kind and gentle criticism, and honesty made this a much better book. I also learned that I really like to overuse the word "beautiful." So, Matt, beautiful job! Finally, I appreciate the meticulous copy editing and proofreading from Ray Braun, who worked hard to correct spelling, grammar, syntax, and capitalization, and give me suggestions for making the book better. His hard work will, hopefully, make this book much more readable for you, the reader.

Finally, I want to thank the people of Jemez Pueblo and the residents of the villages of Jemez Springs, La Cueva, San Ysidro, and Bernalillo, New Mexico, for lending me the canvas and palette of your wonderful home to tell this story.

For my Mom and Dad. Mom gave me the gift of loving to read, and Dad gave me the gift of loving to write

A-stio-lak-wa

There is a secret pride in every human heart that revolts at tyranny. You may order and drive an individual, but you cannot make him respect you.
(William Hazlitt)

July 24, 1694, sometime after midnight

Louis Chiguigui took a moment to feel the unusually warm July wind on his face, looking up to the dark sky in awe of the utter blackness, punctuated by millions of stars. Allowing himself momentary reverie, he took a deep breath. The scent of juniper trees in the wind reminded Louis of the many moments he had spent in his life entranced by how huge the heavens were. He brought his eyes down to meet those of his brother, Francisco, matching the look of distress on his brother's face. Both men looked down at the valley from the top of the mesa to study the unwelcome sight below. The

Spaniards were assembling at the base of the flat-topped mountain, dividing into two groups, preparing to storm the He'mish above them. Louis had been concerned for weeks that this attack was inevitable. He had spent the last two years overseeing the construction of their new pueblo of A-stio-lak-wa, which had been motivated by a need to find a more defensible location for his people to live. Walatowa, the pueblo where most of his people lived, was in the valley below, and although it had free access to the waters of the river, was also vulnerable to attack. Louis castigated himself for being far too trusting of the Spanish. They were kind to tribes who were subservient to them, and ruthless to those who were not. The Spanish were well-armed, well-trained and determined to defeat the He'mish.

As the morning star appeared in the sky, both groups of men in the valley began struggling up the steep slopes of the mesa toward A-stio-lak-wa. Louis counted at least one hundred men, perhaps 120, in addition to Tunndagee and Ceya-kwa tribal members, fellow Puebloans, who were aiding De Vargas in his quest to attack the He'mish in retribution for their revolt against Spanish rule and the murders of several friars along the way. The Spaniards had grown tired of the He'mish tribe, which they called "Jemez" and the once friendly relationship had gradually turned sour over the last forty-two years of Spanish domination.

In past years, the Spanish had found the He'mish useful. The Navajo and the Apache were enemies of the He'mish, and they worked with the Spanish in opposing them. But increasing taxation from the Spaniards in the form of corn and other vegetables had escalated steadily, depleting the food available to the tribe. When the He'mish complained, the Spaniards imprisoned a number of the He'mish leaders, eventually hanging over thirty of them. The Spanish accused them of being sorcerers. They spread lies among the other pueblo tribes that the He'mish were in alliance with the Navajo and Apache. Finally, after years of attempting to accommodate the rule of the Spaniards, the He'mish had enough, and they, along with several of the other pueblos in New Spain, revolted. The revolt came at a significant cost.

Louis turned to Francisco, a look of desperation on his face. "A-stio-lak-wa may fall today, my brother," he said, looking sternly. "I must trust you to perform an important task. You are not just my brother, but also my most trusted friend." From around his neck, Louis removed a magnificent necklace made of black polished obsidian, as shiny as glass, oddly shaped in the form of a human heart and the size of a man's fist, with a small natural hole in the top. The amulet felt cold in Louis' hand despite the warm evening. Although obsidian was common in their lands, this was the most beautiful stone anyone in the tribe had ever seen. Louis had run a leather lace through the amulet. The amulet had been given the mark of Louis' breath, called in their Tanoan language, *'hing*. The talisman was sacred, and Louis, as War Chief, was given the duty of protecting it. Stories of its spirit powers were spoken of in hushed tones around He'mish campfires. The stories explained that it had been found by a former war chief hundreds of years before. In the wrong hands it could wield great evil, and, likewise, in the right hands, it had the power to protect and heal.

Louis put the amulet in a leather bag and he tied the bag with a leather lace. "You must take this to the Shrine of Ma'sewi, brother, and bury it at its' base," he said, handing the necklace to Francisco. "You must do the dance of the Great Spirit. When you have buried it, you must knock down the rocks of the shrine so the Spanish will not recognize it as sacred. It may give us the blessing of Huu-vu-na-tota, so we might prevail. Remember, Francisco, do not remove it from the bag and do not touch it." Francisco reluctantly held out his hand. Louis placed it in Francisco's open palm, squeezing it shut with both of his hands. Francisco stood for a moment, looking at his brother in silence, then scrambled away with the necklace. He stopped and turned back toward Louis. Francisco touched his forehead with his fingers while looking at his brother, then turned back and ran in the direction of the Shrine of Ma'sewi.

As the sun rose on that July day in 1694, the Spaniards and their allied Indians reached the top of the mesa. One group had climbed one side, and another the opposite side. The Spanish attacked from their side and the allied natives attacked from the other, squeezing the He'mish in the middle. The He'mish men did their best to assault the Spaniards by raining rocks down upon them with slings and firing arrows, which, in large part, were thwarted by the armor of the Spaniards. Louis knew his men were strong and resolute and he stood shoulder to shoulder with his tribal brothers relentlessly fighting the Spaniards with all their might. A conquistador charged Louis with a sword and Louis dodged the point, clouting the Spaniard on the side of his head. The man fell to the ground, his temple bleeding. Louis looked up and yet another Spaniard was mounting an attack against him. The harquebus in the attacker's hands hit Louis in the middle of his chest, and Louis fell to the ground. The Spaniard rammed his boot on Louis' head, crushing his skull, and the war chief's spirit left his body.

The desperate attempt to defend themselves did little to impede General Don Diego de Vargas. In less than an hour, the Spaniards, with their swords, crossbows and harquebus, murdered 84 of the He'mish and took 361 women and children prisoner.

The Spanish believed their conquest of A-stio-lak-wa meant they had also defeated the He'mish tribe and their nine pueblos scattered throughout the Jemez Mountains. Time would settle this differently.

1

So This is Archaeology

The British Museum is great for seeing how excellent we were at stealing things.
(Russell Howard)

June 5, 2002

As the sun was rising over the top of Pico Butte, a 1992 Chrysler Town and Country Minivan traveled east on Highway 4. Once blue, the minivan was now a combination of faded paint, rust, and crumpled bumpers. The van passed the Jemez Pueblo on its left, continuing to head east past the pueblo. As the driver headed east on the highway, he regularly checked for the distinctive trucks driven by Jemez Ranger District Law Enforcement Officers (LEO). The Ranger District Office was outside of Jemez Springs, almost to Soda Dam, so he assumed he probably would not encounter them on their hike. On the winding two-lane highway, the van continued north. The driver strained to see out of the dirty window of the van, looking for the spot in which he wanted to park. "I know it's along here somewhere, on the left. It's not more than a mile or so," he said to the other three occupants of the van. "Ah, there it is," the driver said, laughing. He turned left at a sign that said, "La Casitas Fishing Site," and parked the van in a designated spot.

The three men and one woman exited the van, each putting on a knapsack. From the back of the van, the driver pulled out two shovels and a pickaxe. "I hope you're ready for a real hike," said Professor Sinclair Delano III, pushing his thick black plastic glasses back in place on his bulbous nose. Sinclair was an older man with shoulder-length gray hair tied in a ponytail and sported a scraggly beard. While his belly betrayed a taste for rich food and too much alcohol, the man's body was fitter than most men his age. Both his face and his arms were deeply tanned and textured like leather, a side-effect of spending too much time in the sun. The man's two male companions, in their mid-twenties and, unlike the older man, owned bodies more suited to watching TV and eating junk food, looked at one another, then back at the man. The woman who was with them, who appeared slightly older than the young men and in much better physical condition, smiled at the older man.

"Um, sure, professor, no problem," answered one of the young men, sounding less than certain he had made a good decision to come along.

"Excellent, that's the spirit, Jason!" said the older man. "If we are lucky, today will be a day of exciting discovery." Jason Trumble, an undergraduate student at the University of New Mexico, was successfully extending four years of study into six or more, provided his parents continued paying his expenses. Of medium height, Jason was in his mid-twenties, with long, dark hair and a pockmarked face, betraying his adolescent struggle with acne. Jason's idea of exercise was playing beer pong, which had become popular in the last few years on college campuses across the nation.

The other young man spoke up. "We are still getting extra credit for this, aren't we, professor?" he said, seeking to be assured that the disruption of his normally sedentary life would be worth the reward.

"Danny, not only are you going to get extra credit, but you may make enough money for next year's tuition," said the professor. Danny Goldman had just finished his sophomore year at UNM. Far from a stellar student, Danny kept his head far enough above water that his father, a rabbi in Scottsdale, Arizona, would allow him to continue at UNM. His father had dreamed of Danny attending Yeshiva University in New York, where he could get a good Hebrew education. Unfortunately, Danny's pathetic GPA in high school forced certain compromises. Danny was not a drinker, but his girth betrayed a passion for Twinkies and chili dogs. *Lots* of Twinkies and chili dogs, in addition to a lack of concern for eating kosher. Exercise of any kind, and especially hiking, was foreign to Danny. He had reluctantly agreed to come along at the insistence of his archaeology professor, coupled with the promise of financial reward and much-needed extra credit to bolster his lackluster GPA. The professor grabbed a shovel and a backpack and turned to the others, performing his best imitation of a marine drill sergeant, saying, "Now, let's head out!"

The four walked down a path at the fishing site to the edge of the Jemez River. The Jemez was a gentle, meandering river, clear and cold, with its headwaters in the Valles Caldera as a small winding stream in a vast crater. On its way to its confluence with the Rio San Antonio, the river passed through the heart of the Jemez Mountains' most popular recreation areas, and irrigated the farmland of the Jemez Pueblo. At this time of year, this portion of the river was shallow and narrow, no more than a couple feet deep.

"I didn't bring waterproof shoes, professor," said Danny.

"Well then, it'll be soggy hiking until they dry," said the professor, stepping into the river ahead of the others.

"Can you tell us where we are heading, professor?" Danny inquired.

"I told you already, Danny. Naomi, why don't you 're-brief' our companions on the mission today?"

"Certainly, professor," Naomi replied. Naomi Canneloy was a tall, slender woman with bleach-blonde hair, high cheekbones and a small nose which turned up at the end, making her appear elf-like. Naomi was a graduate student in anthropology at the University of New Mexico in Albuquerque and would complete her master's degree in a few months. Her plan was to continue toward her PhD degree, then teach at a university in the southwest. Her emphasis was on the ancestral natives of the southwest. The early Puebloans particularly interested her, although she would have preferred to be working in Inca archeological sites where there were more interesting artifacts, which to Naomi, was synonymous with *valuable*.

Rolling her eyes and speaking to the two young men as though they were five years old, she said, "We are headed to the ruins of Astialakwa and Patokwa. We'll just pass through Patokwa, but it's already been picked over, so it's not worth our time. Actually, picked over is an understatement. It used to abut several ranches, and it was scavenged beyond imagination. Someone even took a backhoe into the ruins and dug holes looking for treasure. Some of the locals were convinced that there was a golden bell buried there, but it turned out to be a myth. Because of the damage created by fortune hunters, the Forest Service took possession of the land surrounding Patokwa, along with the entire Guadalupe Mesa.

"Our rush is that the Pueblo of Jemez Department of Resource Protection and the Department of Anthropology at Harvard are planning a comprehensive exploration of the ruins of Astialakwa beginning next month. So far, it has been relatively untouched. They are going to take six years on this project and there won't be one decent artifact of any value when they get done. I aim to see we get the good stuff first, before they have that chance. And I'd like to know why the Jemez are working with friggin' Harvard. Don't they know there's a world-class anthropology department at the University of New Mexico?"

The professor interrupted Naomi. "Astialakwa is on top of Mesa de Guadalupe. It's a pretty tall mesa, and we'll be gaining a thousand feet of altitude in less than half a mile, so you boys are going to get your cardio in today."

"Although there is a trail to the top, you can't get to it from here. To reach the trail, you have to wade across the Jemez River, which we are about to do right now. Be careful because the brambles next to the river can grab your ankles like an octopus, and you'll have much more than wet feet. Next, we'll work our way through the thickets that line the creek on the other side, and then we'll climb to the top of the small mesa that is south of the tall mesa: Guadalupe. Once we reach the top of the small mesa, then we will start looking for the trail. Once we find it, we can take it all the way to the top, but we'll have to pay attention the entire way as the trail can become very faint in some places and very steep in others. In some places, the footing can be loose. What an adventure, huh?"

The five treasure-seekers had traveled no more than a hundred yards when Jason spoke up. "Tell me, professor," he said between pants, "Why don't you just let the Indians and Harvard find the shit?"

"You know how they say that there is no such thing as a stupid question? Well, good question, Jason," said the professor. "Stupid, but good. But let me answer your question with a question. Have you ever heard of Hiram Bingham? This is a trick question because we discussed him in class."

"Um, could you refresh my memory?" Jason said, a bit chagrined.

"How about this question: Have you ever heard of Indiana Jones?"

"Of course. He was like a badass archaeologist from the movies," Jason said, proud that he could answer the professor's question.

"Well, Hiram Bingham was a *real* Indiana Jones. I shit you not. He was the *real* deal. He was a Yale University history lecturer and in 1911 he climbed to the top of a remote area of the Andes Mountains in Peru and discovered one of the most extraordinary set of ruins on Earth: Machu Picchu. In the abandoned city, he found truckloads of priceless artifacts of the Incas, *some* of which ended up in the Peabody Museum in New Haven. I'm pretty sure that he kept several of the best for himself, because he ended up a full professor at Yale and died with a hefty bankroll."

"Didn't the Incas or the country of Peru deserve to have them?" Jason chimed in.

"Nope," said the professor. "Yale has had them for over a hundred years, and many of the artifacts ended up on the private market. No, son, the rule in this business is, 'finders, keepers.'"

"So, you think there's gold and shit up on that mountain?" asked Jason.

"I've been studying the Pueblo Indians for over a decade," said the professor, "and I'm pretty sure there's no gold, unless some coins fell out of the conquistadors' pockets. Coronado didn't find any; de Vargas didn't find any and Oñate didn't find any. But that doesn't mean there aren't some pretty impressive artifacts that have value up there. There are many rumors of breastplates of conquistadors, weapons, jewelry, pottery and more, all of which have significant value in today's market. And that will be great if we find them. But we are primarily here to find ourselves a genuine treasure in Astialakwa. It's a very special and very rare thing that could be worth, if not a fortune, enough to put a great big smile on all of our faces."

"What's that, professor? Is it like, the Cross of Coronado in the Indiana Jones movie? And, um, can we stop for water?" asked Danny. "I'm, like, dying!"

"Danny, we have just barely started our climb, but, OK, I don't want to give any 23-year-olds heart attacks," the professor said reluctantly.

As the two were gulping water and trying to catch their breaths, Danny asked again. "What are you looking for, professor?"

"Much as I would like to find the Cross of Coronado like Indiana Jones, we are looking for the Jemez equivalent of that cross. We are in search of *El Corazón Negro de Dios*. The Black Heart of God. It's steeped in myth among the Puebloans. Stories have been told about it for hundreds of years. It's a baseball sized piece of obsidian and the Jemez legends talked of it having mysterious powers to empower its holder to perform miracles and other hocus-pocus. It was feared and revered at the same time. During the attack of the Spanish on Astialakwa, I believe the ancestral Puebloans hid it. I've spent years reading the stories and myths of the Jemez tribe that tell of the Black Heart. There is a story that at one point the Navajo stole the amulet from the Jemez and all of the pueblo's crops failed until the Jemez stole it back. There are also stories of miraculous healings, enemies dropping dead without being touched and other aboriginal hogwash. I've talked to a number of the Jemez people, and I've made five trips to Astialakwa in search of it, to no avail. I've read all the records of De Vargas, and official records of the friars in the area. But it wasn't until just a month ago, when I made a trip to *Museo Arqueológico Nacional*, the National Archaeological Museum in Madrid, that I found an overlooked document detailing de Vargas' own search for the Black Heart. A little torture, which they euphemistically called *Interrogatorio*, of several Jemez people revealed what De Vargas considered reliable information of its resting place. After the slaughter at Astialakwa, De Vargas became the Governor of New Mexico. He stated in several writings that it was his intention to return to the Jemez to search for the Black Heart, but, fortunately for us, he died of dysentery in Bernalillo before he could put together an expedition back to Astialakwa.

"As far as I know, I'm the only one who has ever found this information, and now, I think I have a pretty good idea exactly where it is. OK, well, not quite exactly, but pretty damn close. Between the Jemez myths, my conversations with tribal members and the document in the museum, I'm almost certain I've got it nailed.

"So, we'll climb the mesa, this time with more knowledge, we'll gather up a bunch of shit for the University, and we'll find El Corazón Negro de Dios. You'll each get five percent of the proceeds when I sell it, and I'll take the rest and wallpaper my meager bank account in green."

"And I'll get a teaching assistant position and a glowing recommendation for my Ph.D. program for all the hours that I have put into researching the Black Heart," Naomi interjected.

"No offense, professor," Jason said, "But why are you taking us along, and cutting us in?"

"Because I'm going to need you to do some heavy lifting of stones, a shit-ton of shoveling, and a lot of sweat," said the professor. "And that's worth a little something in my book." Sinclair thought to himself, *and I primarily chose you two to help because you're too dumb to think of backstabbing me.*

Jason looked at Danny and whispered, "Did he say anything to you about shoveling?"

Danny simply shrugged.

The professor stood up and said, "OK, we're not going to find treasure sitting here bullshitting. Let's go!"

Naomi popped up and started walking toward the first trail that would eventually take them to their destination. The two boys took deep breaths and stood to join her. "I'll follow up the rear," said the professor. "Good thing I kept a cattle prod to keep you moving," he said. Danny looked back at the professor, just to be certain he was joking.

Professor Sinclair Delano III had been a tenured full professor at the University of New Mexico for twenty years. Born into an east-coast family of moderate wealth, his father had pulled significant strings to place his passably intelligent son into an Ivy League school. Sinclair had a couple of weaknesses. The first was alcohol, and the second was sloth. The alcohol would have been acceptable at practically any college in the 1960's, but the sloth led Sinclair down the path to perdition. Faced with weak grades and an even weaker attendance record, Sinclair was faced with academic probation, which led him to plagiarize a classmate's term paper. He was caught and expelled. His father, Sinclair Delano II, promptly cut his son off from even the most modest stipend, which forced Sinclair III to, if not abandon alcohol and sloth, at least to channel them into opportunities which allowed him not to exert too much energy or ambition at succeeding in life. Enrolled in community college, Sinclair fortuitously caught one of his teachers in a "compromising" position with a student, and replete with photographs of the teacher, unexpectedly graduated with honors. He transferred to Montana State University, and, with the glowing recommendation of another extorted professor, completed his baccalaureate degree with honors, mostly because of his unscrupulous talents. A class trip to Peru and Machu Picchu solidified his desire to make a living as an archaeologist. Fortunately, his applications arrived many years before the internet, and because of his extorted and glowing recommendations, he found himself in graduate school at the University of Arizona, where he gained a master's degree and Ph.D., not in small part, based upon his effective tools of blackmail and plagiarism. Sinclair was offered an Associate Professor position at the University of New

Mexico in 1982. The next year, he published his seminal work, "Ancient Puebloans of New Mexico." The text was a combination of the papers he strategically assigned to and plagiarized from his students, along with substantial passages from a book written in 1920 by a long-dead author, from whom more than half his "seminal work" could be attributed. It didn't matter much as academia celebrated the book as a "monumental achievement in anthropology" by several respected academics with whom Sinclair had, as the mafia says, "the goods" on. That book was published in 1984. The UNM Department of Anthropology promoted him to full professor with tenure, and it was the last significant academic work Professor Sinclair Delano III wrote in the last eighteen years. "Publish or perish" apparently has an extortion exemption.

Sinclair enjoyed his "digs," forays into ruins to dig for answers to humankind's many questions about their past. Each summer he took his students to field schools which included Bandelier, Tskankawi, Chaco Canyon and others. He enjoyed being in the New Mexico sunshine in the summer, watching his students work their fingers to the nubs to contribute to his success.

Sinclair had tripped across references to the Black Heart by accident. He had the habit of burying his Penthouse magazines on his desk under supposedly academic works for afternoon solo entertainment. One afternoon, once he was done with office hours, he was reading his usual fair of letters to Penthouse. Just as he was getting to the part where the guy writing the letter was detailing an incident in which he was accidentally with his wife and two nymphomaniac sorority sisters, one of his academic books fell on the floor. It fortuitously opened to a page where the author was discussing the myth of El Corazón Negro de Dios. The passages mystified him. Penthouse be damned. The article sent him on his quest to find fame, fortune and the Black Heart of God. Nymphos were no longer a significant part of his quest. Sinclair was on a mission from God.

After some degree of suffering by Danny and Jason, the four walked the trail higher and higher onto Mesa de Guadalupe. As they were passing through the ruins of Patokwa, Naomi, now known as "Naomi the Fat Face," secretly between Jason and Danny, felt compelled to vaunt her pretentious reserves of uninteresting knowledge to the boys. "Do you dweebs know what Patokwa means in Towan language?" she said, raising her tiny nose in the air. "It means 'Turquoise-moiety place.' Interesting for a place that has truly shitty turquoise. The early Indians had been here since about AD 900 with pit houses and rudimentary structures. Too bad you don't get to check it out. The main Pueblo structure has almost 600 rooms. But here's the thing. It wasn't here when the Spaniards conquered Astialakwa. The Jemez built the buildings in 1680 right after the Pueblo Revolt. The dumb Jemez burned their current Pueblo of Walatowa out of spite just because the Spanish required them to live there. The construction of Patokwa was pretty much an obvious attempt by the Jemez to get back to their prior way of life, higher on the mesa tops, giving the finger to the Spaniards. At one time, there were probably a thousand people who lived here.

You can see who won that battle by the fact that the Jemez are now all cooped up down in the valley in their little Pueblo of Walatowa, just like the Spanish wanted."

"Now, Naomi," said Sinclair, "Don't you think that's a bit jaded?"

"Fucking Indians," Naomi replied, with a sneer. Jason thought it was interesting that to Naomi, both Harvard and Indians merited the adjective *fucking*.

The trail gradually gained incline, and Jason was just about to tell the professor he was going to hurl when they topped the mesa. It was a truly incredible view from the top of the mesa, and he immediately understood why the Jemez would have wanted to live here. From this vantage, they could see enemies coming from miles away. Although they were a thousand feet above the Jemez River below, they could hear the sound of the water as clearly as if they were next to it. The air was fresh and warm and smelled clean. Far below was the Jemez River, and on the other side of the mesa the Guadalupe River. He could see them merge into one river at the base of the mesa. Looking south, they could see the entire Jemez Pueblo with Jemez High School and fertile fields of corn and other vegetables beyond. To the north they could see the Village of Jemez Springs and beyond that, more mountains. Jason was stunned at the spectacular view.

The feeling didn't last long. Professor Sinclair got them immediately to work. "Now listen up. Here's the thing. You are going to look out and not see a single artifact or remnant of the pueblo.

The dust and dirt of the ages buried the good stuff. I have the skill to point out where you should dig, so listen to me and don't waste energy on a mound of dirt unless I say so. OK, let's break into two teams. Naomi and Danny, you start looking for shiny shit to collect. You've got lots of room in your backpacks, so load up." He turned to Jason and said, "Jason, you come with me. We'll start in the center of the village. When I read about the attack and listened to the myths of the Jemez People, I knew that there would be a shrine somewhere outside of their pueblo, and everything I've put together suggests it is toward the north end of the mesa. Now I know you don't know how to recognize a pile of rocks from something of archaeological interest, so follow me, and we'll see what we find."

As Naomi and Danny began their search for artifacts, Sinclair and Jason gradually walked north. The professor, with a compass in one hand and a notebook in the other, looked left and right. He knew from his previous trips what he was *not* looking for, and what, now that he had read Oñate's journal, he *was* looking for. Two hours later, they reached the end of the mesa with nothing to show for their efforts.

"Let's take a break," said Sinclair. "It's not on the immediate path, so we can go left or right heading back. I think left." Jason shrugged and followed as the professor walked slowly, with purpose. It took no more than a hundred feet of walking to see his goal. "There!" he said. "That's a shrine. I'm sure of it!" Jason looked at the pile of rocks that looked like a hundred other piles of rocks they had passed without the professor giving notice.

Meanwhile, Naomi and Danny were gathering artifacts like super shoppers at Walmart. “This is amazing!” said Naomi. "We’ve only been looking for two hours and we have found three intact pots, about a hundred pieces of chain mail, and at least five spearheads.” She stopped in front of a pile of rubble, which to Danny looked simply like a pile of rubble. “Start shoveling, chubs,” Naomi said. "There is no doubt great shit under here.” A half hour of digging and Danny hit metal. “Take it easy. No damage, dweeb!” Naomi shouted. She started digging with a trowel and uncovered a conquistador’s breastplate, and under the breastplate there appeared to be a ribcage. “I guess some of the Spaniards got the wrong end of an arrow,” she said. “Good for us! Now, dig some more, Chubs,” she said. “If we find a skull, I’m keeping it!”

“I’m getting tired, and maybe even the mouth sweats,” Danny said.

“What in the fuck are mouth sweats?” Naomi said, a look of looking incredulous.

“You know, you work so hard the inside of your mouth gets all sweaty.”

“Fucking undergraduates,” Naomi said. “Now, dig, or ‘mouth sweats’ will be the least of your problems.”

Sinclair looked at the pile of rocks in front of him. In his mind’s eye, he could see a shrine. He just knew it was here. “OK, Jason, my friend, pull off those rocks and pile them to the side. I'm sure it will be fairly deep, so don't start digging until I say so."

Jason rolled his eyes and sighed, unnoticed by Sinclair. An hour later, he had removed fifty stones. "OK, now it's time to dig. But SLOWLY, and with care," he said. "You can't damage any treasure underneath." Jason started digging, not really understanding what 'slowly with care' actually meant. The dirt was soft, and within fifteen minutes, they hit more stones. "Now, remove those stones," Sinclair said. They each did so, one at a time until Sinclair shouted "Stop!"

Sinclair rushed in, pushing Jason out of the way. He had a trowel in his hand and a paintbrush in the other. He gradually dug, an inch at a time, until he hit something solid. He started digging with his hands around the object. In an instant, he felt it. It took a moment to register in his brain, but he was sure that was it. Slowly, he pushed his hands into the ground, and grasped the object, carefully pulling it out of the dirt. As he raised his hands out of the pit he had dug, he shook what looked to Jason like a rock. Four hundred years of earth fell off to reveal a ball of obsidian, shaped like a human heart, with a hole in the top. The leather portion of the necklace had long since deteriorated, but the Black Heart of God was, at long last, in his hands. Sinclair could barely believe he had the treasure in the palm of his hand. As he touched it, a tingle went through his hand, up his arm then throughout his body. He felt lightheaded and as though he was starting to hyperventilate. "I've found it!" he shouted. "It's mine at last!" Sinclair held the Black

Heart, sensing the centuries that had passed since its creation, the many ceremonies that had been focused on it, and the hands of so many generations of humans who had held it with reverence.

A clapping sound began from behind him. He looked over his shoulder to see Naomi applauding, with a broad smile on her face. Jason and Danny followed suit. "Bravo, professor," Naomi said, which sounded to Sinclair almost bitter. "*We* did it!"

Sinclair felt an overwhelming sense of accomplishment. Reluctantly, he handed the stone to Naomi. She took it and cupped it with both hands. "It's amazing! It feels ... almost alive!" she exclaimed. The others watched with surprise as Naomi's eyes rolled back in her head, then closed, her head raised to the sky. Her entire body began to shake for a moment, then stopped as quickly as it came. She stood motionless for a few moments, then her eyes opened and the apparent distress she felt was replaced by a smile. It didn't appear to be a smile of happiness to Sinclair. It was one of malevolence. Danny and Jason stepped away from her in fear. Naomi shook her head as though she was attempting to clear her head, oblivious to the others watching her with concern. "What a rush!" Naomi bellowed.

As Naomi's expression and postured returned to normal, Sinclair touched Naomi's arm. "Are you OK, Naomi?" he asked.

Naomi paused for a moment, staring at Sinclair. "Ye—yes, sure. It just moved me, I guess," she replied.

He held out his hand to Naomi to retrieve his prize which she returned grudgingly. He tucked the stone into his backpack and, in an unsuccessful attempt to sound nonchalant, said, "OK, now we need some shiny shit to bring back to UNM."

"No worries, professor," Naomi replied. "I found a bunch of good artifacts while you were finding the holy grail."

"I helped," said Danny, quietly.

"Fucking undergrads," snarled Naomi.

The four had a late lunch on top of Mesa de Guadalupe, scavenged numerous items that Sinclair knew would make the Anthropology Department's Dean squirm with pleasure. It amazed him at how Patokwa had been scavenged for so many years and yet another half mile yielded treasures unimaginable. Finally, Sinclair stood and said, "Thanks to you three for helping to make this a most profitable day. Let's head down the mesa and get back to Albuquerque."

The four headed back down the way they had come. Jason was in the lead, followed by Sinclair, then Danny and in the rear, Naomi. As they walked Danny and Naomi, unnoticed by the other two, gradually lagged behind until they were out of sight. They had been walking for fifteen minutes when Jason looked back and saw that Danny and Naomi were nowhere in sight. "Professor!" Jason shouted with consternation. "Where are the others?" A moment later, Naomi came into sight running. "Something terrible has happened," she said. "Danny fell off the edge!"

"What?" Sinclair said. "When? Where?"

Sinclair noted that Naomi's voice sounded inappropriately relaxed. "He was in front of me as we were walking. I stopped to check out a small petroglyph, and then I heard screaming. I began running down the trail, and then I saw him. A couple of hundred feet down the mesa. He's face down, not moving, and looks all bent up, like one of those fucking Gumby toys."

The three ran back to the spot Naomi said Danny had fallen. They looked over the edge, and at the bottom was the broken and twisted body. Sinclair was silent for a minute, then took a deep breath. "Oh my God," Sinclair said, staring down at the body of his student. "This is bad. This is really bad," he whimpered.

He sat down on the ground, putting his arms over his head. "I'm going to be in so much trouble when the department finds out. Students aren't allowed to die on field trips!" He sat still for a few moments muttering.

"What to do? What to do?" Taking a deep breath, he said, "OK, we have to call the Forest Service and let them know what has happened,"

"Sinclair," Naomi said quietly, "We'll get fucking arrested with all the antiquities we have in our packs. We can't do that. There will be too many questions."

Sinclair thought for a moment. His career, his professorship, and not to mention, his freedom were all at stake. "Naomi," Sinclair pleaded, "What should we do?"

The incongruous smile Naomi had displayed while holding the Black Heart returned. "OK, we'll call when we get back to the van. We'll stash our artifacts before they arrive. We'll tell them we couldn't call from Astialakwa because we had no cell service on the mesa, which is probably true. Cell service sucks around here."

The three walked the rest of the journey in silence. When they got back to the van, Sinclair placed the call to let the authorities know what had happened (in a highly edited fashion).

2

Dreams

Trust in dreams, for in them is hidden the gate to eternity.
(Khalil Gibran)

The vision of her face was unfocused, as though he were looking through a dirty window, but he knew it was her. It was Randy. He could see her radiant smile, those beautiful green eyes, and her long red hair. She was wearing a yellow sundress and tennis shoes, and she was running toward him from the large pasture behind his home. The sun was glowing, and the sky was a deep cerulean blue. In her hand was a bouquet of mountain wildflowers, an array of beauty from the Jemez: delicate Western Blue Flags, mounds of white Yarrow, Mountain Goldenbean and Columbine. Randy approached Matt, holding out the bouquet. "These are for you, my man," she said, turning her eyes coyly.

Suddenly Matt was no longer on the ranch. He was in the Church of Our Lady of Kazan in Yaroplets, Russia. The dilapidated building, which at one time had been majestic, was abandoned, with high ceilings and columns, many toppled to the floor. Behind him, Matt heard an explosion. He spun to see what it was. Randy was hanging from a rope tethered to a dome in the ceiling. Matt saw a box attached to the ceiling explode, caving in, sending Randy down through a hole in the floor, followed by tons of concrete, granite, and mortar. He screamed, "NO!"

Matt awoke covered in sweat, tears running down his cheeks, his pulse and breathing both racing. It took him a few moments to realize, yet again, it was a nightmare. A familiar dream he had had far too often since he lost Randy. He attempted to bring himself back to reality, consciously slowing his breathing, and gathered himself as much as was possible. After a few minutes, he took a deep breath, let out a sigh, and sat up on the bed. Putting his robe on, he stumbled to the kitchen to turn on the coffee pot, placing both hands on the counter, and dropping his head as the coffee percolated. *Another dream. Damn.*

It was quickly approaching two years since he lost Randy in that horrid church in Russia. The nighttime passion play had plagued him since the actual affair, more frequently in the beginning, diminishing as of late. Yet they were no less intense. He relished the part where he could see Randy smiling, but it always ended in the church. "Things weren't supposed to happen that way, Randy," Matt said quietly, sending his words to the universe. "I just don't seem to be able to stop re-living that moment." He could have sworn he heard her reply in his head, *I'm sorry, Matthew. I will try to help.* The words almost sounded audible as he wiped tears from his eyes.

Matt pulled the pot from the coffeemaker and filled his favorite mug, relishing the smell of fresh-brewed coffee, which helped him to gather himself. His dog, Jake, always accompanying him, was standing particularly close, waiting for his own morning ritual.

Matt had found Jake soon after buying his ranch, the Circle R, named after Randy. Jake was a gorgeous Australian Cattle Dog, well-muscled with a striking blue-gray mottled coat and black fur surrounding one of his eyes. Jake had boundless energy, was true-blue loyal, famously smart, tenacious, and ever alert. Although many cattle dogs are wary of strangers, Matt and Jake had an unspoken agreement that Matt would tell Jake if a person was "friend," or "evil," and Jake would usually follow Matt's lead on the assessment despite often having better sense than Matt on that.

Matt went to a cookie jar, handed Jake one of his favorite cookie biscuits, and walked to his front window. The view of the field in front of his home, which spanned 500 yards down a gentle slope to the east fork of the Jemez River, never failed to inspire his awe. He looked past the river that meandered through the bottom portion of his ranch, to State Route Four, across the highway to the Las Conchas Trailhead. It calmed him to breathe in this view and it always brought him back to earth. The first light had just birthed for the day, and he noted it was quite foggy in the valley through which the highway meandered. *That's weird*, he thought. *It's hardly ever foggy here in the summer.*

As Matt relaxed, enjoying watching the growing light of daytime, Jake growled, low and guttural. Matt looked out to see if there was a bear or mule deer in front, and his eyes traveled to the edge of the highway. He blinked twice as the image he saw didn't make sense. Standing by the highway, immersed in the fog, was a woman, dressed in traditional He'mish native attire, holding her hands out toward him, pointing to the slope above his house. For a moment, he thought he must still be dreaming. He rubbed his eyes and opened them again. She was still there, arms out, pointing. Jake continued his low growl. Matt walked to the front door and opened it, Jake running out, down the porch, and toward the highway. Matt followed Jake onto the front porch, watching in wonder. As Jake got nearer, the woman disappeared slowly into the fog. Jake stopped, looking and sniffing, then looked back at his companion, asking with his expression if he should pursue. Abruptly, from where the woman disappeared, flew a golden eagle, sailing out of the fog and flying toward Matt's home. The eagle ascended above his home and as Matt watched, the majestic bird flew up the side of the hill behind Matt's house, disappearing in the distance. Matt sat down on his rocking chair on the porch and took a deep breath. "Come, Jake," Matt said quietly, and the dog reluctantly returned. *Maybe I need to get a psychiatrist,* Matt thought, walking back into his lodge, shutting the door behind him. This was the third time in several weeks that he had seen the woman, always followed by an eagle. Eagles were a relatively uncommon sight in the Jemez. Old native women by the side of the road were much less common. The woman's first appearance had been astonishing and Matt had run down to the road to find no one there. He had come unglued at the sight, and in the two appearances since the first, Matt had started to think he was having a nervous breakdown.

"Pay attention," said Randy, from behind his shoulder. "She's telling you something important."

Matt whipped his body around in the direction of Randy's voice. "What the hell?" he said. "Randy?" Like the woman by the road, there was no one in the room. Matt's heart began racing. He shouted to the empty room, "Randy? I heard your voice!" *What in the hell is going on with me?*

"I'm here, Matt," came Randy's voice.

"Where? Where are you?"

"I'm somehow with you, Matt. I don't know myself. I'm seeing the world through your eyes, Matt. Matt? What's going on?"

No, I'm having a nervous breakdown. It's a delusion, Matt thought.

"You aren't going crazy, Matt. I know you're thinking that. But I know I'm with you."

Matt collapsed in his chair by the fire, bewildered by what he was experiencing. After a minute, Matt falteringly said, "So you're here, and you saw the woman by the road too?"

"I am, Matt. I don't know what's going on any more than you do, but I saw the woman, and, more importantly, felt her there. I could sense her feelings and emotions, and I know she's trying to tell you something important."

"Coming from a ghost, Randy, I'll take it seriously," Matt replied, as though Randy was actually there.

"Who says I'm a ghost?" Randy replied.

"I don't know if you're a ghost or a hallucination, Randy. But I love hearing your voice."

"We'll figure it out together, my love," Randy whispered.

Matt showered, combed his hair, observing that his hands were shaking, and put on his khaki-colored uniform shirt and green trousers. Officially not in compliance with the Sandoval County Sheriff's Department, he put on dark brown cowboy boots. He spent so much time off the beaten path, they were a necessity. He put on his Stetson buffalo felt silver mine cowboy hat, which also did not comply with the department's uniform code, but one he had negotiated with his boss as a condition of employment. He pinned his deputy sheriff's badge to his shirt and put on his duty rig. He stood at the mirror, looking himself in the eye. At 46 years old, Matt considered himself to be in good physical condition. His hair was greying, but he was in good shape and the years had been kind to his face. He had been thin his entire life, and his six foot five inch body accentuated his slenderness. He poured another mug of coffee, sat down in front of the fire and called his office.

"So, Lieutenant, what's on the agenda for today?" Matt asked.

Lieutenant Horacio Villanueva was Matt's Patrol Lieutenant. Because of the remote area he was in, Matt had no office. The

Sandoval County Sheriff's Office had been looking for a suitable office for Matt and the other deputies who passed through the area since Matt came aboard the year before. Although Matt's beat was not known for much in the way of crime, arrests were occasionally necessary. For the time being, his office was his den. When he made arrests, the Jemez Ranger District Office had two small holding cells which Matt borrowed until transportation could be arranged to the Sandoval County Jail. From Matt's perspective, he would be happy to wait to be tied down with an office. Until that happened, however, morning roll call was a call into the office for any specific orders of the day.

Because Horacio was a tough name, the Lieutenant's nickname since childhood had been "Lacho," not uncommon for such a name. Lieutenant Villanueva had two outstanding characteristics that caused a substantial degree of conflict with Matt. First, Lacho believed Matt was wearing a shield purely because of his relationship with the elected Sheriff, Hector Vigil. Matt and Hector had been long-time friends since they served together in the navy. The second was that Lacho knew about Matt's two dozen years with the Naval Criminal Investigative Service and was threatened by Matt's significant experience as a law enforcement agent and investigator. Their relationship above the line was cordial, but Matt had a deep concern that his lieutenant was not in his corner. Lacho was a good cop, however, and his sense of duty usually trumped any petty grievances he might have had with Matt. Lacho abided with the uniform exceptions with little complaint, mostly because he knew it would accomplish nothing. Nevertheless, it created an uncomfortable tension between the two.

"I'm sending you a fax as soon as we get done with this conversation. There have been several cabin break-ins in SB3." SB3 was Sandoval Sheriff's office designation for the Jemez Mountains patrol area and was the region Matt handled. "I need you to put this on the priority list," Lacho continued. "Additionally, the people in Jemez Springs are complaining about speeders coming through town. It being June and all, the tourists are gathering steam. So, I want most of your day today to be speed enforcement in and around Jemez Springs, Battleship Rock and Soda Dam. Got it?"

"Yes, Lieutenant, I've got it," said Matt. Matt had been ambivalent about taking the deputy sheriff position. When he had walked away from a 24-year career with the Navy Criminal Investigative Service, he wanted to wash his hands of law enforcement. With the loss of Randy, his reasons for staying with NCIS also evaporated. All he had wanted to do was to come home to the Jemez and try, somehow to move on without the love of his life.

His new position as a patrol deputy was very different than his experience with the NCIS. By the time he gave notice that he was leaving the service, he was a Supervisory Special Agent and had been offered the job of Special Agent in Charge of the San Diego Office, which was a position that oversaw over 100 staff and special agents. His experience, first with NIS, which eventually became NCIS, was valuable, but when Randy Glasscock was, he believed, murdered by a former KGB agent outside of Moscow two years before, his life took a cataclysmic change. He resigned from the NCIS, bought a ranch in the Jemez Mountains, and had intended to live a simple life without his sweetheart. Instead, at the unrelenting persistence of his lifelong friend and shipmate, Matt took the job with the Sandoval County Sheriff's Office. Lacho, as his supervisor, was not happy about the accommodation. And what? He got to wear his own boots? He got to wear his own hat? This was simply *not* satisfactory for a man who had spent his 26 years in the Sandoval County Sheriff's Office, completely squared away. Not satisfactory at all.

For Matt, taking the job had been a good thing. It was mostly undemanding, actual crime was minimal, and he had a reason to get up in the morning. He didn't have to think much, he had no subordinates, and he was far enough away from SCSO headquarters in Bernalillo that he wasn't involved in the politics of police work. It was a good place to be, and he could do the job with his eyes closed.

3

Actually, Something Interesting

Life is very interesting… in the end, some of your greatest pains, become your greatest strengths.
(Drew Barrymore)

Matt went to his gun safe and extracted his Sig Sauer P226. It was, once again, not the service weapon sanctioned by the Sandoval County Sheriff's Office, but it was a sidearm he trusted, and that meant more than the reprimand he might receive upon discovery. Matt had carried this model since his days at NCIS. Over the years, Sig Sauer earned a loyal following by selling strong, durable, and reliable handguns to law enforcement, the U.S. military, and firearms enthusiasts nationwide. His P226 had never jammed, was accurate and durable.

He slid the pistol into his duty rig, called Jake, and out the door they went to enter Matt's sheriff's vehicle. The 2000 GMC Jimmy was perfect for his patrols. He used the four-wheel drive more often than two wheels, and it had enough power to convince a speeder to pull to the side for a citation. Jake almost always went with Matt on patrol, yet another break from SCSO protocol.

Matt's patrol area, SB3, was a 707 square mile territory inhabited by about as many people. It ran throughout the Jemez Mountains with a tiny carve-out for Los Alamos County, and to the north about 30 miles passed Cuba, New Mexico. It was an area much too large to patrol, yet, because of the lack of population and the winding roads through the Jemez Mountains, it was manageable for one or two deputies. As with everything in Northern New Mexico, however, populations were shifting, and more people each year moved into Sandoval County.

Although Los Alamos County, very small in its own right, was not part of Matt's area, it had an influence, potentially large, on Matt's job. Los Alamos was where he grew up, went to high school, and where his parents had lived most of their lives. Los Alamos was unique in many ways. It was the site chosen by Robert Oppenheimer to locate the secret laboratory that would build the atomic bomb during World War II. Better known as the "Manhattan Project," Los Alamos was an anomaly on the face of the earth, and most especially, New Mexico. With the highest number of Ph.D's per capita of any city in the world, the town was filled with scientists. The school system was one of the best in the country, due in large part to the demands of the Ph.D. parents. The town also had more millionaires than any town in the world. Los Alamos was, by any definition, weird.

The scientists of the 1940's and 1950's were happy to live in government housing. But they also used slide rules. The scientists of the 2000's were "outdoorsy" and wanted to spend their leisure time skiing, hiking, and even living in more remote areas. Consequently, the Jemez Mountains were a perfect respite for people with more money than common sense. Cabin communities flourished, and the land that a mere thirty years earlier was only good for harvesting timber became communities of highly educated, highly paid people who wanted to escape the "urban life" of Los Alamos, a town of, give or take, 15,000 people, depending on which party was in office in Washington DC. The colorful history of the Jemez Mountains, a place of Pueblo people, Spanish conquest, logging companies, mining companies and ranchers, was quickly becoming gentrified by people with numerous initials after their names and calculators hanging on their belts.

Because so much of the Jemez was in Sandoval County, the elected Sheriff, Hector Vigil, needed to be certain there was a qualified presence in the Jemez. His old friend and former shipmate, Matt Bertram, was the perfect mark. Matt had all the qualifications of a detective and yet was unmotivated to be anything more than a patrol deputy.

Matt and Jake got into the Jimmy and headed toward the village of Jemez Springs. The village was the closest thing to civilization that one could find in the mountains. A hamlet of four hundred people, if you counted the goats, a fantastic bar, a couple of restaurants and some tourist stores, was Jemez Springs. Although it was small, the community had a very rich history, one that even many of the locals weren't aware of, and the residents of the village were diverse, some to the point of being downright odd. In the summertime, the local businesses earned their livings for the entire year, as tourists descended from Albuquerque to visit the Jemez Mountains, enjoy the outdoors and soak in the hot springs.

Being in proximity to the world's largest extinct volcano, the Valle Grande, made the area geologically fascinating to scientists, naturalists, and tourists. Besides the beautiful caldera of the Valle Grande, a prize ranch for over a hundred years, the area was alive with hot springs. Jemez Springs had been "discovered" by the conquistador, Juan Oñate in 1599. After visiting the area, he wrote numerous letters to the king and queen of Spain that the waters were health giving, and thus started the first population boom in the area. From 1600 until the present, people came from around the world to soak in the sulfur springs to give them life and heal their many maladies. In the early 1900s, the springs were marketed as the fountain of youth by entrepreneurs intent on cashing in on the natural wonders. Colorful stories abounded about "Guest" ranches, owned by Chicago gangsters who used the area as hide-outs from the feds, and one rumor, which persisted to the present, was that Al Capone hid out in the dude ranch to avoid capture. Among the many vestiges of Spanish rule, the Catholic church was one of the largest landowners in the area, owning over 2500 acres of land in proximity to Jemez Springs.

Matt spent the first two hours of his day setting speed traps and ticketing snarky yuppies in BMW's who were driving far too fast and complained even more quickly about police harassment. Matt knew that if they fought their ticket, it would come to court when the traveling judge came once a week, and, of course, they would be long gone to Los Angeles or some other far-away place, so he would stand back, let the driver rant and rave, then give them an envelope to mail in their check.

Having done his duty of speed patrol, Matt decided it was time to take a break and begin his work investigating the "crime spree" that had descended upon the area. It is a tribute to how little crime there was in the area when one deputy had responsibility for over 700 square miles of territory. He drove into Jemez Springs, stopping at Las Águilas Bar for a cup of coffee and a danish. Although it was a bar, it was also a morning coffee house and a community gossip center, long before coffee shops became ubiquitous. Las Águilas Restaurant and Saloon was an icon in Jemez Springs and had been in business since just after World War II. Bikers and tourists flocked to the bar in the summertime to enjoy their famous New Mexican food, a variety of live music, and dancing on the weekends. The décor alone was enough to bring people in to see for themselves the animal skins, buck trophies, antique rifles and odd bric-a-brac stuffed in every corner.

As Matt walked into Las Águilas, he was greeted by the proprietor, Maximillian Chavez, known to the locals as "Chavy." Matt brought Jake in with him, and, as usual, Jake was the first to be greeted. "Jakey, my friend, you brought this flea-bitten deputy into my bar?" said Chavy.

"Shut up and bring me coffee, pendejo," Matt responded.

"Oh, no, mi compadre," Chavy said. "I'll bring you coffee, but first, our only K-9 patrol in Jemez must feast!" Chavy brought out a plate of leftover chicken from the night before and gave it to Jake, who truly did feast.

"You know, I don't even have to feed this dog at home," said Matt.

"You better, hombre," said Chavy. "Or me and my friends will cut you."

"Shut up and bring me a coffee," Matt said, without a moment's reflection.

Just like the bar, Chavy was also an iconic personality in Jemez Springs. He loved to tell stories of living out of his VW Microbus in the 1960's, smoking too much dope and being free. His father had started the bar in 1947, and when he became ill, Chavy returned from his "Free Bird" life to buckle down. Chavy was a savvy business owner and ran the bar well. The bar had been featured in several national magazines, and Condé Nast had named it as one of the ten best bars in America. His bar was a place not to be missed on any tourist's itinerary. Chavy, besides being a good friend, was also Matt's greatest source of local gossip and leads in the sparse and relatively trivial crimes in the area, as well as a source of practically unbelievable sea stories of his early years.

"We are having a party tonight, my friend," said Chavy. "It's some full moon or something. At least it's an excuse to drink. We're going to have *Los Reyes* here doing music. I know how you like them!"

"OK, Chavy," Matt replied. "I'll come by if I'm not too busy catching criminals."

"Speaking of criminals," Chavy said, suddenly looking serious, "I hear two more cabins were broken into last week."

"We both know who it was," replied Matt. "I'm going to have to spend my day hiking in the mountains to find the Funk brothers."

"I know, Matty. I don't know why we can't just pool our money and buy them a one-way bus ticket to Florida."

The Funk brothers, Dory and Chuchu, were a subject of much consternation in Jemez Springs. Matt had arrested them over a dozen times for various crimes, and due in part to the fact that the Sandoval County Detention Center was overcrowded, and the local magistrate seemed to have a complete lack of concern for the citizens of the village, they were always out on bail the next day, wreaking havoc, stealing from everyone, not just the weekend scientists. They had stolen from the Los Alamos Labs, and they had even broken into the Jemez Ranger District office and stolen gun holsters and Chinese-made 'genuine' Jemez Indian souvenirs and T-shirts from the gift shop. The Funks were getting annoying enough that Matt knew he was going to have to spend the day trying to find them and arrest them. His lack of motivation stemmed, in part, from the reality that they would be on the street and back at it the next day. He sometimes felt like Bill Murray's character in the movie *Groundhog Day*. It was just another day in the life of a Sandoval County, based in Jemez, deputy sheriff. Get up, eat breakfast, arrest the Funk brothers. Rinse and repeat.

Matt and Jake said goodbye to Chavy, got back in Matt's Jimmy and headed back east for the next stop of the day. Matt's regular daily stop was at the Jemez Ranger District Office. There were two law enforcement officers based in the office who covered the entire Jemez District of the Santa Fe National Forest, which was a quite impossible task. Sworn and trained officers, the "LEO'S" were the closest thing to law enforcement protection, other than Matt, that the area had, and they were often called to assist in matters in which they technically had no jurisdiction. The same was true for Matt. Much of the land in his patrol area was National Forest land, and yet much of the work he did crossed those boundaries. Matt and the LEO's at the Ranger District had an informal yet strong agreement to assist one another. Besides the LEOs, the New Mexico State Police wandered through occasionally, but not enough for Matt to count on their help. The bottom line was that none of his colleagues stood on jurisdictional pride, and everyone accepted everyone's help in getting the public safety job done.

The Jemez Pueblo was a separate issue for law enforcement. Unlike many of the pueblos, Jemez had no police force, although the tribe had applied for and was waiting on approval to form one. In the meantime, the entire Jemez Pueblo was covered by the War Chief's staff, the SCSO and the National Forest Service LEO's.

It was jurisdictionally tough, considering the Pueblo would not allow outside law enforcement on the reservation. Under Federal law, the FBI had jurisdiction over major felonies, but they were few and far between at the pueblo and the FBI had their hands full in Albuquerque.

Matt pulled into the USFS District Office, shut down the engine, and opened the door so that Jake could get out. As this was another regular stop for Jake, it meant a potential snack and adoring fans. Matt walked to the office, opened the door, and Jake dove in, looking for his second favorite person in the world. He stopped and hunched down, growling. Up from behind the counter popped his prize, LEO Paul Toza, who jumped up, holding his hands in a sort of zombie-esque position. Jake ran for Paul and jumped into his arms, licking his face. Paul collapsed on the ground shouting, “I surrender! You win, Jake!”

“You would think that he hadn’t seen you in weeks,” Matt said.

“He knows I have tamales,” Paul said, reaching for a bag on the counter.

“That dog is going to die of heart disease before he’s ten,” replied Matt.

“Yeah, but what a way to go.”

Paul Toza was a member of the Jemez Tribe. A graduate of Oregon State University, he began work with the US Forest Service as a Park Ranger in Glacier Bay National Park in Alaska, very far from the home in which he was raised, as rookie rangers go wherever they are assigned. He worked hard and excelled, never giving up his ambition to come home to where he grew up in Walatowa, the Towan name for the Jemez Pueblo. He still lived in the Pueblo and had raised his family there. He was a family man and coached the high school's long distance running program. Running was to the Jemez Indians what football was to Texas small towns. The tribe had a long history of running and had been competing both with themselves and other pueblos for centuries. Several Jemez families had sons and daughters who received track scholarships to universities. Paul was also a very devout Catholic, and even though Paul didn't speak much of it, Matt suspected Paul was a committed participant in tribal religious ceremonies and dances. The only alcohol that touched Paul's lips was communion wine, and Paul spoke fondly and with respect for his wife, Miranda.

USFS Law Enforcement Officers go through virtually the same training as the FBI, the NCIS and the Federal Marshalls, and they are sworn and armed law enforcement officers. Paul was dedicated, highly trained, and never lost his passion for his people. Because the Jemez Indians had never been displaced to artificial reservations in places far away, the Jemez children grew up speaking their native Towan language, and only learned English when they started school.

Paul was respected in his community, his tribe and his family, and by Matt. Although squared-away in most respects, a point of contention with Paul's superiors was the fact that he wore his hair in a traditional "Chongo," long and tied back behind his head, which was a contrast to the Northern Pueblo members who braided their hair much like the plains Indians. He was willing to wear the uniform in compliance with the regulations and do his duty as the USFS dictated, but he was *not* willing to cut his hair in the Anglo way. Sometimes, when you are the best and work the hardest, you receive grace. The Chongo was the grace given him by his supervisors. He was a valued member of the USFS law enforcement team, and an active member of his Jemez tribe.

Paul's skills as a copy were invaluable to Matt, as Paul knew the territory inside and out. Even though Matt had grown up in Los Alamos to the east, and had spent most of his leisure time camping, fishing and hiking in the Jemez Mountains, he'd had no idea of the influence of the Jemez Pueblo on the rich history of the area. In the eighteen years Matt had lived in Los Alamos growing up, he never once met a Jemez Indian, and knew virtually nothing about the tribe. Paul was his educator and mentor, as without communication and understanding of this most amazing group of humans, Matt would have been handicapped in accomplishing his mission as a deputy.

"What's new in your world, my friend?" Paul inquired of Matt.

"Same old, same old, I guess," Matt responded. "I gave a bunch of tickets to irate tourists this morning. I had to wash off the "F" bombs and screaming when I was done with some of Chavy's coffee and a cheese danish. Now I'm working up the steam to go track down the Funk brothers and probably arrest them for more cabin break-ins."

"Shit, man. That's got to be arrest number twelve for them!"

"Yeah, probably." answered Matt. "I thought I'd drop by, let you feed my dog some of your tamales and see if you have any info that can help me stop four hours in the woods."

"No, not really," said Paul. "They stay pretty far from me, ever since my trusty taser got them when I caught them fishing without a license and they went all *Jango Fett* on me."

Matt gave a questioning look at Paul.

"What? Star Wars, man! You know, Jango Fett? I just saw the movie last week in Albuquerque!" Paul, besides being Jemez, was a nut about Star Wars.

Matt just shook his head. "I haven't been to the movies since they were in black and white."

The door at the far end of the office opened, and Paul's fellow LEO, Kai Gwinn, came through the door. "Hey Matt," said Kai. "How's tricks in your world? Is Toza on his Star Wars fetish again?"

"We were just talking about my exciting morning trolling for speeders and some badass in the movie, Jabba the Fett or something. How about you?"

"I was coming in to tell you we just got a call. There were some hikers up on Mesa de Guadalupe, and apparently one of them took a fall off the mesa. They think he's dead. The other folks in the party are at Las Casitas Fishing Site, waiting for us."

"You want to come along, deputy?" Paul said.

"Sounds like the most interesting thing that's happened all month, man. I'm in," Matt replied.

Kai called the Regional Headquarters in Albuquerque to let them know what was happening and to ask that they put a helicopter on standby in case they needed to extract someone with injuries. As they were walking out the door, Paul said, “It’s *Jango* Fett. And you need to get to the movies more often!”

The LEO’s jumped in their vehicles and Matt and Jake got in the Jimmy. Lights flashing, sirens screaming, the three trucks headed for something, anything, a little bit more interesting than the Funk brothers.

4

Just a Sightseeing Trip, Officers

Half a truth is often a great lie.
(Benjamin Franklin)

Sinclair and the others had stashed their backpacks filled with artifacts, in the back of the van, along with the shovels and picks. As he finished, he turned to the others, and particularly Jason, who was inconsolably crying, snot running down his face, his eyes red. Sinclair sat down next to Jason, his eyes also welling up with tears.

Naomi walked over to the two, hands on her hips, and sneered at them. "OK, now this is going to be very simple for us. We will tell them exactly what happened; that we were separated on the way back, and it took a while to notice Danny was gone. That's the simple part to remember. The most important thing to say is that we were just on a class field trip to look around. If they ask if we took anything, the answer is 'no.' Got it?"

Sinclair stifled a desire to start sobbing and said, "Of course, Naomi. You're right. We've got it."

Jason, unable to speak cogently, just nodded.

The unmistakable sound of sirens approaching meant they would soon have law enforcement visiting. “Hopefully,” Naomi said, “they’ll be focused on a fucking rescue mission, and not on us. But this can’t screw up our plans, understand? There’s too much at stake for all of us, and none of us wants to go to jail.”

“I thought you said *finders, keepers*, professor,” said Jason, between sobs.

Sinclair paused to gather himself, then said to Jason, “True, but there is this little federal law these days called the *Archeological Resources Protection Act*, which might be a bit of a problem for us.”

“Oh shit,” Jason replied, his sobbing increasing in intensity.

The three trucks sped along State Highway Four, heading toward La Casitas Fishing area, which was just a few minutes north of the Jemez Headquarters. As they pulled into the parking lot, they saw a dilapidated van in one of the parking spaces, and three people standing next to it. “Looks like it was the van that took the tumble down the mesa to me,” Matt said to himself.

“Tell me about it,” said Randy from the back seat. “Matt, I don’t have a good feeling about these folks.”

“Neither do I, Randy,” Matt replied. *I’ve really got to see a professional about this*, Matt thought to himself, as he pulled alongside the two LEO trucks and parked. Paul approached the three, with Kai at his side. Matt kept a bit more distance, out of respect for the LEO's, as this was their jurisdiction. Sinclair stepped forward and, with a reasonably decent impression of panic, explained the situation, just as Naomi had coached them.

"Do you think the boy is still alive?" Paul asked.

"I couldn't say. It looked to me like he took a 300-foot tumble, and he wasn't moving and didn't respond to our shouts, but it was too treacherous for us to climb down. I would have been risking my students' lives in doing so, so we decided the best thing to do would be to call you for help."

Paul pulled out a map, and unfolding it, said, "Can you tell me approximately where this happened?"

Sinclair pointed to an area on the west side of the mesa. "We were following the old Potokwa trail up to Astialakwa."

As Paul and Sinclair were talking, Matt walked around to the far side of the minivan and glanced in the window. It was an old habit of suspicion, grown from twenty-six years in law enforcement. As he looked, he saw three backpacks, two shovels, and two pickaxes. The backpacks appeared to be much fuller than a day hike would warrant. He took mental note of the sight, but said nothing.

Paul and Kai approached Matt. "He's on the west side of the mesa, and there are no roads to get even close. I'm going to call Santa Fe and see if they can dispatch a search and rescue team and a helicopter. If they can't, do you think Sandoval County Fire can help?"

"If you can't get them, I'll do what I can. Our resources are pretty limited," replied Matt.

Paul let Sinclair know what they were doing. "We're going to need you to stick around. If he's hard to find, they may need to talk to you."

As Paul and Kai went to their trucks to contact Santa Fe, Matt introduced himself to the three. "So, you were just on a day trip to look at the ruins of Astialakwa?" he inquired.

"Yeah, class field trip," replied Sinclair, beginning to calm down from the accident.

"Not a huge class," said Matt.

"Well, it's optional. Most students would rather study back in Albuquerque or spend their Saturdays doing something else."

"Yeah, I get it. I've never been up to Astialakwa. I grew up in Los Alamos, and camped here in the Jemez all the time, and I didn't even have any idea there were ruins up here, or anywhere else in the Jemez until I started working this area. I used to hike up Battleship Rock all the time, and come to find out there's a shrine right by where we used to hike."

"I know it," said Sinclair. "The Jemez call it Daha-enu. Been there several times."

"Well, I'll be damned," Matt said. "You ever find artifacts on your hikes? Arrowheads, pots, stuff like that?"

Sinclair stared at Matt, trying to decipher whether he was being interrogated was just having a conversation. "We occasionally see arrowheads, and of course, there are lots of pottery shards, but I'm always careful to instruct my students to leave them in place."

"Great," said Matt. "When I was growing up we would find arrowheads all the time. Nobody ever suggested I should leave them there. I've got a shoebox full."

"Well, Deputy, times have changed," Sinclair replied with a smile. It was at that moment that Sinclair realized Danny had fallen with his backpack on. From what he and Naomi said, they had stuffed all kinds of artifacts into both their backpacks. An overwhelming sense of panic surged through Sinclair. If they found that stuff, they were all busted. "Maybe, Deputy," Sinclair said, forcing his voice to sound relaxed, "they should have me ride in the helicopter with them. I—I could be helpful in spotting poor Danny."

Paul overheard the conversation. "That would probably be wise. They've dispatched a helicopter and a rescue team from Albuquerque. They should be here in 20 minutes or so. They'll have to take a look at the parking lot here from the air and see if it's feasible to land here."

Twenty minutes to the second, a helicopter was overhead. The parking lot was large enough to make a safe landing, so they picked up Sinclair and Paul and headed for the west side of Mesa de Guadalupe. It did not take long to spot Danny, face-down, arms and legs twisted in unnatural positions. There was a relatively flat spot just a few hundred feet below him. When they reached Danny, he was dead. From his broken and twisted neck, it was obvious, even to a casual observer, that Danny died upon impact with the ground. They put the body on a stretcher and carried it back to the waiting helicopter. Sinclair shouted to the team, "Perhaps I should hang on to his backpack. I'm sure there are personal items in there his family would want."

"Sir," said the leader of the rescue team, "He didn't have a backpack on, and we didn't see anything around him." Sinclair stood stiffly, saying nothing. He thought to himself, *what in the hell happened to his backpack? Did somebody take it?*

After several hours of interviews and paperwork, they released the three to leave the fishing site. "I'm looking forward to getting back to my dorm for a hot shower," Jason said.

"Unfortunately, we're not going anywhere tonight, son," Sinclair said. "We're going to get a room in Jemez Springs and come back in the morning to retrieve that backpack."

"Well, fuck," said Naomi. "That's just outstanding. We're never going to get rooms on short notice like this."

"I'll treat you to dinner and drinks at Las Águilas. And don't worry about the rooms. I have a friend who will always find room for us."

Matt, Paul and Kai watched the run-down van drive out of the driveway and turn left on State Route Four. "Looks like they aren't heading back to Albuquerque tonight," Kai exclaimed.

"I don't know about you guys, but there's something suspicious about these three," Matt said. "They had shovels and picks and three very full backpacks in their van. Much more stuff than they would need for a simple day hike. Seems to me that they might have been doing a little artifact shopping for themselves."

"Thanks for letting me know," Paul said. "I was kinda getting the creeps from them myself, but I didn't know why."

"You know," Matt said, studying the road, "They turned left toward Jemez Springs, not right toward Albuquerque. Maybe we should head that way and just see what they're up to."

"I know that investigator in you wants to dig something up, and I'd love to oblige, but it's after five, and Kai and I are going to have a mountain of paperwork to get done on this. I don't think there's enough to merit any time, unless something turns up when they do the autopsy."

"I get it," said Matt. "But you guys wouldn't mind if I just sniffed around a little, would you? I promise not to be obtrusive. This is your investigation, not mine."

"Be as obtrusive as you want, deputy," Paul said. "Jemez Springs is your jurisdiction. I think Kai and I may just take a little hike in the morning up to Astialakwa. We'll get some pictures for the report and maybe have a look around the ruins. If they have snatched artifacts, we may see some evidence. Care to go?"

"I'd love to, but I'd have to be back by noon. The lieutenant is going to want me to show some progress with the Funk brothers."

"I think we can make that happen. Meet at seven a.m.?"

Matt nodded, called Jake, who was sniffing out squirrels in the brush, and they headed back toward Jemez Springs. The village was on his way home anyway, so it wouldn't take much to do a little surveillance.

"You're smart to check up on those three," came Randy's declaration from the back seat. Matt was startled hearing her and surprised at how her voice sounded completely audible to him.

"Thank you, words in my head that sound like Randy the Ghost," Matt said out loud.

"What makes you think I'm in your head? And you said yourself that I'm not dead until you see my body. Well, Bertram, did you see my body?"

"I can't believe I'm having a conversation with voices in my head," Matt said. "But thank you for your compliment, Ghost of Randy."

"You're welcome, Matt. That's what I'm here for. And you can just call me Randy."

OK, I'm making an appointment with a professional tomorrow, Matt thought.

Sinclair, Naomi and Jason checked into the Mineral Springs Lodge in Jemez Springs. Sinclair had visited the area many times and had always stayed there. He had even looked at purchasing a cabin in La Cueva, thinking the area around the San Antonio Creek would be a great get-away place. Over the last couple of years, he had become friendly with the proprietor of Mineral Springs Lodge, Maggie Gimple, who had become rather taken by the presence of a professor of archaeology from UNM in their tiny village. Sinclair had, during his stays there, regaled her with stories of exciting adventures, all fabricated, that made Indiana Jones look like a bookworm compared to Sinclair Delano III, Ph.D. It was, despite her adoration, however, June in the Jemez, which meant that lodging would be difficult to come by.

"Oh dear, Sinclair, I completely booked us for tonight," said Maggie, apologetically.

"Isn't there something you could do, Maggie, for an old friend? I would make it up to you by having a drink with you before bed tonight."

Maggie gave the offer some thought. "Well, there is one party that is late checking in. I could tell them that there was some mix-up, and I'll find them a room at my friend's B&B to make it up to them. It's the Kiva cabin, so you would all have to share it, but there are two bedrooms and a sofa bed in the living room, so I'm sure you'll be comfy."

"You are a peach, Maggie," Sinclair said, making his best effort to be suave and charming.

The Mineral Springs Lodge was a historic resort with a colorful history. Jemez Springs, the village, had originally been called Hot Springs, because of the natural sulfur hot springs. Stories flourished of the ancestors of the Jemez Indians soaking in the springs for healing, and even the conquistador and colonial governor of the province of Santa Fe de Nuevo México, Juan de Oñate, espoused the curative powers of the springs. In the late 1800's the area became famous for its hot springs, and people with a variety of maladies came from all over the world, taking a two-day stagecoach ride from Albuquerque to partake of its purported restorative powers. There was no shortage of "first hand" witnesses of people who had been carried in by stretchers, soaking in the springs and miraculously walking out of the springs unaided, people with corns on their feet seeing them visibly disappear and many other accounts, mostly espoused by the proprietors of the "bath houses" which were built over the springs. Mineral Springs Lodge had been at the site of one of the original, and most famous bath houses, which, long ago, boasted of having separate men's and women's facilities for privacy. Although the springs were called 'sulfur' springs, there was, in fact, no sulfur in many of them, and from a marketing perspective, it was much more attractive to call them 'mineral' springs. By 2002, the area had been substantially modernized, but more than a hundred years after people journeyed by stagecoach, some tourists were still making the pilgrimage for cures for their wide and varied maladies. Most people, however, simply enjoyed the hot, relaxing waters and magnificent views offered by the lodge and surrounding area. Several of the springs in the surrounding area were "clothing optional," which drew an interesting nudist eco touristy crowd.

As the three looters entered their room, Jason was still sobbing. Naomi had had just about enough. She grabbed Jason by the collar and pushed her tiny nose against Jason's. "You listen here, you little crybaby," she spat. "You have got to get your shit together and stop your blubbering. We've all got to be cool, calm and collected to be sure that we don't go to prison."

"Prison?" Jason shrieked. "You said nothing about this being a crime. And Danny had an accident, right? I just want to go back to the dorm. Who cares if his backpack is still up there somewhere? Nobody is going to find it!"

Sinclair, sensing that Naomi had taken too hard an approach with Jason, attempted to assuage his agitation. "Look, son, yes, it was an accident. A really unfortunate one. But eventually someone is going to find that backpack, and when they do, who knows what's in it to lead back to us? We have to go find it before someone else does. Now calm down, and when you do, we'll go get drinks, then we'll come back and soak in the wonderful springs." Sinclair looked into Jason's eyes with what he hoped was a fatherly-concerned-empathic look. Jason let out one more small sob, wiped his eyes, and shook his head. "That's my boy," Sinclair offered, attempting to sound calm and confident. "Now go get washed up and I'll take us out for drinks and dinner," Sinclair said, turning away toward Naomi, who was rolling her eyes and mouthing the words, *fucking pansy.*

Jason went into the bathroom to blow his nose and wash his face. Sinclair turned to Naomi. "What has gotten into you, Naomi? I've never heard you swear like you have today, and I just didn't think that you were so mean spirited. I remember that innocent young lady who was in my freshman anthropology class, who was so very interested in the subject. You were my star student. I enjoyed having you in my classes, and I thought we were even developing some affection for one another."

"Look, Sinclair. I grew up on the South side of Chicago in West Garfield Park. Things were tough. My high school had the highest dropout rate in Illinois. I had to fight to make it out of there. Fuck, I've had to fight my whole life, and you don't successfully extract yourself from that kind of an upbringing by being 'nice' and 'innocent.' I finally make it to UNM, and let me tell you I didn't even know New Mexico was a state when I was growing up, and I entered a stunning world of knowledge and success. I thought the world of you, and I was having feelings for you, also. And then, during office hours, you closed the door to your office and in an incredibly awkward way, grabbed my boobs and tried to force yourself on me. I'm sure you remember the kick to your balls, right?"

"Well, um, I don't quite remember things that way, but I'm listening," Sinclair replied.

"So that day our relationship changed. I didn't go to the campus police and report you for sexually assaulting me, and you became my benefactor of good grades, grad school and oh so much more. You contributed to my attitude you pervert. Hence, we now have a business relationship that will compensate me for your appalling fucking behavior and marginal fucking intellect."

Sinclair stared at Naomi for a minute, a look of terror on his face. "You've been different since we were in Astialakwa, Naomi. You've always been an unpleasant person, but you've crossed over into the land of maliciousness."

"Maybe I'm just done with you and your ineptitude, Sinclair. Speaking of which, I haven't seen the Black Heart since we were on Mesa Guadalupe. May I check it out? Please?"

Sinclair shook his head and opened his backpack. Naomi reached in and brought the amulet out, holding it as though it was a small pet. She looked at the shimmering black glass and saw her reflection in it. Sinclair watched Naomi, stunned at the look on her face, alternating between ecstasy and avarice.

"Put it back, Naomi," Sinclair said, a tinge of worry in his voice. "The kid is a weak link in this. I need you to babysit him and keeping him in your sights after we get back to UNM."

"Fucking wonderful," Naomi replied as she carefully returned the Black Heart of God to the backpack.

5

An Obvious Quandary

Truth is ever to be found in simplicity, and not in the multiplicity and confusion of things.
(Isaac Newton)

Matt and Jake cruised into town, Matt on the lookout for the ramshackle van. It took some searching, but he finally spied it in the parking lot of Las Águilas Bar. He turned to Jake and said, "Well, good fortune for you and me, my friend. We get to kill two birds with one stone! Chavy will be happy we came by; we can hear a bit of great Chicano rock and check out the professor and his people at the same time."

Matt pulled his Jimmy into the parking lot and got out, Jake accompanying him. Jake was something of an honored VIP in Jemez Springs. Matt could, with a great deal of stretch, call Jake his K-9 patrol, but the people of Jemez Springs didn't give a crap about state laws if they didn't make any sense. Jake was welcome *anywhere*, while Matt, jokingly, was a bit suspect.

Matt walked in and Chavy was at the bar. Jake looked at Chavy, who looked at Matt, who said a quiet *OK*. "Come here Jake!" Chavy said, holding out his hands. Jake vaulted the bar without touching it, straight into Chavy's arms. Chavy received a thorough dog kiss on his face. "Well, Jake, nice of you to come tonight, my friend. I see you brought someone with you!" Matt smiled, and sat down at the bar, Jake playing bar-back and licking the floor, where someone spilled something enticing to the dog.

Chavy, without asking, pulled down his only bottle of Jack Daniels single barrel reserve and poured Matt a double, neat. "You going to have dinner tonight?" Chavy asked. "Tia's Rellenos with frijoles, correct?"

"Until you put stuffed sopas on the menu, yes, definitely, my friend!"

"We are a bar, here, compadre," Chavy replied. "You want stuffed sopas, go to Rancho de Chimayó!"

"They aren't that tough," Matt said. "Let me get back in the kitchen and I'll stir up a delicacy."

"You'd start a fire, and I would be *fuera del negocio*. You stick with law enforcement, and I promise, I'll figure out how to make your damned stuffed sopapillas."

"Deal," replied Matt.

As Matt looked around the bar, he spied his three UNM folks. It appeared as though food was the least important part of the night, as they had an entire bottle of tequila at the table, and the younger kid appeared to be slamming them down like he was dying of dehydration in the desert, with the apparent encouragement of the other two.

Matt finished his wonderful chili rellenos and his drink. Although he was enjoying the music, it had been a long day, and the three UNM people seemed pretty damn innocuous. "Chavy, what do I owe you, my friend?"

"Fifteen will get you through, Matt," Chavy replied.

Matt laid a twenty on the bar. "I'm sorry, but I'm going to have to take your dog home," said Matt.

"Anytime you want to leave him, I'm happy," replied Chavy. "You, I'm not so sure about!"

"Te veré mañana para un café mi amigo," Matt said.

Chavy smiled. "Your Spanish is getting better, amigo," Chavy replied, "and I'll see you tomorrow for coffee, too, cabrón."

Matt smiled back at Chavy. "I know swear words, too, Chavy!" He turned to Jake and quietly said, "Jake, let's go," and in an instant Jake was on the other side of the bar at Matt's side, ready for his next adventure.

Matt's drive north toward home on NM State Route Four was replete with the mesmerizing majesty of the mountains of Northern New Mexico. Each turn produced another striking location, which also usually resulted in a memory from Matt's youth coupled with memories of enjoying the mountains on vacations with Randy. The first spot they passed was an area popular among tourists called Soda Dam. This unusual geologic feature, which was a hot springs deposit that was at least 7.000 years old, was jammed with tourists this time of year. The dam was primarily composed of calcium carbonate and travertine, extended over 300 feet in length across the Jemez River Valley, and was over 50 feet high. Where the river flowed through the dam, it created a unique natural soda bridge over the stream and a scenic waterfall. Matt remembered the hours he spent climbing on the dam and soaking in the water at the bottom when he was much younger.

After passing other familiar youthful hangouts, including Battleship Rock, San Diego Canyon Overlook and La Cueva, Matt reached home, built a fire in his river rock fireplace, and poured himself a nightcap. Jake settled on his rug in front of the fireplace, his backside pointed so close to the fire that Matt worried it would burn. It was relaxing in his home, and many times he wondered why he had disrupted the harmony he felt there by going back to work. Upon reflection, he knew the answer. He enjoyed law enforcement. He was still relatively young at 46, and as much as he loved his ranch, it would have eventually become dull for him. He had been active since he left home for the navy at eighteen, and he had a long way to go until he was ready to quit.

Apart from the excitement today, Matt was completely on edge about Randy invading his thoughts. Her voice seemed so real, yet he knew it must be some kind of PTSD or, perhaps, a brain tumor, or even mental illness. At best it was unsettling, and at worst, he feared he was falling apart. Yet he couldn't shake the feeling that she was actually there, somehow, in some unexplainable way.

Sinclair and Naomi were busy pouring tequila down Jason in a vain attempt to make him manageable. After a half a bottle of Komos Añejo Cristalino at ninety bucks a pop, Sinclair was wishing he had purchased a bottle of Cuervo. *Cheap* Cuervo. Although Jason was excessively inebriated, Sinclair had to admit to himself, he too, was feeling no pain. It amazed him that Naomi, even though she had out drunk them two to one, seemed as sober as a judge. When Jason finally emitted a complete sentence in which no words made sense, he turned to Naomi and said, "I think, maybe, we need to get this guy to bed."

"Yeah, before he hurls all over us," Naomi replied.

The two helped Jason to the car and drove back to Mineral Springs Lodge, Jason singing his own personal and irritating version of "Blue Eyes Crying in the Rain" repeatedly. When they arrived back at the Lodge, Jason stopped and said, "Wayyyyt a minute. Y-You promise me a soak in the springs anIwanna go."

"OK, Jason, that's fine," said Sinclair. "But we don't have swimming suits."

"Thaas OK," replied Jason. "I can go commmmando."

"No," said Sinclair. "I need to be sure I'm welcome back here, and you are not showing your nards to any of the tourists. At least wear your skivvies."

With some effort, the two successfully deposited Jason in the springs. Sinclair laid back, enjoying the hot temperatures and looking at an almost full moon in the sky. Naomi, for some unexplainable reason, had brought a bathing suit. She was comfortably soaking next to Jason. “I’m heading to bed, you two,” Sinclair said. "We’ve got to get an early start back up to Astialakwa." As Sinclair was getting out, Naomi’s cell phone rang. She extracted herself from the springs, and took the call as she was walking away from Jason.

With Sinclair and Naomi gone, Jason was by himself in the springs. Some moment of cogency made him realize it was time to get out, even though it felt so good. After all the tragic happenings of the day, he was exhausted, drunk, and ready for bed. But for the moment, it seemed like too much work, as he drifted in relaxed bliss.

With little notice from Jason, two hands touched his shoulders from behind. Jason was close to falling asleep and his self-protection reflexes were completely unavailable. The two hands firmly gripped his shoulders and nuzzled his head under the water. His intoxication eliminated most of his natural struggle, as the last of the air in his lungs was consumed. Jason’s last thought was a vision in his mind of a black piece of obsidian, shaped like a human heart.

6

The Paradox of Coincidence

Coincidence is the word we use when we can't see the levers and pulleys.
(Emma Bull)

It was 6 am, and Matt had been up for an hour. June meant early sunshine, and he enjoyed doing his morning chores while the sun was gradually bringing the night into day. He had fed the horses, made sure the chickens had water, was finishing his morning coffee, and packing his knapsack for the hike to Astialakwa. Matt was looking out his front window, as was his habit at this time of day. Once again, the old woman was by the side of the road, pointing up to the ridge behind his house. This was the fifth time the woman had appeared by the highway. She was not there every day, but her appearances were becoming a semi-regular occurrence. He had tried to walk down to the road twice, but she was gone by the time he reached the highway, with the sight of the woman replaced by a golden eagle flying up the mountain behind his lodge. *I can't believe I'm starting to get used to seeing this,* he thought, when the phone rang. It was the SCSO night sergeant. "Looks like someone might have drowned in the Springs at Mineral Springs Lodge last night. An ambulance has been dispatched. We need you to get down there as soon as possible," said the sergeant.

"I'm on my way," said Matt. He buckled his duty belt and retrieved his sidearm from the nightstand safe. "Come on, Jake," Matt said. "I guess your morning cookie biscuit will have to wait."

Matt opened the door to the passenger side of the Jimmy and Jake jumped in. Matt walked around the truck to the driver's side, started the truck, and raced toward the Mineral Springs Lodge. Matt's ranch was about fourteen miles from Jemez Springs. If the highway had been straight, the drive without lights and sirens would have been fifteen minutes, maximum. But State Route Four was anything but straight on the way to Jemez Springs. Negotiating the hairpin curves as quickly as he could, Matt made it to the lodge in twelve minutes. Matt thought back to his interview for the deputy job with his navy buddy, Hector Vigil. Although a job offer was pretty much a foregone conclusion, as a governmental bureaucracy, the Sandoval County Sheriff's Office was subject to certain procedures, including an interview with the sheriff. Hector asked Matt why he wanted to be a deputy sheriff. Realizing saying he didn't really want the job would have been inappropriate, Matt responded with a slightly less inappropriate answer, saying, "Because I like to drive fast." The statement was accurate, anyway. His trip from home to Jemez Springs was now a new, personal speed record for him, but the celebration would have to wait. He pulled into the parking lot and saw the ambulance had already arrived. Maggie came scuttling out of the lodge and met Matt as he opened the door to his truck. "What's up, Maggie?" Matt inquired.

"Oh dear, oh dear," Maggie said repeatedly. "The young man Sinclair brought with him last night drowned in the springs! Come this way, Matt. Hurry!"

Matt wondered why there was a necessity to hurry if the kid had indeed drowned, but he humored an obviously shaken Maggie Gimple and jogged with her to the spring. By the time he reached the spring, the EMTs had already pulled the kid out of the spring and one of the EMTs had a stethoscope on his chest. Matt kneeled to see a body that had no potential for life. His skin was shriveled and pasty white. The young man looked to Matt like a boiled chicken. The EMT turned to Matt, looking a bit embarrassed he had even listened to his stethoscope. "He must have been in there all night," said the EMT.

"Wow, I'd say. I've seen a lot of things in my life, but never I've seen a poached human being before."

The EMT let him know that they had already called for the Sandoval County Medical Examiner. The M.E. was a contractor to Sandoval County and was based in Albuquerque, which meant it would be an hour or more before anyone from the office would arrive. "Can we get a blanket or something to cover the kid?" Matt said. He saw the professor and the lady from their group come out of their cabin, heading toward him, a look of horror on the professor's face.

"You're not going to leave him there, are you?" Maggie said, sounding panicked. "Bodies are not good for business!" Maggie Gimple had owned the Mineral Springs Lodge for fifteen years. She had, as so many people before her, visited the Jemez Mountains on vacation and fell deeply in love with the picturesque locale and the charm of the small village. When she discovered the lodge was for sale, she signed papers on the spot, gave up her career as a body paint artist in Huntington Beach, California, and adopted the life of an innkeeper. Maggie was from Scottish roots, barely stood five feet tall, and looked like she had just arrived the day before from the Scottish Highlands of the 1600's. Although her business management skills were a bit wanting, she made up for the deficit with a dogged determination and an enormous supply of Scottish frugality.

"Just give me a bit of time, Maggie. I want to inspect the scene as thoroughly as I am able, then I'll call into the office and see what they want me to do. I promise we'll get him out of here as quickly as we can."

As Sinclair and the young woman approached, the professor began squealing, "What's happened? What's going on? Oh, my God, it's Justin!"

Naomi looked at Sinclair with disdain. "It's Jason, you nimrod."

Naomi, overshadowing Sinclair, thrust herself full throttle into an emotional public spectacle, sobbing and crying, blubbering and bawling, saying, "My Jason. You lovely, lovely young man." The performance caught Sinclair off-guard as he watched Naomi as though he had never seen her before. He had certainly never seen her display any emotion other than irritation, and he was pretty sure she thought Jason was a wormy little creep.

"I'll talk to you two in a minute. I'll be right back," Matt told Sinclair and Naomi. A group of people was already gathering, so Matt went to the Jimmy and grabbed a camera and some yellow crime scene tape. He cordoned off the area, asking people to give him space, and quickly surveyed the scene. There were no visible contusions on the body and no blood was visible. He could see no signs of a struggle. He took several photographs of the body and the area they found the kid. About that time, Kai and Paul pulled up in their truck.

"We were waiting for you at La Casitas, but we heard the chatter on the radio. I assumed you'd be here. Can we help?" Paul asked.

"That would be nice," Matt said. "I've got to make a quick call to the office and see what they want me to do."

Paul and Kai kept people away from the body while the professor continued his blabbering at the two LEOs. Matt went into the lodge's office and called his office in Bernalillo. By that time, Lieutenant Villanueva was in the office, and the desk sergeant passed Matt's call to him. Matt explained the situation and what he had done to this point. "Should we wait for you to send out a detective, Lieutenant?" Matt asked.

"It'll be afternoon before I can break anyone loose, unless you think we've got a murder on our hands," Lacho replied.

"This is getting out of hand, Lieutenant," Matt said, irritated that SCSO neglected his patrol area. "We have some evidence that this group was in the Jemez to steal artifacts, one of the students died on the mesa and now another student has died. If anything deserves a detective, I think this qualifies."

"I'll be the judge of what qualifies for a detective, deputy, and you are out of order with your tone of voice," Lacho growled. "Besides, you have more investigative experience than any of our detectives, should you choose to employ it. I expect you can at least do the preliminary detective work. It should be a cakewalk for someone with your qualifications."

Matt got the message and was not going to challenge his superior, even if he was berating him. "I haven't talked to his friends yet, but it's not looking like there was any kind of struggle. I saw them drinking pretty heavily at Las Águilas last evening, and I'm guessing the kid may have passed out in the springs. Let me wait for the M.E. to arrive, and I can interview his friends. If I dig up any evidence that suggests foul play, I'll call you back and you can advise me on how you want to proceed."

"Sounds bueno to me, deputy," the lieutenant replied. "It would be a bitch to break a detective out of here today."

Matt went back to Kai and Paul. "It would be great if you guys could stick around, at least until the M.E. arrives. I need to talk to the professor and his companion. I'd love it if you'd have a look at the body and the scene and let me know your opinion."

"Estariamos felices de ayudar," Paul replied. While Matt's Spanish had improved since he arrived in the Jemez, it was much more rudimentary than his colleagues believed. He was pretty sure Paul said he'd be happy to help, but he wasn't admitting to ignorance until he had to. Although Matt had taken Spanish in high school, the years had stolen all but about ten nouns and five verbs, not including swear words. He had been studying Spanish almost constantly since he took the new job with SCSO. A large percentage of the local population spoke Spanish, but they were almost always bilingual. Matt felt that if he could at least have a working knowledge of the language, it would help him connect with the people he served.

Matt's conversation with the professor yielded little more than he thought it would. "We drank too much last night, that I'll admit," said the professor.

"I'd say," Naomi chimed in. "A couple of fucking drunks."

Matt noted he hadn't heard a person use the "f" word with such a frequency since he was in the navy, and especially not from a woman. He recalled the day before, her potty mouth was the most distinctive characteristic he had noted, other than her surgically enhanced mammaries.

The professor explained to Matt that they had come back to put Jason to bed. Jason, instead of going to bed, had insisted on soaking in the springs. The professor had soaked for a few minutes, then had gone back to their cabin, leaving Naomi and Jason. Matt looked at Naomi and said, "Perhaps you can pick it up from there, miss-"

"Canneloy. Naomi Canneloy, but please, deputy, call me Naomi," Naomi interrupted.

"OK, Naomi, the professor went to bed and left you two there. And?"

"Um, a few minutes later, I got a call. I have to admit I forgot about the little shi—um student, after the call, so I walked around the grounds for a bit and just went to bed. My bad."

"That's it? 'My bad?' That kid is dead."

"Yeah, well, I feel badly and all, deputy, but I didn't really know him that well, and if he didn't want to die, he shouldn't have gotten drunk and gone in the springs. Whatever happened to personal responsibility? Duh."

"Yesterday," Matt said, "I was just hanging out with the Forest Service Law enforcement officers, so I didn't get any personal information. I'm going to need your full names and contact information, and I don't know if you were planning on heading home today, but I'll ask you to wait until the Medical Examiner has a chance to look at the body."

Matt went back over to Paul and Kai, and they suggested it looked to them as though he had simply passed out in the springs. Paul looked down at the corpse of the student. "Half a bottle of tequila and 104-degree water is a poor combination. You have any idea how many people die in their hot tubs each year?" Matt shrugged. "Me either, but I'm sure it's a lot."

Paul and Kai decided they would not be much more help. "We're going to head out to Las Casitas without you, Matt," Kai said. "We need to have time to get up to Astialakwa before it gets dark." Matt thanked them for their help and wished them luck in their search.

Two hours later, the M.E. arrived in a large van. He performed a quick examination, pronounced Jason officially dead, and put him in a body bag. "We'll do an autopsy, probably tomorrow, and I'll let your office know the results," he said, with no more comment.

"Any more observations, doctor?" Matt said, trying to garner some sort of statement.

"Nope. Even though I'm not a coroner, it's pretty evident that we have a cooked dead kid. Interesting."

Matt finished surveying the scene and walked to Sinclair's cabin and knocked on the door. The professor opened it, still retaining the look of horror on his face. "I think we have as much as we can get for the moment," Matt told them. "They've taken Jason to the M.E./Coroner's office, and they'll be doing an autopsy tomorrow or the next day," Matt said. "I've got your contact information. If we need any more information, someone from my office will be in touch."

Sinclair and Naomi went back to their cabin. "Oh, my God," Sinclair said. "I've lost two of my students in two days on my field trip. This is a complete nightmare! I never should have brought them along. Now their families will probably sue UNM and me. Do you have any idea what kind of explaining I'm going to have to do?"

"Yeah," Naomi replied, matter-of-factly, "It might not go too well for you. Fucking Karma. Seems to me there's a little Darwin in action here. Look Sinclair, at least the good side is that we don't have to split the sale of *our* Black Heart with those two dweebs."

"That's completely out of line, Naomi. Don't you have any compassion? You're really showing some empathy, Naomi. Wow."

"Hey Professor 'High and Mighty,' it's just a coincidence. These things happen, and they are explainable. I'm just glad I'm not the one who is going to be doing the explaining!"

As the door shut, Sinclair looked at Naomi. "I'm going to need your help explaining to my department head what happened," he said.

"And what's in it for me?" Naomi replied.

This girl is a bastion of sensitivity, thought Sinclair, not recognizing a similar trait in himself.

"I'll make sure you get that teaching fellowship immediately, and I'll get at least a couple of my colleagues to write *glowing* letters of recommendation for your PhD program. A couple of them owe me some favors."

"And you'll guarantee that I'm 4.0 in all my classes with you, too, right?" Naomi added.

"Um, sure. No problem. Our dilemma right now is that there's a backpack up there on the mesa somewhere, and we have got to snag it before anybody else does. I'm not sure how we go about doing that. Those two rangers said they were headed to Astialakwa. That means we can't go today. We'll have to spend another night here and head out tomorrow."

"Fucking wonderful," Naomi replied.

7

TIME FOR A FUNK (OR TWO)

If there were no bad people, there would be no good lawyers.
(Charles Dickens)

It was nearly noon by the time Matt wrapped things up at the Mineral Springs Lodge. He drove up to the Jemez Ranger Station as he could use their phone to call into the office without the hassle of sketchy cell phone service issues, and they were always happy to loan him an empty desk. It surprised him to walk in and find Paul and Kai there. "I thought you were going to head up to Astialakwa to have a look," Matt said. "

"Our day is not always our own," Paul replied, looking to the back office. Matt took a peek to see a man in a suit talking on the phone. "A Special Agent from Albuquerque," Paul said, almost whispering.

"For a fall off of a mesa?" Matt inquired.

"No, nothing like that. He checks in every three or four months just to be sure we're not selling fry bread from our trucks and taking three-hour siestas. We'll have to put off our trip until tomorrow, which leaves an open seat if you are still interested."

"Of course I am, Paul," Matt replied. "I've got a strong feeling that the deaths are related, and I want to see Astialakwa for myself."

The US Forest Service had a well-designed and functioning law enforcement component. The Forest Service was a part of the US Department of Agriculture, and was separate from the Department of the Interior, which managed the National Park Service, Fish and Wildlife Management, and the Bureau of Land Management. Since the National Park Service took over the operations at the Valles Caldera National Preserve, there had been nothing but conflict between the two agencies. USFS Law Enforcement and National Park Service Law Enforcement did not play well together, and there was an ongoing battle of jurisdiction of many of the areas in the Jemez Mountains.

"He's here this time because he got a call from the LEO with the Valles Caldera Preserve saying that we were overstepping our jurisdiction. Now it's a giant clusterfuck of bureaucrats sorting things out. What they don't realize is that *they* are the newcomers, here. We've been patrolling areas that, until two years ago, were our jurisdiction. I don't really care what they work out. I'm just tired of the infighting. Enough of that," Paul said. "You up for hiking with us tomorrow?"

"Your special agent won't be going along?" Matt replied.

"Look at him, Matt. The guy is wearing a wool suit and wingtips. He's going to have to spend an hour shining his shoes just from walking from his car to our office!"

"As long as I don't create a jurisdictional nightmare for you," Matt replied. "Oh, and I have got to bring in the Funks before I do anything else."

"Well, good luck on that," said Paul. "I'd help you out, but, you know, Big Brother in wingtips is watching!"

Matt made his calls to the office, letting them know he would fax his report that evening, and assuring the lieutenant that he was on his way to capture the desperado Funk Brothers. When he finished, Matt walked out to the truck. Kai and Paul were throwing a frisbee for Jake, who was entertaining them with behind the back catches, whirling catches, and even his specialty move, the backflip catch. "You should put him in a competition, Matt," said Kai.

"What, and take all the fun away from you guys?" he replied, smiling. He called Jake, jumped in the truck, and rolled the window down. "Hopefully this won't take too long," said Matt. "I know they are going to want me to transport to Bernalillo, and that's an hour each way. Looks like microwave burritos for me tonight."

"Go get the bad guys, deputy," Paul said, "And if you need to hold them for a few hours here, we've got two empty cells."

Matt and Jake headed back on Highway Four, past Soda Dam. About a mile further on, he turned east on a dirt road, shifting into four-wheel drive and headed up the road toward where the

Funks hung their hats, a glaring euphemism for what they were actually doing: squatting on someone else's property. When the road turned into a path, he pulled next to a beat-up pickup truck that, to the casual observer, looked abandoned. He knew from experience it belonged to the Funk brothers, as he had pulled them over more than once while they were driving it. He parked the Jimmy and he and Jake got out, Matt grabbing a small pack, and started walking on the path. It was a fairly rugged trail which dissuaded hikers and law enforcement from venturing too close to the Funk's cabin. Matt had made at least five visits to the Funk brothers in the past year, so he knew the trail pretty well.

About a half mile up the trail, the trees cleared a bit as he walked past dozens of marijuana plants. The Funks had placed a makeshift trip wire fashioned from fishing line across the path and had attached glass bottles and pieces of metal as an intruder early warning system. Matt bent underneath the wire without causing a sound and continued to walk toward the Funks' cabin. To describe the Funks' abode as a *cabin*, was much like calling a prison cell a mansion. The main "quarters" was an ancient camper with a blue tarp covering what remained of the roof. Over time, the Funks had remodeled their cabin, building several rooms onto it from scrap wood, corrugated metal, and from the looks of things, stolen bricks. The landscaping was primarily old beer cans, bottles, and an assortment of rusting metal.

As Matt approached, he could see both Dory and Chuchu Funk lying on pink cushioned outdoor chaise lounges. Matt had a list of items stolen in the latest cabin heist, and he remembered seeing the lounges on that list. The two were engaged in a discussion on who was hotter, Shania Twain or Britney Spears. The debate continued as they passed a doobie between themselves. Each brother held a quart sized A-1 beer in his hand. Chuchu, the younger of the two, was wearing a worn-out ball cap backwards with the Chevron Oil logo on it, pink heart-shaped sunglasses and a pink feather boa. Chuchu was far from what anyone, other than himself, would consider "hot." He was tall and skinny with a blotchy, reddened face and a long, thin and pointed nose. His lips were so thin that his mouth appeared to be a slit below his nose. Under the boa, he was wearing what Matt imagined had once been a white t-shirt, grimy blue jeans, and pink flip-flops. Dory, the older of the two brothers, was shirtless, allowing his hefty belly to lap over once gray sweatpants, which may have been washed at some point long ago, but for which there was no visible proof. Dory's features and physique were a contrast to his brother. He was a big man carrying at least fifty pounds more weight than Chuchu. Dory was bald on the top of his head with a ring of hair just above his ears, grown long into a bizarre mullet, but what he lacked on top of his head was present in great abundance on the rest of his body. He had a beard that he had not trimmed since perhaps the 1960's, and thick black fur on his shoulders and chest. Complimenting his ape-ish exterior, Dory sported a tattoo on his corpulent belly that read, "Never don't give up."

"Afternoon, boys," Matt said, walking up to them, completely surprising the two.

"Whoa, deputy, you have some super ninja skills, dude," said Chuchu.

Dory quickly stashed the doobie they were smoking in his mouth, lit, immediately spitting it out with a whimper. "Ouch. Shit!" Dory said, taking a swig of his A-1 in a careless attempt to put out the fire in his mouth.

"Seriously, man," Chuchu said. "We got all kinds of alarm systems, and you, like, floated in like a superspy, man."

"By the way, dude, we don't know anything about those pot plants you passed by," said Dory. "I think some hippies planted them or something. We were going to report them to, um, somebody, man."

"I'm not here about the pot plants *this* time," said Matt. "I'm here more about cabin break-ins that have the Funk Brothers' M.O. stamped all over them."

"We don't know what you're talking about, dude deputy," said Dory. "Like my great Uncle Dory, the world-famous professional wrestler used to say—um, Chuchu, what did Uncle Dory used to say?"

Dory smiled, a look of fond remembrance on his face, "'I don't know what the *funk* you're talking about, man,'" replied Chuchu, laughing at his only and highly overused joke.

Uncle Dory, to whom the younger Dory referred, had been a professional wrestler who gained fame in the 1960's and retired from professional wrestling to start a wrestling academy in Humptulips, Washington, maladroitly called "The Funking Conservatory." Dory and Chuchu never failed to bring up their "famous" relatives, Dory and Terry Funk, whom Matt was certain would disown Dory and Chuchu if they even knew they existed. Matt had been regaled over the last year about the famous Funks from the infamous Funks, usually handcuffed and in the back seat of his Jimmy, who had plentiful stories of the exploits of the wrestlers the two considered to be gods.

"What's on today's agenda, gentlemen, is a discussion with you about the burglaries of a number of weekend cabins up here over the last few weeks." Matt pulled out his notebook and opened it to a list of stolen items. "We can start with the pink lawn chairs you're sitting in, the pink boa and sunglasses that look so glamorous on you, Chuchu, the mountain bike parked next to your home and the TV set I can see through that sort-of window part of your cabin." Matt stopped taking a second look at their cabin. "Do you guys even have electricity?"

"No, man," said Dory. "We were gonna sell that TV, dude."

"Shut up, man," said Chuchu. "I don't want to go to jail tonight, Dory."

"Well, too late, guys," said Matt. "I need you to stand and put your hands in the air," he said. Simultaneously and with surprising hustle, Chuchu started running at Matt, full speed, as Dory took off the opposite direction toward the woods. Matt yelled to Jake, "Jake, cow!" and Jake took off after Dory. As Chuchu approached,

Matt stepped to the side, stuck his leg out, and Chuchu face-planted beside Matt, who cuffed him while he was still conveniently on the ground. Jake took a leap for Dory's butt and latched on, bringing Dory face-first to the ground, also.

"Not fair, man!" shouted Dory. That dog doesn't look like a police dog. You faked me out, dude! That's like, unconstitutional, man."

"He's *not* a police dog," Matt replied as he was placing the handcuffs on Dory. "He's just a very undiscriminating cattle dog. Whatever I suggest to him is a cow is fair game to Jake. You're lucky I didn't say 'squirrel!'"

"Well, it still not fair, man. If you're going to have a police dog, it needs to be a German Shepherd or one of those Rotweaners, or whatever you call them."

Matt walked the handcuffed Funk Brothers down the path to the Jimmy, putting them in the back, with Jake between them. "Jake, keep an eye on those two," Matt said. Jake replied with a low growl and an impressive showing of teeth.

Once they got to Jemez Springs Matt once again had cell service. The dispatcher directed him to bring the prisoners to Sandoval County Detention Center. Matt sighed at the thought of an hour drive to Bernalillo, then an hour back. "We're headed to Bernalillo, guys," Matt said.

"Shit," Chuchu explained. "Why don't we get to go to municipal court like usual?"

"Because this isn't Tuesday, when the magistrate is here, and you have graduated to a felony this time, guys. No nice Municipal Court Judge to take pity on you and let you go home."

"That sucks, man," said Dory. "We had a party planned with the beer we stole."

"I advise you dorks to exercise your right to remain silent," Matt said, shaking his head.

By the time Matt finished transferring his prisoners and completing the mountain of booking paperwork, it was after 6 pm. He headed home, stopping first at the Sanchez Taco Truck at the Chevron on US 550. Matt had a passion for Sanchez tacos, and it was his one consolation in having to drive to Bernalillo.

By the time Matt finished his tacos, the Funk brothers had been arraigned, and with the help of a public defender and an overcrowded jail, were released on their own recognizance, had stolen a motorcycle in downtown Bernalillo, and were driving home on their new motorcycle. They would arrive a half hour before Matt walked into his own home.

8

Serendipity

I think we consider too much the good luck of the early bird and not enough the bad luck of the early worm.
(Franklin D. Roosevelt)

Matt was standing by the front window of his house, as he had become accustomed over the last few weeks, waiting to see the old woman by the highway. As she once again appeared, wearing a striking turquoise necklace, a long blue linen skirt, a white buttoned blouse, and a crown made of fir fronds, Matt said out loud, “What do you want, woman?”

“She wants you to take some action above your place on the side of the hill,” Randy said.

“Two ghosts in one morning are too much for anyone, Randy,” Matt replied.

“There is such a thing as good ghosts,” Randy said. “And besides, I’m *not* a ghost. At least I don’t think so. I just feel a strong connection to this woman, Matt. It’s important.”

"Then what are you?" Matt said, turning to face the voice, hoping to see her behind him in the flesh. He could see nobody.

"Well, I'm not quite sure. Let's just say I'm Randy until we figure this out."

Matt smiled. "OK, Randy, we'll go with that until I can get in to see a psychiatrist and get myself medicated."

"By the way, I haven't said it to you, but I love your place," Randy said.

"I consider it our place, Randy. There will never be another woman for me. Ever."

Matt called his office and explained to Lieutenant Villanueva his success in bringing in the notorious Funk Brothers the day before. Villanueva replied by letting Matt know the judge had released the two criminals on their own recognizance pending trial. "Great," said Matt, "another wasted day."

"Not really," said Lacho. "Next time, you can arrest them for failing to appear at trial, which you know is coming, right?"

Matt explained to Lacho he would like to accompany the LEO's this day up to Astialakwa. "There's just something that doesn't work for me with this scenario," Matt reflected. "I know the autopsies have not come back yet, but the kid who drowned was up on the mesa earlier in the day along with the kid who died on the mesa. I'm not a believer in coincidences like this. I'd like to see the place for myself as my suspicion meter is off the charts in this matter."

"OK, but I think it will be a waste of time," replied the lieutenant.

"Unlike busting the Funk Brothers," said Matt, more than a little sarcastically.

Matt packed his hiking pack with lunch, water, and cookie biscuits for Jake. He always kept the pack ready, as he was off-road more often than not in this job. The pack was probably a little over-full, but he liked to keep extra ammo magazines, a compass, waterproof matches, a survival knife, emergency blanket and some high protein bars, just in case of unexpected delays in the mountains. One night without a fire, even in June, was uncomfortable, and unexpected things happened in the mountains. Matt called Jake, who was out on the property chasing chipmunks. Jake came running, ready for the day's adventure. Once Jake was in the Jimmy, they set off for La Casitas Fishing area.

Dory Funk was sitting in his new pink chaise lounge eating a bowl of Fruit Loops. He didn't have any milk, so he poured a part of his beer on them, took a taste, smiled, and dug in. Chuchu came out of the camper in his underwear, stretched, farted, and lit a cigarette. "Man, I'm bummed," Chuchu said to his brother.

"How frumm?" Dory asked, his mouth stuffed with Fruit Loops and beer.

"This cabin gig is getting old, dude. The cops are onto us. We need to find a new gig to make money."

"You don't mean, like getting jobs, do you, man?" Dory questioned, showing great anxiety.

"Oh, hell no, man. That's for losers. We're the Funks! I mean, like a new way to rip people off."

"Oh, good," replied Dory. "I was starting to get worried, man." Dory furrowed his brow as though he was actually pondering the issue. "We could make a still and sell moonshine," Dory suggested.

"Do you know how to make moonshine, dude? I definitely don't, man. Besides, that would be way too much work."

"We could sell our pot to tourists," Dory said, still attempting to be helpful.

Chuchu shook his head. "We've barely got enough pot for ourselves, man. But, dude, I think tourists might be our ticket, my brother. I've been thinking that we're getting pretty good at breaking and entering. It's just that the cabins don't usually provide much of the good stuff we can pawn. No jewelry, hardly ever a gun. Mostly coffee makers and TV sets.

"But I was thinking, Jemez Springs has lots of tourists who stay in the resorts and lodges. They bring their fancy jewelry, cameras and expensive hiking shit. That's all really easy to haul off and pawn, man. How about we try our luck at a resort or two, man?"

"Dude, you sure got the brains in the family, Chuchu!" Dory said. "Where should we start?"

"Let's start with the Mineral Springs Lodge," Chuchu suggested. "It's spread out, there's a bunch of separate cabins, and that Maggie Gimple has been on my ass since I was in third grade." Chuchu once again furrowed his brow. "I made it to third grade, didn't I?"

"You joker," Dory said, "Of course you did, man. You made it all the way to sixth grade before they permanently expelled you. And your idea is off the chain, dude! It is the ultimate coolness!"

"Yeah, I thought we could flip the script a little bit, dude," said Chuchu. "Hand me a *J* and let's blaze that shit before we go. With any luck, we'll be smoking some *kind bud* tonight. Maybe even blow a little *krell*." Chuchu had been a Mötley Crüe fan since he was a teenager and loved the word 'krell' from the movie *Heavy Metal*, which was slang for cocaine. Chuchu had never come close to being able to afford cocaine, but it didn't stop him from talking as though his kilo was arriving any minute.

Sinclair and Naomi locked the door of Kiva cabin, got in Sinclair's minivan and drove a couple of blocks north on State Route 4. They stopped at Las Águilas Bar for coffee and enjoyed some huevos rancheros. Sinclair rationalized they would need their energy for the hike they would be taking. When they finished their breakfast, they drove on to La Casitas Fishing area.

As they pulled into the parking lot, Sinclair shouted, "Shit!" At the far end of the parking lot sat a Forest Service LEO truck and a Sandoval County Sheriff's truck. "I thought they said they were going yesterday!" He slammed on the brakes, watching the trucks. It was apparent to Sinclair the cops had arrived earlier and were already on their way up to Astialakwa. Sinclair pulled into the parking lot, finding a space on the other side where they wouldn't be as noticeable if the cops returned. "Shit! Shit! Shit!" Sinclair said, while smacking his palm on the steering wheel. Naomi remained silent and calm.

Once Sinclair had calmed down a bit, Naomi said, "Look, Sinclair. They are up there now, and there's nothing we can do about it. We certainly can't follow them. Now just let someone with some brains work this out for you. We'll just pull out of the area and drive about a hundred feet down the road. We can park out of the way where nobody will notice us, then walk back up to the area. There are picnic tables on the other side where they won't see us, and we can just wait until they get back. If they don't have the backpack, we're fine. We'll just go have a look ourselves up on the mesa.

"But here's the reality, Sinclair. They trained those cops in fucking searching skills. If they don't find it, I doubt anyone will until long after anyone cares about fucking Danny. If they *do* find it, we'll just tell them that Danny must have gone back to Astialakwa to grab some artifacts without telling us, even though we both lectured him about leaving everything intact. We'll say he must have fallen when he was rushing to get back to us. Easy-peasy, Sinclair.

Cops are stupid and lazy, and they'll eat it up like chocolate, as long as we stick to the fucking story."

Sinclair took a deep breath and let the air out with a sigh. "Wow, you are incredibly underhanded, Naomi. I'm not sure what's gotten into you, but it's a little scary. Anyway, I guess at this point we really don't have another solution. I'm just going to hope that they don't find that backpack."

The Funk brothers finished their doobie and grabbed a couple of A-1's for the road. As they walked down their path, Chuchu ran into his own trip wire, setting off a cacophony of clattering bells, broken beer bottles crashing into one another and clanging metal pipes. "Man, you made the shit outta that alarm, dude!" Dory said, proud of his brother's impressive perimeter security skills and ignoring the fact that he had caught himself. The two reached the road, spent their customary ten minutes trying to get the pickup to start, hood up, Dory spraying starter fluid into the carburetor, which had no air cleaner on. The truck, giving in to the Funks' relentless efforts to start it, surrendered, and the excessively loud, muffler-less vehicle came to life. Dory slammed down the hood, jumped into the passenger seat, and off they went, two fatuous pirates bent on finding plunder in the form of expensive tourist possessions in Jemez Springs.

The two brothers drove into the village, passing the Mineral Springs Lodge and parking in front of a vacant store a few hundred feet further down the highway. As they started to walk toward the lodge, Dory said, "Wait, Chuchu. I gotta get my lock-picking tool." Dory went to the bed of the truck, grabbed a sledgehammer, and returned to Chuchu. "Ready to get our game on, dude?"

The Funks circled around to the back of Mineral Springs Lodge. Most of the guests were already gone for the day, out to hike at one of the many spots in the Jemez, picnic along the East Fork of the Jemez River, or to explore the Valles Caldera National Preserve. The two thieves peaked around the corner of the lodge to be sure there were no housekeepers or other staff present. Seeing none, they found the closest cabin to break into that would provide them with a quick getaway. They walked up to the front door of the cabin and knocked. Hearing no sound, Chuchu took his "lock picking tool" and slammed the sledgehammer into the doorknob. The force cracked the latch bolt as the door flew open, and the two walked in. Looking around, they could see there were not any valuable personal possessions in the cabin. Had they been a bit more observant, they would have realized the cabin had just been cleaned and was awaiting new guests for the evening. "Shit, I shoulda thought this through," said Dory. "The touristas are going to be taking their cameras and shit with them when they go out for the day. That's my bad, dude!"

"Hey, no worries, Dory, man, we'll figure this out. Let's try another cabin, just to be sure, dude." They shut the door as much as they were able, then moved to the cabin next to the one they had just broken into. Looking around the grounds, there were still no staff or guests to be seen. They walked onto the porch of the second cabin. Above the door was a sign saying "Kiva." Once again, they knocked and hearing no answer, Chuchu used his lock picking skills in the same manner as before. As they walked in, this cabin, too, at first blush, appeared to have a dearth of pawnable treasures. Then Chuchu spied three backpacks on the couch, which screamed *expensive and pawn-worthy camping gear.* Outside the door, they heard a housekeeper talking to someone. Chuchu grabbed a backpack and handed it to his brother, then lifted the other two. "Let's make like horse turds and hit the trail, man!" Chuchu said to his brother. As they walked out of the cabin, they could see the housekeeper, but, fortunately for them, her back was toward them. They slipped around the corner and ran for their truck, hoping for an enormous trove of pawnable booty.

9

A Return to Astialakwa

I'm a very firm believer in karma, and put it this way: There's a reason I get a lot of good parking spots.
(Al Jourgensen)

Paul, Kai, Matt and Jake reached the crossing of the Jemez River, less than a quarter mile from the parking area. Jake took the lead and enthusiastically dove into the river. With two hops, he was on the other side, shaking his body like an epileptic seal. As they crossed, Paul showed the others the way to the trail.

"Have you ever been up here before, Matt?" asked Paul.

"Not only have I not been up here before, but I had also never heard of Astialakwa before I took the job with the SCSO. You know I grew up in Los Alamos, not more than an hour from here. I spent the vast majority of my summer weekends camping all over the Jemez, fishing at Fenton Lake and San Antonio Creek, climbing the wall at Las Conchas, inner tubing in the winter at Sawyer's Hill, but I knew nothing about the amazing history of the area, and especially not the Jemez Pueblo. I had never met a Jemez Indian until I met you."

"Not the first time I've heard that, Matt. People don't realize that my people had nine pueblos in these mountains at one point or that we grazed horses in the Valles Caldera. They do not know that, unlike the plains Indians, we have never been 'relocated.' This has always been the land of the Jemez Indians, despite the machinations of the Navajo, Apache, Spanish, Mexicans, and the US Government. The government never took our Tanoan language away, so it is still the first language of our children, unlike so many tribes who were forced into an 'Indian School' to learn English. By the time our children are ten, they are usually tri-lingual: Tanoan, Spanish and English."

"Your ancestors. Were they the Anasazi?"

"Now that is genuinely funny, my friend. You probably do not know where that word came from."

"I thought it was a word from some ancient language."

"Sure it is. Our former enemies were the Navajos, before they settled down in pueblos and stopped raiding other tribes. The Navajos called the Pueblo People 'Anaazaja.' When anthropologists were studying the history of the first people in the area, they came across the word, and, not understanding it, turned it into 'Anasazi,' which they thought meant 'ancient ones.' It was actually a pejorative term, and most certainly didn't mean that."

"Wow. I had no idea," Matt said. "What do you think is the secret of your people flourishing so long, surviving the purge of the pueblo revolt and being a strong nation today?"

"It's tough to put into words, my friend," Paul said. "We have no word in our language that translates into the word 'religion.' Although we accommodated the Spanish and became Catholics, I would say that we still keep our original view of the world. Unlike traditional western religions, we are concerned with the continuity of a harmonious relationship with the world in which we live. Our spirituality is twenty-four hours a day, seven days a week, 365 days a year. If there's a secret to our existence, it is that we came face-to-face with nature, but did not exploit her."

"One more question, Paul, I promise," Matt said. "Why don't you allow non-tribal members into your pueblo, and why don't you allow photographs of your ceremonies?"

"Good question, and I know a frustrating one, sometimes even for ourselves. If we were like the Taos Indians, we could have a thriving tourist industry in our pueblo, inviting tourists in to spend their money and watch scheduled dances each day. The reason we have chosen to be private about our lives goes back to the pueblo revolt in 1692. We took our spiritual lives underground because of the harassment of the Spaniards. We have public dances that people can come to on certain days, of course, but our sacred dances and the unique ceremonies of Jemez Pueblo are ours, and we guard them and our people from outsiders so we will never lose them. In fact, we never ever reveal to the public who our tribal spiritual leaders, what you might call 'medicine men' are. It may not look like it, but we have already lost so much. Look at where we are going today. We'll pass through the ruins of Patokwa, then on to Astialakwa. Neither are on pueblo land. The Forest Service administers dozens of our people's shrines, and we have to have permission to visit them for sacred ceremonies. Several are on private property, and some the landowners refuse to allow us to visit. We aren't even sure where all the sacred sites are, as their locations were passed down by word of mouth from each generation to the next."

Paul's explanation sparked Matt's imagination.

"Go ahead, Matt, ask him," Randy said. "He might be able to help."

Matt paused, thinking, *great, my schizophrenia is following me.* "Paul, I know I told you that was my last question, but I have one more, and it's kind of hard to ask."

"You can ask me anything, my friend. I might not answer, but you can ask."

"For the last several weeks, in the morning, and not every day, I see a woman, dressed in a long, blue linen skirt, a white shirt and a crown of fir fronds on her head. I know it sounds pretty crazy now that I say it out loud."

"What? Where, Matt?" Paul said with interest.

"She is down by the highway, turned toward my property, and she points at the hill behind my house. When I try to go down, she disappears. Coincidentally, an eagle has been flying over at the same time she disappears. I don't know what she's pointing at, but she seems to implore me to do something."

"Wow, Matt. That isn't crazy at all. In fact, you may be a witness to something very special. I think I might know what and whom she is, but before I say anything, let me speak with some of our pueblo's spiritual people. They may be able to confirm it."

"OK, so I'm not crazy?" Matt inquired.

"Definitely not. Not even close. This could be very exciting, Matt. It's actually pretty incredible. I'm glad you told me. I have a feeling the elders will be keen to know about this."

Matt was enjoying the hike, and Jake was enjoying it even more. Jake would tear off in front of the three men, just out of sight, then race back to them, sometimes with the present of a horned toad or skink, delicately held between his teeth without harming the animal. Jake had no cattle to herd, so he continually attempted to herd the three men, barking at their heels, then running in front of them, looking back and running full speed up the trail.

"Jake is turning his hike into a twenty miler when I think it's less than a mile to the top of the mesa," Kai said. "He's going to be one tired pup!"

The mesa they were climbing was called Guadalupe Mesa. The mesas to the west of the Valles Caldera and to the east where Matt grew up were easily identifiable and unique monoliths rising out of the valley. The finger mesas had been formed into volcanic tuff, essentially fused volcanic ash, that erupted from the Valles Caldera about a million years ago. On the mesa top, the tuff formed colorful cliffs and created a rolling terrain. When Matt was young, he enjoyed climbing the faces of the mesas, which always possessed small caves and soft rock, and very often had footpaths that had been carved deeply into the tuff over many years of travel by ancient Puebloans.

Paul had a map with him marking the spot they believed Danny had gone over the edge. As they came closer to it, they stopped, all three men looking down, imagining the terror of falling off the edge of the mesa. It wasn't a sharp precipice, so Matt was trying to understand how he could have fallen so far. It was steep, however, and if he had tripped or slipped, it is conceivable that the momentum would have carried him the entire way down to the valley below.

As the three men approached the general area where Danny went over the cliff, Matt noticed a spot on the trail that was scuffed by the soles of boots and shoes. "I think this is where he went over," Matt said.

"Wow, Matt, I didn't know you had American Indian blood in you," Paul said, impressed. "I sure wouldn't have seen it if you hadn't pointed it out to me."

"I'm Irish and Scandinavian, Paul. Frankly, I think the Vikings don't get nearly enough credit for their tracking skills," Matt replied with a smile.

"You should get a picture of this, Paul," Matt said. "It looks to me like two separate sets of shoes in this little entanglement. I don't have enough expertise to know if it means there was a scuffle or not, but it's worth adding to our investigation."

Paul took pictures, and they then continued up the trail. When they reached Astialakwa, they spotted what looked like tracks made from relatively fresh footprints. "I don't know anything about what to look for," Matt said, "but it sure seems like there are several shovel holes around here."

"The USFS trained Kai and me in this, Matt. One of our jobs is the investigation of artifact thieves. Are you aware of the Archeological Resources Protection Act of 1979?"

"Never heard of it," Matt replied.

"Over the years, thousands of truckloads of artifacts have been stolen from tribal lands across the country, including the remains of the ancestors. Many of these were 'appropriated' by 'legitimate' university archaeologists, taking them to study the history of ancient people on our continent, and then put on display in their museums. Much of it remained in those museums and their basements for many years. In 1979, the US Congress decided it didn't belong to them, and so they passed a law making it a crime to steal artifacts from places such as Astialakwa. You can do some serious prison time for that. Many tribes from all over the Americas have had to file lawsuits in an attempt to have their property and the bodies of their ancestors returned to where they belong."

"I had no idea," Matt said. "But it sounds like a reasonable law to me."

"Well, we as USFS Law Enforcement Officers, are all trained in spotting it and tracking down the criminals who steal artifacts and the precious remains of our ancestors. It still goes on today. Astialakwa is … was … pretty much untouched by thieves. But what we have here is an active artifact pilfering site. And it didn't happen long ago. What's truly sad is that our Pueblo and Harvard University were about to begin excavating and preserving this site in just a month. Who knows what these thieves got. It doesn't take a super investigator, however, to build a theory about this incursion. It's very suspicious that these holes are fresh, just at the time a UNM archaeologist happens to take students on a field trip here."

"Paul, I'm thinking about the backpacks I saw in the back of the professor's minivan. They looked to me to be too full for them to just be hiking day packs. I'm thinking we may have found the people who did this," said Matt.

"Thanks for bringing that up," Paul replied. "I think we have suspects."

The three walked around the footprint of Astialakwa, photographing areas that had been dug up or disrupted. As they reached the outmost perimeter of the ruins, there was a larger pile of rubble with squared-off blocks. Someone had shoveled the base of the rocks out a couple of feet down. Matt had no expertise in archaeology or artifact pilfering, but even he could see they had moved the blocks, a hole had been dug out, and there was an impression in the soft dirt where it appeared something had been removed. Paul was particularly interested in this spot and took multiple photographs. "I'm not absolutely sure of what this is," Paul said, "but it sure looks like the remnants of a shrine of some sort. Quite often, my ancestors buried valuable tokens in the shrines as offerings to the spirits. We will take this back to my pueblo's Department of Resource Protection and I'll get our district office involved in the forensics. They will know what it is, I'm sure."

Once Paul and Kai were satisfied they had seen everything they needed to, the three started heading back down the mesa, Jake leading the way. As they once again reached the spot Matt believed Danny had fallen, the three stopped. Matt leaned as far over the edge as he dared, looking for anything that might help them understand more about the death of the student. "Wait a minute. Paul, look down here. Do you see something?"

Paul leaned over the edge, while Matt pointed in toward a thistle bush growing out of a rock on the side of the mesa. "Yeah, I think so. Looks like it might be a black bag to me."

"Hang here, guys. It doesn't look like a tough climb down. I want to see what it is." Matt proceeded to find his way down the side of the mesa about a hundred feet or so. When he reached the spot, he yelled up, "It's a bag of some sort. I'll bring it back up." It took fifteen minutes for Matt to climb back to the top. When he did, he handed Paul a pack. "Your honors, ranger!" he said, proud of himself that at 46 he could make the climb without becoming too winded. "If I'm not mistaken, this pack is very similar to the bags I saw in the van."

Paul set the pack on the ground, and the three huddled around it. As Paul opened the rucksack, he gave a whistle. "¡Santa mierda!" Paul said, as he began pulling intact pots, metal spear heads, obsidian arrow heads, a metal breastplate and more out of the bag. "Well, I hate to possibly destroy any evidence, but we will have to carry this back to the truck and then we can get it to the forensic lab for analysis. But it seems our professor and his field trip group have a little *splainin'* to do."

"What's left of them," Matt added.

Jake was the first to come out of the river trail at La Casitas. Sinclair and Naomi were sitting at a table at the far side of the area, waiting for the three law enforcement agents to return. As soon as they saw Jake, Sinclair said, "They're coming!" and the two jogged back to the bushes behind the table. Jake saw the two and interpreted their actions as needing a bit of his herding skills, so he started running toward them, barking. "Oh shit, oh shit!" Sinclair said, whispering, "Stay! Sit! Scat!" to the dog, who was only encouraged by his flailing arms and erratic behavior.

Matt, Paul and Kai soon emerged from the brush, and Matt spied Jake running away from them, barking. "Not a good time for chipmunk hunting," Matt said, giving a whistle and shouting for Jake to come. Jake stopped, looking back at Matt, then looked back at the two people hiding in the bush as though to say, *don't you see those suspicious people?* When Matt didn't give in, Jake turned and ran back to the three.

"We'll get this to the lab ASAP, Matt, and I'll let you know what they find," Kai said.

"I'll be very curious, but my brain wants to jump to one conclusion. Because of the death of the kid in the springs, I think we are a little bit, how did you put it? Intertwined jurisdictionally?"

"Aren't we always?" Paul replied, smiling. "I'll let you know as soon as I know."

The three men parted company, Jake taking his wingman position in the front passenger seat next to Matt, still eyeing the bushes where he had seen the strange people.

Matt checked in with the office on his cell phone, which barely had enough bars to engage in a broken conversation with his patrol sergeant. The sergeant informed him that there had been a break-in at the Mineral Springs Lodge and requested Matt to proceed there immediately.

As the two trucks left the parking lot, Sinclair and Naomi came out from the bush. "We are truly fucked," Sinclair said, holding his head with his hands.

"Fucking professors," Naomi mumbled. "Sinclair, we are so far from fucked right now. Yes, they'll be coming around asking questions. But the answer is simple and explains two concerns at the same time. Danny must have intentionally lagged behind us to grab some artifacts without our knowledge, and he tripped as he was trying to re-join us, taking one giant leap for Dannykind."

"Alright, I think it might be plausible enough. Let's head back to Jemez Springs, pack up and get the hell out of here and back to Albuquerque. At least we can force the cops to come to *our* turf to ask more questions."

10

A Deep Funk

Desperation is like stealing from the Mafia: you stand a good chance of attracting the wrong attention.
(Douglas Horton)

As Matt pulled into the parking lot of the Mineral Springs Lodge, a virtually inconsolable Maggie Gimple met him at his truck. "Oh my God, Matt!" Maggie shouted as he was getting out of the Jimmy. "This never happens here. We've never had someone die on the property, and we've never had a break-in! What am I to do? That poor young man. He seemed so nice."

"Now, Maggie, calm down a bit, and explain to me what happened," Matt said, using his most mellow sounding Zen master-like voice.

"How can I calm down? This is terrible! This *never* happens in Jemez Springs. We have a quiet village here," Maggie continued unabated. Matt gave up, and simply followed Maggie as she waddled into the lodge and out the door to the plaza.

"They broke into two of my cabins. It looks like they smashed in the doors. That's going to cost a fortune to fix!"

Maggie showed Matt the first cabin. It looked to him as though someone had used a battering ram against the doorknob. "It was an unoccupied cabin?" Matt asked.

"Yes! Who would break into an empty room?" Maggie asked. "There's one more cabin that was broken into as well. The professor and his group occupy it. I don't know where they are, but they've been gone since early this morning."

They walked over to the professor's cabin and Matt walked in, looking around the rooms. There were toiletries on the bathroom counters, but the cabin did not appear to have been rifled-through.

At that moment, Sinclair and Naomi arrived. "What in the hell?" Sinclair shouted, scanning the area.

"I'm sorry, Sinclair, but somebody broke into your cabin," Maggie said.

Sinclair stared at Maggie, an incredulous look on his face, his lips moving, but no sound was being emitted.

Matt turned to Sinclair. "Professor, I need you to take a look around and see what they took."

Sinclair stepped into the cabin, searching the room with his eyes. He immediately looked at the couch where they had left the three backpacks. They were missing. Sinclair gave a small, involuntary yelp, turning to look at Naomi, an appearance of complete helplessness on his face. "Well, professor, what's missing?" Matt said.

Sinclair, unable to form a coherent word, looked pleadingly at Naomi, who took the challenge. "Well, deputy, we didn't bring much stuff. We had some water bottles and a hiking staff, but we really hadn't planned on staying over, so we don't have much. Do you have any idea who would do this?" Naomi gave Matt her most amatory look, batting her eyelashes.

Matt stared for a moment, bemused at Naomi's incongruous behavior. "It's a bit early to say who might have done this, Miss Canneloy."

Naomi smiled, tilting her head down, and raising her eyes to meet Matt's, doing her best impression of a seductress; a skill she had developed as a means to accomplish her ends. "Please, deputy, call me Naomi."

"Are you kidding me?" Randy's voice came from behind Matt. Although he was becoming less astonished when he heard Randy, it still startled Matt at audibly hearing her. "And I'm *not* jealous," Randy continued. "She's devious, Matt. Watch your back–and your watch."

"Well, I'll tell you who did it," Maggie chimed in. "Those malicious, nasty, wicked, mischievous pot smoking twits, the Funk brothers did this."

"I agree that it fits our local hoodlums, alright. But do you have any hard evidence it was them, Maggie?"

"Oh, come on, Deputy Bertram, who else would do it? They are the only low-life, brain-damaged, scumbag criminals we have around here. And besides, my head housekeeper, Romi Botello, said she saw their piece of crap pickup parked across the street this morning. I think that's enough to lock them up right there."

"Good to know, Maggie," Matt replied. "I'll definitely have a visit with them."

Maggie turned to the professor and Naomi. "I'm so sorry about this, Sinclair. If you would like to spend another night, it's on the house. My handyman is in Bernalillo right now, getting new doorknobs. The door should be all fixed up in a couple of hours."

Sinclair squeezed a semblance of a smile from his ashen face. "Thanks, Maggie. I think, given all that has happened, one more night here would be nice."

Matt and Maggie went back to the front desk to complete the paperwork, and Sinclair and Naomi went inside their cabin. "Another fucking night? I didn't plan to spend my entire fucking summer vacation in fucking Jemez Springs, and especially not fucking you, er, I mean fucking with you. Oh fuck, you know what I fucking mean!"

"Naomi, don't you see? We've *got* to get the backpacks back, and especially the Black Heart. I can't allow all that research and time spent finding the Black Heart to be wasted. We have no choice. It is riches or jail. And that means we have to find these, Frank brothers, as quickly as possible, and negotiate the return of our property."

"It's Funk, Sinclair. And, fuck," was Naomi's response.

Matt and Jake finished their paperwork with Maggie and climbed into the Jimmy. "I don't know about you, Jake, but I could use a drink."

"I could use one too, sailor," came Randy's voice from the back seat.

"Can ghosts be jealous?" Matt replied.

"Oh, don't bring that up, Bertram. That lady is up to no good, and if you don't recognize that, you aren't the investigator I thought you were. You've got a growing list of evidence that points toward those two raiding Astialakwa. To think for a minute that the deaths of the two boys is a coincidence is a mistake."

"Oh, I have her number, Randy," Matt replied. "I'm just not completely sure if they are up to something, or if she's just an abrasive, unpleasant person."

"You mean a bitch?" Randy replied.

"Randy, I think you *are* jealous!" Matt realized that he had completely adjusted to the fact that he was conversing with the disembodied voice of his partner. It was helping him to return to the world of the living himself.

11

Holy Fire Water

Religion is what keeps the poor from murdering the rich.
(Napoleon Bonaparte)

Jake perked up when Matt pulled his Jimmy into the parking space in front of Las Águilas. Matt changed from his deputy sheriff's shirt into a black t-shirt and put his duty belt in a locked box in the back of the truck. Matt had discovered that sitting at a bar in uniform not only made the patrons uneasy but also pressured him to have an iced tea instead of something a bit harder. Jake sat next to Matt waiting for his signal, which came as a quiet "OK." With permission, Jake jumped in the air, spun twice, and headed to the door of the bar. As a customer opened the door to leave, Jake pushed inside and ran behind the bar and into the open arms of Chavy. One man at the bar said, "Hey, what the hell is a dog doing in here?" just as Matt walked through the door.

Chavy stood up, Jake in his arms and said to the man, "This ain't no dog, man. He's the Jemez Springs K-9 patrol!"

"I never saw a cattle dog that was a police canine," the man said gruffly.

"Well, now you have. This is Jake. *Deputy* Jake, to you!"

Matt sat himself at the bar without commenting on the interaction. Without asking, Chavy poured Matt a drink from the special bottle of Jack Daniels Single Barrell Select he kept out of sight from the other patrons, and set it in front of him, then opened the bar refrigerator and pulled out a steak bone. He held it up to Matt with questioning eyes. Matt simply nodded. Chavy smiled and kneeled down in front of the dog, bursting with anticipation. "Jake, you feast tonight, amigo!" Chavy said, holding the bone out for Jake.

Jake stood in front of Chavy, looking at Matt for permission. Matt obligingly said Jake's favorite word: "OK." The feast was on.

An enormous man sitting next to Matt said, "That's quite a well-trained dog you've got there."

"You know," Matt replied, "I'm pretty sure he's the one who has trained me."

The man smiled. A side-effect of being in law enforcement is the nagging habit of constantly observing the surrounding people. Matt took a quick inventory of the man. He was tall, most likely in his sixties or early seventies, with broad shoulders and hands the size of baseball mitts. He had a kindly face, but his wrinkles and mottled nose informed Matt the man had spent a good deal of his life over-consuming alcohol.

Chavy walked up to Matt and the man, "Matt, I see you're talking to the father," he said. Matt looked at Chavy with a confused expression on his face. “Matt, meet Father Amos O’Sullivan, Las Águilas Bar’s resident priest.”

“Nice to meet you, Father,” Matt said, holding out his hand. “I’ve seen you in here before but haven’t ever had the opportunity to meet you. I’m not much of a church-going man. Are you the priest here at Our Lady of the Assumption?”

“I’m not much of a church-going man, either, deputy. I live at Saint Frumentius of Aksumite, down the road.”

“Oh, that’s the place where wayward priests go, right?”

“I think wayward is a bit kind. It’s been mostly us alcoholic priests since the 1940’s, and it was founded for good purposes. The ministry has helped a great number of priests over the years who might have otherwise been forced to leave their calling. In the early ‘90’s, however, the diocese started importing the pedophile priests the church needed to make disappear from public view, and the place went to heck in a handbasket. The ministry lost its insurance, and the church had to close it down. The diocese gave most of the property to the Sisters of Perpetual Indulgence—I’m kidding, that’s not their real name, it’s just what I call them, in jest, of course, and they left four of the ‘wayward’ to maintain the facilities.”

“So, you’re an alcoholic?” Matt asked.

“I’m a *recovering* alcoholic,” Father O’Sullivan responded.

“But you’re drinking,” Matt said.

“I’m recovering very slowly. And please don’t call me ‘Father.’ You can call me by my given name, Amos, or my nickname.”

"Which is, let me guess—Sully, right?"

"Coach."

Matt took a drink. "Well, Coach, you can call me Matt. I haven't had a nickname since I was in the navy, so no point in resurrecting one now. If you don't mind me asking, how did you get the nickname *Coach*?"

Amos grinned. "In my day, I was the coach of the men's shooting team at St. Rigobert College in Belfast, Maine."

"Colleges have shooting teams?" Matt asked, a bit astounded.

"It's a big thing in a large number of colleges. Depending on the college, they do skeet shooting, indoor range shooting, trap shooting, rifle and handguns. It's an official NCAA sport," replied Coach, "although it will probably never replace football."

"I had no idea," said Matt, "but this just brings up a whole bunch of questions. You don't have to answer if I'm getting too personal, but how does a Catholic Priest become coach of a shooting team at a presumably Catholic college that has a very improbable saint's name, and then end up in some sort of permanent alcohol rehab in the Jemez Mountains?"

"Just lucky, I guess," Coach said, smiling. "I tell you what, you buy the next round and I'll give you the Reader's Digest condensed version."

"Worth it," replied Matt, who motioned to Chavy, raising two fingers. "What are you drinking?"

"The only thing an Irish Catholic priest would drink, except for pilfered communion wine: Jameson." The priest knocked back the drink Chavy just handed to him. "That was on my friend, here," he said to Chavy. "Next round is on me."

"If you don't mind, I'll take a raincheck on another drink. It's not good for my career to drink and drive. But, please, go on. I can't wait to hear about your life."

"Keep in mind, this is the short version," Coach said, "I can give you details another time."

Amos took a sip of his whiskey and smiled. "I'll start with the stuff that's stereotypical. My family lived in the town of Donegal in the North of Ireland. My mother and father, as good Catholics, obeyed God's command to populate the earth, presenting the world with seven Sons and Daughters. My parents sent me to the US to live with my mother's sister when I was the age of thirteen. I had been 'selected' by my father and mother to be the priest of the family, as all good Irish Catholic families require at least one. The common theory is that it hedges your bets on making it to heaven. As a good and dutiful son who was dubiously called to the priesthood, I did my part and was preparing to please my parents and live that life. Unfortunately for my career, there was a little intervention, perhaps divine, perhaps not. The Vietnam war was re-shaping a lot of kids' plans for their lives, and mine was just one of them. A month after receiving my US citizenship, my new country drafted me into the Marine Corps. Seminary would have to wait for the government to be done with me, and my life took a slight departure from my family's plans. Once I was in the Corps, they recruited me to Force Reconnaissance, or FORECON. It's the special operations arm of the Marine Corps. The FORECON battalions had two kinds of missions, which we called 'Key Hole' and 'Sting Ray.' Key Hole was intelligence gathering mostly, and Sting Ray was 'Direct Action,' which you probably know better as 'Black Operations.' I had the chance to join a Sting Ray Battalion in Vietnam and picked up quite a few 'secular' skills along the way.

"When I finished my hitch, I headed back to seminary, along with my bag of PTSD and a bottle of Jameson's Irish Whiskey. I somehow managed to graduate, was ordained and assigned as a chaplain at, you guessed it, St. Rigobert College in Belfast, Maine. The college lost their shooting coach when he shot himself in the head, showing off his cowboy pistol-handling skills to his team. The team was obviously traumatized, so they brought me, the chaplain, in for counseling. When they found out I had some shooting skills myself, it was a foregone conclusion that I would assume the deceased coach's duties. Unfortunately, their new coach was a full-blown alcoholic, which doesn't mix well with guns.

"So here, Matt, is where I have to digress just a bit. You said that St. Rigobert was an unlikely name for a saint, right?"

"Yeah, I vaguely remember saying that," Matt confessed.

"Well, the namesake of the college, St. Rigobert's claim to fame was also interesting and unlikely. The story goes that he had been given a live goose to take home for his dinner. Rigobert gave the bird to a servant-boy to carry home with him. Along the way, as Rigobert was reciting the divine office, the bird broke free from the boy's arms and flew away. The boy was inconsolably despondent about losing the goose, but Rigobert comforted him, urging him to trust in God. It was at that point that the miracle happened. When Rigobert resumed his prayers, the goose flew back to them. Thereafter, Rigobert, who was the archbishop, decided not to have him for supper but kept the bird as a pet. The goose would walk with him to church where, as the tame bird patiently waited for him, he celebrated Mass, and when Rigobert was done, the bird would follow him home."

"So let me get this straight," said Matt, "And I don't want to sound like I'm making fun of your religion, but that was enough of a miracle make Rigobert a saint?"

Coach shrugged his shoulders, saying, "It would astound you the kinds of miracles that have gotten people into the Catholic hall of fame!" He continued, "Now, you might ask, how does that calculate into your story, Amos? Well, here's the thing. I, a man who was inebriated most of the day, every day, was assigned duty as a shooting coach. I'll bet you can't figure out what the mascot of St. Rigobert's College is."

"Tell me it's not a goose," Matt said.

"You guessed it. And it just so happens that I had been counseled several times about my alcohol use, and, most likely, the provost of the college was looking for a good reason to can me. Well, I gave it to him. We were at shooting practice. I was three sheets to the wind. The mascot, a goose named Portabella, was kept in a cage close to the football field. A mishap occurred and Portabella got out. Oh, I forgot to say that we were in the middle of skeet-shooting practice. Not knowing it was Portabella, I saw the goose fly over, and running with my good judgment tank practically empty, took the opportunity to hunt live game. I was a pretty excellent shot even when I was blitzed. Down came Portabella, and off I went to Saint Frumentius of Aksumite for alcohol treatment. That was twenty years ago. I stayed, and nobody made me leave. And I've had a nice twenty years of rehab, courtesy of the Roman Catholic Church."

"It doesn't look like it's working too well," Matt interjected.

"It's working splendidly, I'd say. I'm caretaking church property, and nobody gives a damn what I do in my leisure time, or any other time, for that matter."

"That's quite a story, Coach," Matt said. He paused, trying to decide if he should bring up his own current situation. With a couple of drinks down, he set his better judgment aside and took a risk. "You said you did counseling?"

"That's a large part of a priest's duties, so, yes, I did quite a lot of it. Is there something you need that I can help with?" Coach asked.

"Well, I was planning on seeing a psychiatrist," Matt said, "But maybe I can bounce something off of you."

"Shoot," said Coach, "Oh, sorry, guess I shouldn't have said that."

Matt smiled. "OK." He cleared his throat and took a breath in preparation. "I hear a person talking to me who has been gone for over two years. She helps me with my work. There. I said it."

Coach took a sip of his Jameson. "I'm assuming you knew this person when she was alive?"

"We were lovers and a committed couple for twenty-four years. We both worked for the Naval Criminal Investigative Service, NCIS. I'm sure you heard the story of the KGB agent who killed all the sailors?"

"You were involved in that?" Coach said, raising his eyebrows.

"I was the reason Makarov was doing what he was doing. He kidnapped Randy, my girlfriend, and took her to Russia, where she died in front of me at Makarov's hands."

Coach gave a whistle. "Wow. That's a lot. And now you hear Randy speaking?"

"I just started hearing her voice recently. Not only does she speak, but we have conversations. She has been giving me a lot of good advice."

"Well, you finally admit I'm helping. I was wondering if I'd ever get an affirmation from you, Bertram," Randy said from some vague place behind Matt.

Because of the pause, Coach said, "She's talking to you right now, isn't she?"

Matt nodded.

"Matt, I've seen a lot of weird and unexplainable things in my life. My time in Vietnam produced more than a few ghosts that I've had to deal with."

"Oh, geeze, he's going with the ghost thing," said Randy. "Walk away, Matt, this guy's a loser."

"I'm not saying you're hearing a ghost," Amos said, almost as though he had heard Randy. "I'm just saying that in the sense of 'unseen things,'" Coach said. "Grief can produce a whole helluva lot of weird things, and everybody grieves in their own way. Losing someone close to you—whether that's because of a death, a divorce, or the even the ending of a friendship—is hard. Along with the initial shock, it's a challenge when you must go on and learn how to navigate the future without them by your side. And because the grieving process is unique for everyone, it can often be lonely and isolating. I heard somebody say once that grief is much like a band-aid being ripped away, taking the top layer off your heart.

"We all deal with grief differently, but yours is unusual, to say the least, Matthew. I always used to ask people who would tell me about the dysfunctions in their lives, 'Is it impeding your life?' If the answer is yes, then you need to deal with it, as it will eat you up."

"That's the funny thing, Coach," Matt confessed. "I'm enjoying the conversations, and it's like I have a partner helping me with life. The only thing that's getting in the way is that when I hear her voice over my shoulder and I turn, expecting to see that smiling face and beautiful red hair, she's not there, and it saddens me. Well, and, of course, the whole hearing voices in my head thing could be interpreted in a pathological sort of way."

"Well, if it's not getting in the way of your life, my advice would be to enjoy it while you have it. Many people wish they could hear the voices of departed loved ones, and you have been given a gift."

"I never thought of it that way. So, I'm not crazy?"

"Son, I know crazy, and you aren't it," Coach said, putting a hand on Matt's shoulder.

"Thanks, Amos. Really. Now, I've got to hunt down my dog, who is no-doubt two cheeseburgers to the wind by now if I know Chavy, and we'll hit the road."

Coach stood up, almost tipping over onto the bar. "I have a sense that we'll see more of each other in the future, Matthew."

"I hope so," Matt replied.

As he and Jake were leaving the bar, Randy said, "You know, I like the guy. Let's keep him."

"I thought you said for me to walk away because he was going for the 'ghost' thing," Matt said.

"Well, I guess that's where people go first. Besides, we're both dealing with the woman by the road, so it's probably reasonable."

"I agree, Randy," Matt said. "I think he's a good guy too. Now let's go home. I'm bushed. Tomorrow's Saturday. I think we should saddle Zany and camp up on the mountain tomorrow night."

12

Who's On First?

Reality is easy. It's deception that's the hard work.
(Lauryn Hill)

Sinclair was pacing the length of the living room of the cabin, his hand rubbing what was left of the hair on top of his head, muttering incoherently. Naomi, appearing a bit more relaxed, had the TV on, and was watching the weather on KOAT in Albuquerque while filing her fingernails. "I wish Weatherman Morgan was still on. He was the best," she said, matter-of-factly.

"How can you be so calm?" Sinclair said with considerable incredulity. "We are in deep shit. Maybe we should just give it up and go back to Albuquerque."

"That's fucking stupid," Naomi replied, not looking up from her intensive nail care session.

"Then what do we do?" Sinclair implored, thinking to himself, *who brings a full manicure kit with them on a day trip to the mountains?*

"Well, first, Sinclair," Naomi said, "you need to grow a pair. You are a university professor, and I am a *gifted* graduate student. We're fucking brilliant. We need to find these Funk brothers, who, judging from their inept burglary, have the combined IQ of a turnip. Maybe a little lower. Step one: You go find that inn keeper who is sweet on you, which, by the way, is so cute at your age. She seems to know quite a lot about the Funk brothers. You find out where we can find them and leave the rest to me."

"To you? What are you going to do?"

"I'm going to be Parthenope to the turnip boys, and they'll lay their little stash they stole in my lap."

"Who the hell is Parthenope?" Sinclair asked.

"Sinclair, that's tenth grade reading. How in the hell did you get a Ph.D.?"

Although Naomi's "plan" seemed dubious at best, Sinclair realized he didn't have a viable alternative, so he left the cabin to find Maggie. "Maggie, sweetheart, how are you doing after such a trauma?" Sinclair asked as he walked into the front desk area of the lodge.

"Oh Sinclair, it's been such a tough couple of days. But what am I saying? You lost two of your students and had your cabin broken into. I should console you!"

"Nonsense, my dear Maggie," Sinclair said, realizing his attempt at being charming sounded more sycophantic than captivating. "I remembered I had offered to have a drink with you. But our series of unfortunate events has prevented that."

"Well, I don't know about you, but I could use a drink right now," Maggie said, pulling a bottle of Hennessy V.S.O.P. from behind the counter along with two glasses.

"I had intended to buy *you* that drink, Maggie," Sinclair said, feeling himself salivating slightly at the sight of good cognac.

"Next time, Sinclair," Maggie said, walking from behind the counter. "Let's sit out in the courtyard."

Maggie poured Sinclair a tall glass, which Sinclair emptied immediately. Taking the bottle and pouring himself another, he said, "You sounded pretty certain it was these Funk brothers who did the break-in today."

"Oh yeah," Maggie replied. "They have been nothing but trouble for several years. Jemez Springs is quiet, and we all look out for each other even though we come from many diverse cultures and backgrounds. We've come to smell the work of the Funk brothers. They usually steer clear of the people who live here and prey on the weekenders and the tourists, but lately they've let that tradition slide. No, I'm sure it's them."

"If one were trying to find them, where do they hang out?" Sinclair asked.

"I know they are squatting somewhere back in the mountains around Soda Dam, but I'm not sure where. There are rumors they have their place booby trapped with explosives and such, so about the only people I know who know exactly where they live are Deputy Bertram and the LEO's from the Ranger station."

"They must come into town occasionally, don't they?" Sinclair pressed.

"We see them in town, but they are pretty much banned from the stores and Las Águilas Bar. I hear that they mostly stay up in their cabin. My housekeeper, Romi, had a crush on one of them for a while. God, I don't know why—it's a small town." She shivered a bit as she said it. "Romi said they head to La Cueva and buy beer pretty much every Friday night when they have money, then go up to Fenton Lake to get drunk and swim in that foul reservoir bursting with algae. She said it's their idea of bathing."

The front door of the lodge opened, and Maggie turned to see who it was. "Oh, it's guests, Sinclair," Maggie said. "Maybe we can finish this later?"

"Of course, Maggie. I'll be looking forward to it." As Maggie went inside to tend to her guests, Sinclair grabbed the bottle of cognac and headed back to the cabin.

"Well, it may be a dead-end, but I've got something," Sinclair said to Naomi upon his return. He explained the recreational proclivities of the Funk brothers at Fenton Lake.

"It's Friday night and happy hour time," Naomi replied. "Let's go do some funking hunting."

Dory and Chuchu had escaped around the back of the Mineral Springs Lodge, circled back to their truck, and put the backpacks in the truck's bed. After their obligatory ten minutes of starter fluid and cranking, the old pickup came to life, and they raced toward home feeling like the James brothers after a train heist.

They grabbed the backpacks out of the truck and started the hike to their cabin. This time they successfully avoided the trip wires, and upon reaching "home sweet camper," fell on the stolen pink chaise lounges, exhausted. "Dude," Chuchu said, "Let's take a look at our score, man!"

With great anticipation, Dory brought the backpacks to the pink lounge chairs. With the care of a surgeon, Dory slowly unzipped the top of the first backpack as they both peered in, hoping for treasures beyond measure, or at least some expensive hiking equipment. "What the hell?" Dory said, staring in the bag. "It's just a bunch of old Indian shit, man!" He began indelicately removing the contents, which included intact pots, spearheads, and more. Several of the pots, which were over 300 years old, shattered as they haphazardly tossed them on the ground.

"Open the other two, Dory," Chuchu said, sounding panicky. Dory did so, and both sat, staring disappointedly at the contents on the ground. Chuchu looked at Dory. "Who in the fuck would have three backpacks of crappy Indian shit, man?" he said.

"Man, we got screwed, Chuchu," Dory replied. "All that damn work just for this. It's not easy being criminal masterminds, dude!"

The two continued searching the pockets of the bags, hoping to find something, anything, that appeared valuable. Just as they were about to give up, Dory shouted, "Fuck yeah, man!" as he brought out a $50 bill. "We scored! It's beer tonight, man!"

Satisfied they had successfully accomplished their mission for the day, Chuchu looked at his brother. "Light a doob, man," he said. "Turned out to be a totally awesome heist, dude. Man, I need a nap. Then we'll go get a case of beer and take a swim at Fenton, dude."

Sinclair and Naomi pulled out of the parking lot at Mineral Springs Lodge, turning left and onto Highway 4, headed toward Soda Dam. Just north of Jemez Springs, the highway climbed in altitude as the pines and other flora gradually became denser and more verdant. They passed the Jemez Historic Site, where one can walk just a few hundred feet to see the ruins of the ancient Gisetowa Pueblo, one of the nine pueblos the Jemez Tribe had once occupied. Further on, they passed the Jemez Ranger District offices. A few miles further, they passed Soda Dam. Another ten minutes driving and Sinclair turned into the parking lot at The Cave, the only convenience store in La Cueva. "What are we stopping for?" asked Naomi, who had been daydreaming during what she considered a completely boring drive.

A sign above the door read, *Bait, BBQ and Beer*. Sinclair replied to Naomi, "We need bait," and went into the store.

In a few minutes, Sinclair returned with a case of Hamm's beer, five Slim Jims meat sticks and a pack of Marlboro cigarettes. "Wow, that's some fancy shit, Sinclair," Naomi said, gushing with sarcasm.

"If you want to catch a bottom feeder, you need to use stink bait," Sinclair replied without making eye contact with Naomi.

Back on the road, Sinclair turned left at La Cueva onto Highway 126, where they began up the mountain, heading for Fenton Lake State Park. Fenton Lake was what most people would consider to be a small body of water, only 37 acres in size. New Mexico was relatively devoid of water in general, and Fenton Lake was the largest reservoir within a two-hour drive. "As I recall, there's a day use area with picnic tables at the park. Let's try that first," said Sinclair.

Sinclair turned left off Highway 126 onto a dirt road with a small sign indicating the day use area for Fenton Lake. As the two pulled into the park, they began searching for a beat-up pickup truck, which Maggie had mentioned when she was talking to the deputy. It didn't take long for them to see what could only belong to the

Funk brothers. Parked in a carve-out was a blue and rust colored 1963 Chevy truck with plumber's racks, a hasp with a padlock for a door lock, and a garbage can welded to the bed of the truck. The bottom side panel was completely rusted through, as was much of the roof, restored to the satisfaction of the Funks with a generous application of duct tape. They parked alongside the pickup and got out of Sinclair's minivan, which, despite its own rather shabby appearance, was show-room beautiful compared to the truck. Sinclair grabbed a six-pack of the Hamm's he had purchased, stuck the Slim Jims and cigarettes into his back pocket, and exited the minivan. "I'm not so sure this was a good idea," Sinclair said to Naomi.

Naomi smirked at Sinclair. "Look, Sinclair, I got this covered," she said as she began walking toward an area with picnic tables. Close to the water, sitting on top of a picnic table in their underwear and chugging beer, she saw her prey. There was no mistaking the Funk brothers.

Chuchu and Dory watched the two people approaching with mild suspicion. This time of year, there were plenty of tourists coming up to the lake. The brothers found they could usually intimidate the tourists into leaving quickly, simply by being themselves. Neither made any attempt to put on pants with the people approaching. Chuchu simply gave one of his thunderous belches, raising his beer can toward the tourists. That was almost always sufficient to scatter intruders. These two, however, simply sat at another table about twenty feet from the Funks. Sinclair handed

Naomi a Hamm's and opened one himself. Naomi cracked the beer and swigged half the can, then let out her own belch.

"Dude, look at that awesome chick with the old guy, man," Dory said.

"And they're drinking the good stuff, too, man," replied Chuchu, staring at Naomi as though he hadn't seen a woman in years.

Naomi stood up and said to Sinclair, "You just stay here. I'll be right back." She turned and started walking over to where Dory and Chuchu were sitting. Still, neither of them made any attempt to put on pants.

"Hey guys, sorry to bother you, but I was wondering if that lake was good to swim in," Naomi said, putting the beer to her mouth and taking another mouthful.

"Oh, hell yeah, we come up here and swim all the time so we can stay in shape," Chuchu said, trying his best to sound erudite.

"I was just wondering about that. I didn't bring a swimsuit, so I'd have to skinny dip."

"Oh, we do that all the time, man," said Dory.

Naomi flashed her finest coy look at the two and said, "Well, I'd have to have a couple more beers in me before I did that." She smiled, brushed her hair behind her ear, and touched the tip of her tongue to her upper lip. "Hey, you guys seem kinda cool. We've got plenty of beer. Can we join you?"

"Well, hell to the yes, darlin'," Chuchu replied, barely able to contain himself. "Mi table-o es su table-o! But won't your boyfriend be jealous of a couple of young, hot dudes around you?"

"Oh, that's not my boyfriend," Naomi replied. "He's my professor at college. We're just up here in the Jemez on a field trip. I'll go get him and we'll get more beer out of the van."

As Naomi was leaving, Dory turned to Chuchu. "Like, a college babe, man. I hear they bang all night long!"

"And they brought beer, dude! This just might be our lucky day, brother!" Chuchu replied, giving his brother a high five.

Naomi returned to where Sinclair was sitting. "OK, this is going to be a piece of cake," she said to Sinclair. "Just don't blow it. Let me do most of the talking and this will go just fine."

The two walked back to the table where the Funk brothers had nested. They had put their pants and shirts on while they had the opportunity. Chuchu smiled and said, "Not sure why we're putting clothes on, dude. We're gonna be gettin' ours with that bootylicious college girl in no time, dog!"

Sinclair went to the van and got another six-pack and the two walked over to the brothers' table. Sinclair held out his hand for the Funks to shake. "Sinclair Delano the Third," he said.

Chuchu and Dory turned and looked at each other, then broke out hysterically laughing. "Sinclair? Really, man? And you got numbers after your name?" Dory managed to gasp out between laughs. "Sorry, dude, I didn't mean to talk shit to you, man. I just never knew nobody who had that name. Actually, I didn't even know that was a name. But my bad, man. You ain't responsible for the shit your parents did to you. Take it from us."

"Not a problem, gentlemen. I get that a lot." Would you like a beer or a Slim Jim?"

The two simply grabbed the beers without hesitation. Chuchu downed an entire beer in one breath, and as he was grabbing for another, said, "Listen to this." He proceeded to belch the alphabet. He got to the letter 'p' in one belch, then called up another from the depths of his belly and finished the alphabet.

"Wow," said Naomi. "I've seen nobody who can do that."

Dory chimed in, "Chuchu can usually do the whole alphabet in one burp. Took him five years to get it all."

The two academics stared and simultaneously repeated, "Wow."

"So, you two are on, like, a field trip for school?" Chuchu inquired.

"Yeah. Professor Delano—Sinclair, is an archaeologist, and I'm a graduate student working with him. We are just exploring some of the Indian ruins as a part of class. You know, hiking and hoping to find a random arrowhead or something along the way."

"Really? People do that in college?" Dory said. "I went to UNM once. Some asshole student there stole a bitch I was banging, so I went there to kick his ass. I had no idea how big the place was, so I just stole a cool skeleton from one of the classrooms and called it even."

Chuchu grabbed another beer, took a slug, wiping the foam off his lips with the back of his hand. "You're interested in arrowheads and Indian shit, huh?" he said.

Naomi jumped in. "It's always kind of cool to find stuff like that in these old ruins. It must be awesome to live up here in the mountains, huh? You guys look like a couple of mountain men to me," she said, attempting a sultry look, which, to a casual observer would have appeared chaste. Fortunately, the brothers were not anywhere close to being experts in the subtleties of flirting. Most of their sexual experience had been in the alleys adjoining Central Avenue in Albuquerque on an irregular and always pre-paid basis.

"Well hell yes, we're mountain men, dude!" Dory chimed in. "We live in the woods in a cabin we built ourselves, and we mostly live off the land. Except we do eat Slim Jims." Dory grabbed one of the meat sticks, opened it, threw the wrapper on the ground, and shoved the entire stick in his mouth. Dory was pretty sure he had Naomi in the palm of his hand, and if mountain men turned her on, then he was determined to go all Grizzly Adams on her in a second.

"That's so cool. I'm really turned on by that rugged outdoors kind of thing," Naomi declared. "You guys must have come across arrow heads and stuff at some point. Maybe you could show us where we could look for some?"

"It's hard as hell to find that shit, man," Chuchu said. "But we have collected some of that stuff along the way. We're a little short on the dineros this month, man, so maybe you'd want to buy some from us."

"Hmm, I don't know," Naomi replied. "People aren't really into it the way they used to be, so it's not worth much. What do you have?"

Chuchu looked at Dory, who gave him the 'OK' to continue. "We got lots of stuff. Pottery, arrowheads, some nice Indian rocks. We could let it go for, oh, say, $300."

Naomi gave a whistle. "I'm just a starving college student, and, frankly, University Professors aren't paid very well. Wish we could, but that's way too much."

"Well," Chuchu inquired, "What could you pay, man?"

"We would have to see it first, but if it's good stuff, Sinclair and I could pool our money and maybe come up with $100. It wouldn't be easy, but I think we could do it."

Dory started smiling. The thought of getting rid of those bags of worthless stuff for $100 sounded good to him. "Cool," said Dory. "We could probably go for that, hey Chuchu, man?"

Chuchu smiled as well. "And you throw in a case of that Hamm's beer, too?"

Now Naomi was smiling. "Great. Can we go take a look at it, and see your mountain cabin that you big, healthy boys built, too?"

Chuchu grabbed the last two beers from Sinclair's six-pack and said, "Follow us. It's kinda in the middle of nowhere, so you'll have to hike a little ways, dudes."

With that, the Funk brothers walked to their truck and began their process of getting it fired up. After the regular ten minutes of cranking, the truck came roaring to life. Sinclair and Naomi followed the truck out of the park on their way to the "mountain man" cabin.

13

SÉÉEH-WAGI

Many of my fellow atheists consider all talk of 'spirituality' or 'mysticism' to be synonymous with mental illness, conscious fraud, or self-deception. I have argued elsewhere that this is a problem - because millions of people have had experiences for which 'spiritual' and 'mystical' seem the only terms available.

(Sam Harris)

Matt rode Zany and ponied his mare, Adobe, up the mountain trail on his way to Peralta Ridge. Matt's current favorite camping spot was in a lush green valley at the base of Peralta Ridge. Although it was forest service land, it was rare to see anyone else. Matt enjoyed camping next to a large pond in the valley. He could watch the sunset over the mountains to the west, and in the morning, he would watch the sun appear over the top of the peak, warming his face as the sunshine reached the valley. It was a place for him to regain his center, calm himself, and reflect. Occasionally, he would have to share his pristine valley with backpackers, but it usually resulted in making new friends. It often surprised Matt at the far-away places the hikers lived. For some reason unknown to Matt, the Austrians were fond of coming to the Jemez, which he thought ironic, considering the amazing mountain beauty they possessed in their own backyard.

Tonight, he, Jake, Zany, and Adobe had the valley to themselves. He pitched his tent and strung a high line between two trees to tie Zany and Adobe. He only tied them as a precaution, as they were both trained to be ground-tied. But a random thunderstorm or the sound of coyotes or bears could send them into a panic, and he had spent too much time playing hide and seek in the forest, looking for his horses when he could have been relaxing.

Matt built a small campfire and then used his saddle and the saddle blankets as a backrest in true cowboy fashion to enjoy the fire. The sun had gone behind the mountains, and twilight was blossoming in the night sky as he watched the stars gradually appear until the heavens became a light show of celestial wonder. "I wish you could see this place, Randy," Matt said, gazing at the sky.

"I see it through your eyes, Matt," Randy replied.

"I just don't understand what's going on, Randy. I hear you as clearly as if you were actually here, right next to me."

"I can't tell you, Matt. I don't know myself. I just know I can talk to you and see what you see through your eyes," Randy said.

"Well, even if it is a little crazy, I'll take it. I love you, Randy, and losing you tore a hole in my soul that will never be filled."

"It's not a hole, Matt," she said. "It's a vessel. For more joy, for more love, for more life, it makes room in your soul for that. It will fill with all of those things if you let it."

"I will never stop loving you, Randy. There is no one else for me, ever."

"I will never stop loving you, Bertram. And let's trust the future on that second part. I want you to be happy."

"Randy, do you remember what happened in Russia?"

"I remember some of it. I remember being in that church, and I remember you and Jake Packer being there, but it gets very fuzzy after that."

"I wish I could have saved you, Randy. I will never forgive myself for that."

"Listen here, Bertram," Randy said. "You did nothing wrong. You went to the ends of the earth to find and save me. Tell me Makarov is dead."

"He's dead alright."

"Good. He was an evil man. Here's the thing, Matt. I see you now grieving so much for me that you can't live your own life. You live in a magnificent place and you've gone through all the motions to set yourself up with a wonderful life. Yet you walk around as though *you* are the one who is gone. You aren't relishing your life. You were one of the best NCIS special agents ever, and now you treat your job with zero dedication and minimal effort. That's not the Matthew Bertram I know and love.

"I don't know why I'm here, Matt. But it seems reasonable to think that, just like you went to the ends of the earth to save me, I've come to save you. You are young, healthy and you have everything going for you."

"Except you," Matt interjected.

"Maybe that's why you are hearing me, Bertram. Perhaps I'm here to help you save yourself this time. To find purpose. To find pleasure, and, don't stop me, perhaps to find love again. This miracle of the two of us communicating must have purpose, and although it sounds strange, I think the purpose is to help you find your own purpose once again. We used to say that we never married each other because we were married to our jobs. A marriage is a supreme commitment. I think it's crucial that you marry life again.

"I know you love me," Randy said, "with all your heart. And because I love you, I can't stand to see you half-way in this life and half-way out. I want you to find that silly Matt Bertram I know is in there. That guy who makes decisions without giving due consideration, who isn't afraid to take risks that put him in situations way over his head, and whose child-like innocence in the midst of a mean and ugly world rises to the top, like cream to milk."

Matt could say nothing in response. It was true. He was lost, uncommitted and living half of a life. Perhaps Randy was right. *If so*, Matt thought, *I'll make certain that she saves me.* As he gave thought to Randy's comments, he looked to the huge black sky dotted by millions of stars. While he stared, a shooting star passed overhead. In the distance he heard the screech of a golden eagle, a punctuation mark to Randy's loving homily.

The next morning, Matt broke camp, put away his camping equipment, saddled Zany and ponied Adobe down the steep mountain trail toward home. It was a warm, sunny Sunday morning. Matt had to admit to himself that he preferred the summer days over winter. Matt's main house on his small ranch was at 8,500 feet in altitude, so even summer days were chilly in the morning.

As Matt re-entered his sixty acres, he could look down and see his home, barns, and corrals below. Jake was ahead of him. He could tell that Jake liked to think he was the leader of the outing, but it also allowed him to find unobservant chipmunks to chase. "Chase" probably was not the best word for Jake's chipmunk hobby. Jake was fast and could easily grab a chipmunk, sending it to its doom with little effort. "Herd" was probably a better word for Jake's pastime. Jake would find a chipmunk, chase it, and whirl around in front of it to force the poor rodent to change course. Jake was a magician in forcing chipmunks to take evasive action against his speed and agility. That was Jake's game. Matt had never seen Jake put a chipmunk in his mouth, even though he could have easily done so.

Matt reached his corral and removed Zany's saddle and bridle and Adobe's halter and put both horses in the corral. He brushed both, feeding them carrots, then put some oats in their feed buckets as a reward. The mountain grass was so lush this time of year that supplemental feeding was an unnecessary, but much appreciated treat.

Matt and Jake went inside the lodge. Matt took a shower while Jake worked on an old bone on his blanket on the porch. When Matt was done, he walked out onto the porch to see if the old woman was there. Matt had not had breakfast and his stomach was growling like a bear. "It's Sunday, Jake. Let's treat ourselves to breakfast at Las Águila. What do you say?" From the tone of Matt's voice, Jake raised his head and his ears stood straight up as though he knew they were going to do something fun. He jumped up, spun in a circle and raced to the Jimmy, waiting impatiently for Matt.

As Matt and Jake walked into Las Águilas, he was reminded by the full house that it was June in the Jemez, and the tourists had descended on the village. There was one open seat at the bar, which he took, saying, "Morning, Coach," to Father Amos O'Sullivan who was in the seat next to him, sipping coffee.

"Why Matthew, how's the craic?" replied Coach.

"It's doing well," Matt replied, not sure what the proper response was to what must have been an Irish saying. "Enjoying a morning cup of coffee, Amos?"

"Of course, Matthew—the Irish kind, of course."

"Of course," said Matt. "Don't you have mass or something to do, Coach?"

"Well, truth be known, it's been quite some time since this old man has taken the sacraments. I feel I did my duty over the many years of service to our Lord. Hey, you would make a great priest, Matthew. You got a confession out of me in two minutes flat!"

"It's also a handy skill for a cop, Amos," Matt said, smiling.

Chavy walked over to Matt, Jake in his arms, a bone in Jake's mouth. "I found this mongrel begging for enchiladas," Chavy said.

"I should know you'd wait on the dog before me," Matt replied.

"He's nicer than you, Deputy," said Chavy. "What can I do for you today?"

"I camped up by Peralta last night and worked up an appetite. Jake talked me into coming here for some of your delicioso huevos rancheros and your café fuerte."

"Coming right up, amigo!" Chavy said, setting Jake down behind the counter to gnaw on the bone. Huevos Rancheros were a Northern New Mexico delicacy, and Matt never missed an opportunity to make them his breakfast. As with most Northern New Mexico cuisine, it was a simple yet flavor-filled dish, comprising a corn tortilla topped with beans, chilies, cheese and a fried egg. There was strong disagreement over the best chili to add to the dish and it drew sharp sides. There were the "red" people who preferred red chili sauce, especially on huevos rancheros, and the people who preferred "green" chili sauce. The debate was so ubiquitous that the New Mexico legislature had passed a resolution making "Red or Green?" the official state question. Matt mostly fell into the green category, but often made the exception for huevos and enchiladas. Chavy called him "bi-chilied," which Matt was fond of hearing.

"So, how's your Randy doing?" Amos asked, suddenly serious.

"We went camping last night and had a delightful conversation by the campfire. You know, Amos, I don't know if I'm hearing voices in a psychiatric sense, if she's a ghost, if it's my grief working itself out, or there's something bigger going on. But I have to thank you for your counsel the other night. Your question about whether it's impeding my life is good, and the truth is that it is not. It is actually enhancing my life. Once you said that, I relaxed. I've stopped worrying about what is going on with Randy, and I'm just accepting it for the time that I'm given. Randy gave me a tongue-lashing last night. A loving one. But I feel like I have an entirely new perspective on life. I have to thank you and Randy for that."

"Ah, Matthew, it's nice of you to say. Just when I thought my calling as a priest was over, you came along. I have to thank you, too."

A hand slapped Matt on the back from behind. "You didn't order me huevos, *anglo*?" Paul said, as he sat down next to Matt.

"I was thinking you were more of a waffle house kind of guy, Paul," Matt replied.

"Now that you mention it, waffles do sound good! Actually, Matt, I had breakfast before church. I hate for my stomach to growl during mass. I stopped in just to see if you were here." he said.

Matt turned around to face Paul. Paul was not in uniform. He was wearing western boots, jeans, and a denim shirt with a striking heishi turquoise necklace. Matt realized he had only seen Paul out of uniform a couple of times since they met. Without the forest service law enforcement uniform and his duty rig on, Paul looked much different to Matt. It embarrassed him that when he looked at Paul, he saw the ranger first, and then, occasionally, Jemez Indian. "So, what's up, my friend? Can I at least buy you a cup of coffee?"

"Sure," Paul replied. "I stopped by because I wanted to have a chat with you about the woman you are seeing on the road."

"You're also seeing a woman by the road?" Amos said. Matt put a finger to his lips in Amos' direction, and in a crude attempt to steer Paul's curiosity away, said, "Paul, have you met Father Amos O'Sullivan?"

Paul smiled and put out his hand to shake Amos's. "Of course. Everybody knows Father O'Sullivan around here. I've given him a lift back to Saint Frumentius a couple of times. Good to see you again, Father."

Matt felt compelled to oblige Amos. "Yeah, in the early mornings several times each week, there's a Jemez woman standing next to the highway, turned in my direction and pointing up the hill towards the mountains. When I try to approach her, she disappears."

Paul looked at Matt with an intensity Matt had not seen before. "I talked to an elder in my tribe, Matt, and he thinks he knows what's going on. He's a wise and respected man, and he wants to come out to your place, perhaps spend the night, and see if his idea is correct. Does that sound like something you would be up for?"

"Of course. I have plenty of room, and would love to meet him, and perhaps learn what is going on. How about you both come? We'll have supper and a quiet evening, and then we'll see if she appears in the morning."

Paul smiled. "How about tonight? Our elder is very eager to see the woman."

"Tonight works just fine. I'm pretty eager to figure out what's going on myself. How about six, and I'll grill some trout for us."

Matt turned to Amos. "Any chance Coach could come too, if you're willing, Amos? He's been very helpful to me in matters that are a little transcendent."

"Sounds intriguing, Matthew," Amos said. "You do stock Jameson at your lodge?"

Matt smiled and nodded. Paul looked to Matt, then to Amos. "Fine by me, but I'll need to check with my elder to be certain he's OK with it. Now, I've got to get home. The kids are having a big foot race this afternoon. We have some great runners this year."

Paul called Matt at home late in the day. "My elder is fine with the priest coming, as long as he's not too drunk," he said. "How is six o'clock?"

Matt confirmed and went to the freezer to pull out some trout he had caught fishing in San Antonio creek. He would have liked to catch some fresh trout, but fishing in the Jemez was a hit-or-miss activity, and there certainly wasn't enough time to catch sufficient fish for dinner.

A few minutes before six, a pickup truck pulled into Matt's driveway. Jake immediately raised his head and growled softly until he recognized Paul's truck. Once he did, he looked at Matt for permission and received the cherished "OK." Jake was off the porch in an instant and waiting at the truck's door for Paul to open it, doing so in his usual way, raising his hands, and making a zombie noise. Jake gave his fiercest growl back, then dove into Paul's arms.

Paul gave Jake his official greeting, then set the dog down and went around to the front passenger door. Paul helped an ancient man from the truck as Matt walked down to help. The man was short of stature and was wearing a ball cap over his gray, shoulder-length hair, tied in a traditional Chongo, with a finely crafted turquoise necklace and a white shirt with hand-embroidered designs at the collar points and his left and right breasts. He was wearing glasses and a pair of Nike tennis shoes. Amos was sitting in the middle of the truck's bench seat, waiting for the man to clamber out of the truck before exiting himself.

"You guys are early," Matt said.

"You sound surprised," Paul responded. "Jemez are always timely, unlike our Navajo friends," he said with a smile. It was a well-used joke among the Jemez who enjoyed a little fun taking a poke at a Navajo stereotype.

"Matthew Bertram, I would like you to meet out esteemed elder, Benny Baca," Paul said, sounding much more formal than Matt was used to.

"It's a pleasure, sir," Matt said to Benny.

Benny smiled, looking at Matt from the top of his head to his boots, as though he was examining every square inch of Matt before responding. "I'm glad to meet you too, Deputy," Benny finally said. "You have been hurt badly, both physically and mentally," he said, almost matter-of-factly. It was true, he had been hurt in both ways. In May of 2000, just two years before, a former KGB agent had shot him twice while he was trying to save Randy. The adversary, a man named Pyotr Makarov, was using Randy as bait to complete his revenge against Matt. Matt had lost Randy in that attempt. While the gunshot wounds had effectively healed, he feared his heart and soul would not.

"This is someone you need to pay attention to," Randy said from behind Matt.

"And it would appear that the person you lost, deputy, is closer than you think," Benny continued. Matt stood, stunned, realizing that Benny could somehow see or feel Randy. Benny left the subject and moved on. "I have always wanted to see this place. I have driven by it many times with wonder and curiosity."

"Please let me show you around, Mr. Baca," Matt said. "Then perhaps we can go inside. I'll get you settled in your rooms, and I'll put on some tea for you."

"Em, Matthew," Amos said, "I'm afraid I'm allergic to tea. Perhaps some of that Jameson would soothe me."

"Of course, Coach," Matt said. Paul just shook his head, not understanding why Matt had bonded to the drunk priest.

Matt's latest project on the ranch was a fire pit he had just completed behind the lodge. While Benny, Paul and Amos were settling into their rooms, he started a fire. He enjoyed wrapping his trout in aluminum foil and burying them in the coals of the fire, along with ears of corn. The four men had an enjoyable meal by the fire while Matt and Benny got to know one another as night descended upon them.

The conversation paused as the four looked to the clear sky to gaze at the stars. Benny said, "Before tomorrow, you should know something about this place and the people who have lived here for millennia. We, the Hemish people, believe the land we inhabit is alive. We call it No-wa-mu, or "Mother Earth." No-wa-mu supports us and gives us life, and sustains us. Because of this, we feel obligated to take good care of her. This differs greatly from the goal of the Europeans. They came to exploit the land; we came to be caregivers. Since we arrived in these mountains, we have set aside places for specific uses. We designate places for our spiritual practices. There are shrines in many places here in the mountains. In a time long ago, forest lands could not be used for hunting, except for the Eagle Catching Society. There were places where our sacred fir trees grew. We harvested firs for our ceremonies but had strict rules about how much we harvested so that our lands would remain lush and green. Our lands are not inanimate. They are alive. And others live among us we cannot see. I am inclined to think the woman you see by the road is one of those. She has chosen to appear to you for a reason. Tomorrow we will hope she comes and tells us her purpose. Now, Paul needs to take me down near the road. I have some things in my bag and a ceremony I will do which will encourage her to speak to us. I'm afraid I cannot allow you to watch, much as I would like to. But Randy is welcome."

The blood drained from Matt's face. He had not mentioned Randy's name to anyone other than Amos, and he was pretty sure Benny and Amos had not spoken. Benny stood, walked over to Matt, and put both hands on his shoulders. He quietly said, "kwaa." He then took his right hand and placed it over Matt's heart and, once again, quietly said, "pe'h." Then he and Paul left to perform their ritual.

Matt sat back down in front of the fire. Amos looked at Matt and smiled. "I don't know what he said," said Amos, "but I saw a change in your countenance. How do you feel?"

"I feel calm. And, somehow about a hundred pounds lighter," Matt said. "Amos, did you say anything to Benny about Randy?"

"I certainly did not," Amos replied. "I think this man may be more than just an elder, however."

Matt woke early the next morning, dressing and putting on coffee for his guests. He looked out the front window at the highway below and was astounded to see that the fog was back. "She's coming this morning," Benny said from a chair in the great room, which gave Matt a start. "I was about to walk down. Let me go alone, but it is just fine if you watch from here."

Benny walked out the door and down the porch steps. Matt noticed Benny moved more quickly this morning than he had the day before, standing more upright, like a much younger man. With each step toward the highway, Benny appeared younger. About halfway to the highway, the woman appeared out of the fog. The two stood face-to-face about ten feet apart. Neither of their mouths moved. They simply stood, looking at one another. The woman raised her arms and pointed up the side of the hill behind Matt's lodge, as he had seen her do several times in the last weeks. Benny touched his forehead with his hand, turned and walked back. With each step, he moved more slowly until he reached the porch, struggling to climb the steps. He had, once again, become his age.

Matt went outside and helped Benny up the steps and into the lodge. Benny sat in one of the overstuffed chairs, and Matt brought him a cup of coffee. Paul and Amos simultaneously appeared from their bedrooms. "Did she come?" Paul said. "I can't believe I didn't wake up to see it."

"You weren't supposed to, Paul. It was for Matt and me to see," Benny replied. Benny took a sip of his coffee while the others poured themselves a cup and sat down and waited until Benny was ready to speak.

"You have seen Weh'ng Péh. She is the mother of the Eagle Catching Society and appeared to you to show us an important place. On your property is a shrine. It is called Séééh-Wagi, or the 'Eagle's Altar.' It is a most holy place and an important ceremonial location for our people many generations ago. When the Baca land grant was issued by the Spanish, this land and our shrine were lost to us. I have heard others speak of Séééh-Wagi, but the location was forgotten by my people before my father's grandfather."

"It is now legally yours, Matthew. But I wish to ask that you consider allowing my people to come, find it, bless it, and perhaps use it occasionally for important ceremonies. I know it is asking a lot, but we would be very grateful if you would grant this to us."

"Would you allow me to take part?" Matt inquired.

"It is forbidden—but, perhaps, there is a way to make a small exception. I will talk to our governor and our war chief."

"Even if you don't, Benny, I'm happy to work this out with you."

Benny smiled. "It is good to know you, Matthew. And by the way, Randy will tell you herself, but she agrees. She liked Weh'ng Péh."

14

Prey Tell

We truly have an ancient part of the brain that was about survival when we were prey, but we seem to have gone past prey. We eat everything and nothing eats us.
(Nick Nolte)

"What are we doing, Naomi? These guys are scumbags," Sinclair said, as they were driving behind the Funk brothers toward their property.

"Grow a pair, Sinclair," Naomi replied. The phrase was getting on Sinclair's nerves. "Look, they're a couple of dumbass yokels. We have intelligence and resourcefulness. This is going to be like stealing candy from a fucking baby."

The truck in front of them slowed, and a hand reached out the window, indicating the driver was turning. Apparently, any turn signals the truck once had were inoperative. The truck turned left on a dirt road and Sinclair followed about a half mile until the road disappeared. Sinclair pulled next to the truck. "Don't forget the beer, man," Dory said to Sinclair.

"I've got that, and even better," Sinclair smiled as he held up the bottle of Hennessy he had pilfered from Maggie at the lodge.

"Dude, I'm liking you," Chuchu said.

The four left their vehicles and walked another quarter mile on a trail into the forest until Chuchu held up his hand as though he were leading a platoon of marines through the jungle. "We've got booby traps out here, and trip wires with alarms to warn us if the pigs are coming, man," he said. "Follow me and I'll get you through safely." Chuchu took two steps and his ankle hit one of the trip wires they had set. A young sapling flew at Chuchu like a jack-in-the-box clown, and he took a direct hit in the face, knocking him to the ground. "See, man," Chuchu said, wiping pine needles from his face, "I just fucking saved your lives, dudes!"

Naomi gave Sinclair one of her classic sneers, and, in a rare act of self-restraint, said nothing in response. As they reached the brothers' "cabin," Sinclair was astonished at the ramshackle shelter before his eyes, replete with an old camper, corrugated metal roofing and an assortment of tarps that formed their palace of the derelict. Surrounding the shelter were dozens of black garbage bags filled with beer cans. "Home sweet home," Dory said. "Wanna doob?"

Sinclair pondered for a moment whether it would garner the brothers' trust for him to smoke marijuana with them and decided he could find another way to accomplish that. "Sorry, guys, but I'm allergic." A poor excuse, but the brothers didn't seem to mind.

"More for us, then, dude," Dory said. "Hey, how about the bottle of booze, man?"

Sinclair brought out the bottle of Hennessy. "Do you guys like cognac?"

"Let me see," Chuchu said, grabbing the bottle and take a large, long gulp. "Woah, guess I do, dude!" He passed the bottle to his brother, who did the same.

"I don't know if you guys indulge," Naomi said, "but I've got some Xanax if you want some," she said.

"Wow, fancy booze and drugs, too, man!" Chuchu responded. "We're going to have us a party!" Naomi handed each of them three of the pills, which they each washed down with an entire beer.

"Well, before you get too fucked up, let's take a look at the Indian shit you have," Naomi interjected.

"Oh, yeah, dudes, I almost forgot," Dory said. Already relaxing in his pink chaise lounge, he pointed near the steps to the camper. "Chuchu, you wanna get them for me, man? I'm already buzzing."

Chuchu retrieved the bags and set them down at Sinclair's feet, then flopped on the second pink chaise lounge, took another swig of the cognac and a hit on the joint Dory passed over. Sinclair made a production of looking at the contents of the bags, confirming the Black Heart was still among the artifacts. As he reached in the bag and took hold of the Black Heart, he suddenly felt a sense of strength and courage that was a surprise. He wanted to keep holding it, sensing a power he had never felt before. Forcing his hand to return it to the bag he turned to the brothers. Trying to make a disappointed face, Sinclair looked up at the brothers. "Yep," he said, "You're right about the Indian shit. It's not worth much of anything. I'm not sure we want to buy it."

"Hey dude," Dory snarled, "We made a deal, man."

Sinclair raised his hand as a gesture of peace. "You're right, Dory, we did. Even though it's not worth it, a deal's a deal."

The brothers were quickly heading for that place between intoxication and catalepsy. It amazed Sinclair, however, at the capacity the men had for alcohol and drugs. Within fifteen minutes, Chuchu was snoring and solidly unconscious. Dory, with great effort, managed to stand up. He wobbled a bit, but with an abundance of effort, walked over to Naomi. "I think we ought to throw a little more in the deal, man," Dory said. "I think pretty girl here and me needs to play a little game of 'hide the sausage.'"

"No fucking way, 'Dude,'" Naomi spat.

Continuing to walk toward Naomi, Dory pulled a .38 revolver from his back pocket, pointing it first at Sinclair, then at Naomi. "Professor, man, you need to give me some privacy." Dory's advance now included the start of unbuckling his pants. Sinclair stood up and Dory pointed the gun in his direction. "Just cool your jets, man," Dory said. "This won't take long."

"You're right, you fucking hillbilly," Naomi said as she let go a full-throttle roundhouse kick to the side of Dory's head, folding him in two and putting him on his knees. She followed her opening salvo with a knee to his nose, as Dory screamed at Naomi to stop.

Naomi took a three-step jump and mid-air, once again, kicked Dory's head, putting him on the ground, unconscious.

Dory's scream had awoken Chuchu, who rolled off of his chaise lounge onto the ground and was struggling to get up. Naomi lunged into action once again, giving Chuchu a swift kick to the face and a roundhouse kick to the side of his head. Chuchu fell face-first onto the ground. Both men were not moving.

Sinclair, having witnessed Naomi in action, was in a paroxysm of panic. "Oh my God, Naomi. You've killed them!" he cried. "And where the hell did you learn to do that?"

Naomi gave Sinclair a look of disgust. "I'm a fucking black belt in Taekwondo. Been doing martial arts since I was seven. How do you think I survived my upbringing?" She reached down and checked each of their pulses. "These fucking brain-damaged Neanderthals are going to be fine. I hit them in their heads. They don't have anything in there that can be damaged. And, by the way, thanks for all your help, Sinclair. Now, let's grab the bags and get the fuck out of this hellhole and back to Albuquerque before they wake up."

Naomi snatched one bag and Sinclair grabbed the other two. He put the bags on his shoulder. Before turning back to the truck, he put the bottle of Hennessy in one backpack and grabbed up several of the joints, while Naomi grabbed Dory's handgun and stuffed it into her backpack. The two began running in the direction of Sinclair's minivan, occasionally hitting a trip wire which mostly caused hundreds of beer cans to clatter together. Twilight was descending, making the path much more difficult to follow, forcing the two to stop several times to orient themselves in the direction of the minivan. After several failed attempts, the minivan came in sight. "Oh, thank God," Sinclair said, putting the packs in the backseat and starting the van. They followed the dirt road back to the highway and turned left, intending to travel nonstop back to civilization and the safety of Albuquerque.

They had been on the road for about ten minutes when the radiator light buzzed to life on the dash. "Don't worry," Sinclair said, "that happens all the time. We'll be fine." A few minutes further on, the engine began making a horrific sound as a small plume of steam billowed from under the hood. Sinclair hit his fist on the steering wheel. "Shit," he said. "We'll have to find a place for the night and hopefully get it fixed in the morning."

"Don't you know how to work on cars?" Naomi chided.

"Hell, I don't even know how to open the hood," Sinclair unabashedly responded.

"Where in the hell are we going to find a place? It's got to be miles back to Jemez Springs," Naomi responded.

"I don't know. I just know we have to get off the road because when the Funk brothers wake up, they are going to be pissed. I don't think we want to be anywhere within fifty miles of them, and certainly not on their turf." Sinclair managed to keep enough life in the engine to pull onto a dirt road with a mailbox at the street. He drove up the road, hoping to find someone who could help them secure a tow truck. At last, they came to a cabin. It had no lights or a vehicle in front. Sinclair looked at his cell phone. "I've got no service," he said. Naomi confirmed the same situation with her phone. "Let's hope they have a phone," he said, getting the minivan to limp close enough for them to walk to the cabin.

As they approached the cabin, they confirmed it was empty. Sinclair tried the front door, which was, unsurprisingly, locked. "Wait here," Naomi said as she went around to the back. Sinclair heard glass break, and Naomi opened the front door to let Sinclair in. "They're going to have some repairs to make," was all she said.

There was power to the cabin, and upon turning on the lights, the two searched for a telephone with no luck. "It's dark. We're tired, and we'll need someone to help with the van. I think maybe we ought to spend the night here, and we'll figure out what to do when it's light."

Given the circumstances, Naomi reluctantly agreed with Sinclair. The two found bedrooms and fell onto the beds. They were safe for the night at least, and could sort things out in the morning.

Sinclair awoke as the sunlight peeked in his bedroom window. He opened his eyes, spending a moment trying to remember where he was. As the events of the last evening came into focus, he got up to see if the owners of the cabin stocked any coffee. He came into the kitchen, and Naomi had already raided the pantry. Coffee was made, and she handed Sinclair a cup. "You know it's Saturday, right?" she said.

"Yeah, I thought about that when I woke up. I don't know if anyone fixes cars in Jemez Springs, but odds are good we'll have to wait until Monday."

"You also know that those fuckwits are going to be looking for us, right? And we can't go to the sheriff for help, right? And they know we have the artifacts, right? And if they tell anybody, then we are completely made, and we'll be arrested for stealing the artifacts, right?"

Sinclair sat down with the cup of coffee and pressed it to his forehead. "I don't think we have to worry about them reporting the theft. I would have written them off as a couple of harmless small-time crooks, but after seeing Dory pull a gun and try to rape you, I think they are more dangerous than we gave them credit for. I'm sure they are going to try to find us, and I know we can't go to the cops. Let's just sit tight for now and think about what our options are. At least we are safe here."

"I'll sit tight for a little while," Naomi said. "But you and I both know that the Funk brothers are a problem; a problem that needs to be purged."

Chuchu awoke to the sun shining on his face in the pink chaise lounge. "Wow, dude, I got sozzled last night, Dory." He heard no answer coming from the other pink chaise lounge. Chuchu made several attempts at opening his eyes before he managed to get one partially opened, sufficient for him to take a quick glance at his surroundings.

"Dory? Hey dude, where are you?" he asked. He heard moaning coming from beside the camper. With utmost effort, Chuchu forced himself up and willed his other eye to open. Dory was on the ground. He walked over to Dory as he attempted to turn himself off of his face and onto his back. "Woh, man, I thought *I* got tanked last night. You don't look so good, man."

Dory's forehead had been cut open and his eye was swollen shut. Much of his face was a dazzling shade of purple. "It wasn't the drugs, my brother. It was that professor dude and his ninja turtle girlfriend. She, like, fucked me up with all kinds of kung-fu shit, man."

Chuchu helped Dory onto his pink chaise lounge and handed him a beer which Dory chugged in one breath. "I need a joint, man, like *stat*," Dory mumbled through his swollen lips.

Chuchu went to their stash box. "Dory, man, you're not going to like this, man, but our last three doobs are gone." Chuchu looked around the camp. "Oh, man, Dory, those bags of Indian shit are gone, too!"

Dory felt in his pants for his .38. It was not there. "Chuchu, look over where you found me, man, and see if my gun is over there."

"No, dude, your rod isn't here."

"That is badong, dude. We been ripped off, man."

"What are we going to do, Dory, man?"

"We are going to make them pay, man. Nobody, but nobody, rips off a Funk!"

15

A Time For Detective Work

The police are not here to create disorder, they're here to preserve disorder.
(Mayor Richard J. Daley)

Matt saw Paul, Benny and Amos off, realizing as they were driving away that it was Monday morning, a workday, and he was late for his daily roll/phone call. He went inside and dialed the office, waited on hold for a few minutes until Lt. Villanueva was on the line. They went through a few ministerial issues regarding office procedures. "We've decided that we want you to come into the office here in Bernalillo on Monday mornings from now on," Lacho said.

"Is there a problem?" Matt asked, concerned that they were dissatisfied with his work.

"No, no, not a problem," replied the LT. "The sheriff feels, and I agree, that we just need to give you more exposure to the office as a whole," he replied. "As you know, funding is a big hassle right now, and the area here is exploding with people. We only have three detectives in the entire office, and it's not enough to cover the area within Bernalillo and Rio Rancho. We'd like you to spend a little face time with our detectives because there will be occasions when we need a detective in your area, and unless it's a mass murder or something, there's no way we'll be able to dispatch someone. We're not going to *officially* make you a detective as we need you doing what you're doing. But unofficially, we may need to call on you to do the job. Now I know, you've got a couple of dozen years as an investigator, and you can probably teach our detectives a thing or two, but we would like you to be aware of the Sandoval County way of doing things so we're all on the same page."

Matt paused for a moment. "OK, I think I've got it. I'll still be a patrol deputy, unless I'm not?"

"Yep, deputy you've got it crystal clear," replied Lacho. "And," the LT cleared his throat, "Your first assignment just happens to be today. They did the autopsy on Jason Trumble on Saturday. Toxicology will take a couple of weeks, but the Medical Examiner has determined that the cause of death was drowning, which we all knew. He found some suspicious bruising on the kid's shoulders and has tentatively concluded that his death might be in the realm of 'suspicious.' He wasn't willing to say he was murdered, but it merits further inquiry. So, part-time detective Bertram, we're going to need you to do some investigating. If you come up with something that indicates a potential murder, we will assign a detective to the case. I'd like you to call Sergeant Bobby Hanson before you head out today. He heads up the investigations division, and I want you to get to know him. Plan on being at roll call, in person, at 8 am each Monday, starting next Monday, here in Bernalillo. OK?"

"Sure thing, Lieutenant," Matt replied. *A two-hour drive each Monday*, Matt thought. *That's a helluva use of my time.* "One more thing, Lieutenant," Matt said, "I know we've had some tensions between us since I came on. I want you to know that I've had a difficult time adjusting to life since I moved here, but I'm feeling much better now. I want to be a team player and a valuable asset to the office. Anything I can do to make that happen, I will."

There was a pause on the line. Finally, the LT spoke. "Thanks for saying that, Deputy Bertram. I've been a little judgmental myself. I'll put in some effort on my side, too. My beef with you, deputy, is that you could be such a valuable asset and you just seem to be sleepwalking through life. I grieve for the loss of talent like yours."

"I understand, Lieutenant," Matt replied. "I've had something of a wakeup call in the last few days. I agree with your assessment up to this point, and I expect you'll see a few changes. But I'm still wearing my hat and boots."

Lt. Villanueva smiled and told Matt he would fax the autopsy report to him, then he transferred Matt over to Sergeant Hanson.

"Matt, I'm looking forward to meeting you," Sergeant Hanson said. "The Sheriff has told most of us about your amazing career with NCIS, and that you're kind of a double-legend there for bringing down the largest spy ring in navy history, plus eliminating the Russian guy who was responsible for the largest mass murder in US history, until Bin Laden and 9/11 last year, of course. I think we're lucky to have you aboard, and I hope that you and my detectives can learn a thing or two from each other."

"That's very kind of you, Sergeant," Matt said. "I'm sure this will be a good experience." The two talked about the death of Jason Trumble and the autopsy findings. "Suspicious may just stay that way, Matt, but it will be good to get statements from everyone who has a connection with the incident, and maybe just look into the backgrounds of the four people involved.

"There is another matter that has been moved over to Investigations Division, too, and that's the break-in of the hotel in Jemez Springs. This is the kind of thing that we would ordinarily send a detective to investigate, but, frankly, that won't ever happen with our staffing shortages. Good thing it happened at the same place where the kid died. You don't have to make two trips. Who knows, they might be related. I'll leave that up to you and your investigative skills."

The conversation completed, Matt showered, dressed for work and he and Jake were off to Las Águilas for morning coffee and gossip. After the ritual greeting between Jake and Chavy, Jake returned and curled up under Matt's bar seat and began crunching on a bone. Chavy walked over with coffee for Matt. "What's the news?" Matt asked.

"It's June in Jemez Springs," Chavy replied, chuckling. "Tourists are a two-edged sword. The summer months pretty much pay all my bills for the year, but there's this phenomenon that I like to call 'tourist brain.' I'm sure most of these people are reasonably intelligent and hold down good jobs back in Chugwater, Wyoming or Choccolocco, Alabama, but they lock the door to the house on their vacation and leave their brains at home. They forget rules about crossing the street and forget their belongings in, oh say, bars and such. Oh, and I'm not sure what's up, but the Funk brothers have been driving up and down State Road 4 and all the back streets around here since Saturday. They've got *un palo en sus traseros* about something."

"Wonderful," Matt replied, shaking his head. "I'll keep an eye out for them."

Matt finished his coffee and headed for his second regular stop, the Jemez Ranger District office. Once again, after a ritual Jake greeting, Paul, Kai and Matt sat in Paul's office chatting. "We got the autopsy results on Jason Trumble," Matt said. "Looks like the M.E. thinks his death is borderline suspicious. He found some questionable bruises on the kid's shoulders. I've talked my LT into letting me to do a little more investigating."

"That's interesting," said Paul. "Sure looked to me like the kid just passed out in the hot water. But then, what do I know? The autopsy of Danny Goldman is scheduled for today in Albuquerque. After the strange footprints we found on the mesa, I'm wondering what they'll find."

"I'll tell you truthfully, Paul. Things are starting to form a pattern for me. I brought you the autopsy report that my office faxed me this morning. Do you want to make a copy for the pathologist who's doing Danny's autopsy?"

"Yeah, seems like they ought to have all the info. I'll do the same for you when we get the report."

"OK, my friends," Matt said, standing. "I guess I'm out on my appointed rounds. I need to go have a chat with the UNM folks and have another chat with Maggie about the break-ins. It probably means another trip out to see the Funk brothers, too. Another fun day in paradise."

Matt and Jake's next stop for the day was the Mineral Springs Lodge. As Matt was parking his Jimmy, he spied Maggie shuffling toward him from the office. As he stepped out of the truck, Maggie approached, wringing her hands. "Oh dear, oh dear," she said. "I was just about to call you, Matt. Something else has happened here. I think I've been cursed or something."

"Now, slow down, Maggie. Let's go inside and you can tell me what's up."

Maggie poured Matt some coffee and gave Jake a dog biscuit. "Now, what's happened, Maggie?" Matt said.

"Professor Sinclair and that Naomi lady are gone," she said.

"You mean they checked out?"

"No, they just left. They drove out of here heading north on Friday evening, and they haven't been back. They left their belongings in the room, and they didn't check out. Sinclair has stayed with us many times and he always pays his bill and checks out. I tried calling Sinclair's cell phone, but it goes straight to voicemail. Oh, bears must have murdered or attacked them, or, or ..."

"Now hold on, Maggie, let's don't go jumping to conclusions. I'll head out east in a bit and see if maybe I can find them. I'm sure there's a logical explanation. And you know how sketchy cell service is here. You don't worry yourself, OK?"

Maggie nodded, but was obviously not feeling assured by Matt's words of comfort. "Now, Maggie, I have a few more questions about the break-in on Friday and the death of the young boy, and then I'll go see if I can find the UNM folks." Matt asked his questions, but, unfortunately, Maggie was not much help. She was completely convinced that it was the Funk brothers who broke into the rooms and would not be dissuaded from that belief. Matt had to agree that they were the prime suspects. As far as Jason went, Maggie was no help. She saw nothing and knew of nobody other than the UNM people who saw or heard anything. She was open to Matt interviewing staff and getting the names and numbers of the guests who were staying at the lodge the night he died.

"You told me that your housekeeper had seen something, um, Romi is her name? Can I have a talk with her if she's around?"

"Sure, Matt," Maggie said. "She's working on one of the cabins right now."

Matt walked out to the courtyard, looking for a cabin with a housekeeper's cart in front. He approached Romi as she was picking up clean towels for the room. Matt introduced himself, asking if she was open to answering some questions.

"Yes, deputy, I saw the Funk brothers' truck across the street at the old thrift shop that's closed that morning," Romi said in response to Matt's questions. "I didn't tell Maggie, but I saw them walking back to their truck and one was carrying a sledge hammer."

Matt walked back to his truck to look for the Funks, assured that they had, indeed, been the burglars of the cabin.

Sinclair and Naomi set out in the morning on Monday walking along the road toward Jemez Springs, hoping they would find cell service before the Funk brothers found them. They reasoned that their best chance of avoiding the Funks was to leave in the morning. Sinclair's guess was that they were not early risers, which was a correct assumption. Walking along the side of the highway, Sinclair was vigilantly listening for the sound of cars coming. Each time he would hear a car, he would shout "Car!" and jump into the bushes at the side of the road until the car passed them. They performed this maneuver four or five times in the first ten minutes they were on the road. Naomi followed Sinclair along the road, checking her cell phone every few minutes, hoping for a signal. Sinclair, once more, gave his "Car!" shout.

Naomi looked into the sky, rolled her hands into fists and shouted back to Sinclair, "Fuck this! I'm flagging it down!" Much to Sinclair's distress, Naomi stood in the middle of the road waving her hands at the truck that was headed toward them. As the truck got close enough to identify, Naomi said, "Fuck. It's the sheriff's deputy." She paused for a few seconds and said, "Sinclair, come out of the bushes. We can make this work. But let me do the talking." Sinclair crawled out from the bushes, several branches sticking to his wispy gray hair, and resigned himself to what would happen.

Matt slowed his Jimmy down as he saw the two walking along the side of the road. He pulled up next to them, rolling down his window. "Oh, thank God, Deputy Bertram," Naomi said. "You are our guardian angel!"

"I was actually out looking for you two," Matt said. "Maggie at the lodge let me know you hadn't been in your room since Friday. She was worried you had been eaten by bears."

"Could we have a ride back to town, Deputy?" Naomi said. "I'll explain the adventure we've been on."

The two got in the rear seat of the Jimmy as Jake in his position as wingman, watched them like they were desperados, occasionally giving them low, guttural growls. "Friends," Matt said to Jake, which stopped the growling but not his wary eye.

Naomi went into full flirt mode with Matt. "You are definitely our savior, deputy," she said, batting her eyelashes at Matt. "We went up to that beautiful Fenton Lake and were just enraptured with the beauty of the mountains. Sinclair has some camping equipment he keeps in his van, so we just thought, 'what the heck, we'll just camp here.' We enjoyed it so much that we decided to stay another night. Then, late yesterday, as we were heading back, Sinclair's minivan broke down. It was so late, and we were so far from town that we decided just to spend the night in the van. My back will never be the same."

"So, how far have you walked this morning?" Matt asked.

"Oh, we just started about ten minutes ago," Naomi replied.

Matt smiled. "You know you broke down just a mile from Jemez Springs, don't you?"

If looks could kill, the look Naomi gave Sinclair would have boxed him up and cremated him all at the same time. "It was dark, and we just don't know this area, so we really did not know," Naomi said, stifling an urge to pull her gun out and shoot Sinclair on the spot.

"We just need you to drop us off at the local mechanic and arrange for a tow truck to come get the van," she said.

"That's a taller order than you know, Miss Canneloy. You see, they don't have a garage here in the Springs, and certainly no tow trucks. You'll have to get the van towed either to Los Alamos, which is about an hour east, or Bernalillo, which is about an hour south. And you can expect to pay a premium to get a tow truck out here."

"My God," said Sinclair. "Towing that piece of junk would cost more than the van is worth! There must be an alternative?"

"Well, no guarantees, but there's a guy who lives in town and fixes cars on the side at his home. He doesn't have a tow truck, but he might be willing to put a tow strap on and limp you into his place. Like I say, no guarantees, but we can stop and see."

"We appreciate your help, deputy," said Sinclair. "I guess we'll be staying in the area for a few more days."

"That's actually good for me, professor," Matt replied. "The autopsy results came back on your student, Jason, and the medical examiner had a few concerns. We don't have any detectives available to come out this way, so I've been asked to look into it."

"Oh my, deputy," Naomi said, "How could that be? It seems pretty cut and dried what happened. And, no offense, but shouldn't a *real* detective be 'looking into it?'"

"I think they just want to be sure all the 'i's' are dotted and 't's' are crossed, Miss Canneloy. And besides, I was a Special Agent with the Navy Criminal Investigative Service for twenty-four years. I quit NCIS a couple of years ago and thought I was going to be a rancher, but the Sheriff of Sandoval County is a friend, and he talked me into getting back in the saddle, so to speak. I think a little investigation like this is within my wheelhouse."

It suddenly became silent in the back seat. Matt continued, "So, even though I'm sure you're in the mood to head home, I'd appreciate it if we could sit down and go through things a little more thoroughly before you leave. If you get your van fixed quickly, I can always drive out to UNM and we can go through my questions there, if you like. I'm sure your dean wouldn't have a problem with that."

"No, no, we would be happy to stick around and answer your questions," Sinclair said, after making a slight gurgling sound. "It's summer vacation, and another few days in the beautiful Jemez won't be a problem."

Matt drove into Jemez Springs and turned at Mooney Boulevard, traveling up a dirt road until he reached a dirt driveway. He turned onto the driveway, passing a mobile home, and stopped in front of a large metal building. A tall and rotund man wearing coveralls and a beat-up ball cap came walking out. Matt got out of the Jimmy with Jake close behind. "Matthew, you brought Jake to visit," the man said in a heavy Turkish accent, kneeling down and scratching Jake's neck. Sinclair and Naomi exited the truck and walked up to the men.

Matt introduced the man as Nazar Onut. "My friend Matthew says you have a little car trouble," said the man. "I may be able to help, but you need to know I am not professional mechanic. It is mostly hobby for me."

Sinclair explained the problem, and Nazar offered to take them back to the van and he would see if he could fix it there. "If not, we just put tow strap on and bring to my garage. Is against the law, but I know when the local deputy goes to lunch," he said, chuckling at his own joke.

"Are you going to be staying at Mineral Springs tonight?" Matt asked.

"Um, yes, I guess we will, provided I can convince Maggie to get us a room," Sinclair said.

Matt handed Sinclair his card. "Call me when you get back to your room and I'll come by for a chat. Mineral Springs Lodge is just a couple of blocks away, so you can walk if you need to. If it's after five, we can do it in the morning. I'll just be doing patrol duty the rest of the day."

Matt left the two in the care of Nazar and headed out to his regular duties. He decided he would interview the UNM people before talking with the staff and people in the surrounding businesses about the break-in and Jason's death.

As Matt resumed his patrol duties, Randy said from the back seat, "I don't know about you, Matt, but those two just seemed to act very suspiciously. The professor said he's been in the area several times, so why wouldn't he have known that his room was just a mile down the road? And why did they get very quiet when you informed them the kid's death was suspicious? You need to keep an eye on them."

"I will, Randy. Although I can't imagine what kind of motive they would have for murder, things are adding up. I can't help but think that something happened at Astialakwa to provide that motive. From the way they acted after the break-in, I'd bet dollars to donuts that the Funks found something of interest in the professor's cabin which might help me to put the pieces together. They had three backpacks in their van at La Casitas. I need to take a look in their van and see if they are still there. Anything else?"

"Do you see either of those two as people who go camping?"

"Good point."

Matt decided to drive up the highway and see if he could locate the van. No more than a mile east, there was a dirt driveway.

He turned up the driveway and spotted the van tucked behind a tree. As he inspected the minivan, he could see it had overheated, and there was antifreeze spattered on the windshield. He looked through the dirty windows and could see the three small backpacks in the rear. They could have contained camping equipment, he supposed, but they were also the same size as the backpack he and the rangers had recovered from Mesa de Guadalupe. The shovels and picks he had seen at La Casitas were still there. The door of the van was locked.

At the end of the drive was a cabin, so Matt took a look around. He knocked on the door and there was no answer, so he walked around to the back of the cabin. There was a broken window in the back door. He knocked again, and not receiving an answer, went inside. The cabin was tidy, and he could not see any obvious theft. He made a note to look up the owners and call them to let them know of the break-in, and left, hoping to be out of the area by the time the UNM people arrived with Nazar to take the van back to Nazar's garage. *Well, that contradicts the camping story*, he thought.

Matt spent a few hours writing tickets to speeding tourists, giving directions to tourists who were lost, and chastising tourists who were standing in the highway, oblivious to oncoming traffic, attempting to get that "perfect" photograph for their family back home. At 1pm he and Jake stopped in at Las Águilas to get a bite to eat. When they were on the road, Jake usually took the opportunity to snooze in the back seat, but whenever Matt slowed down, Jake was at his position as Matt's wingman, hoping they would get out of the truck for an adventure, or at least a stretch. As soon as Matt turned into Las Águilas, Jake was upfront, ears raised, anticipating a stop at his favorite restaurant and bar.

Matt walked in the front door of Las Águilas, Chavy and the other regulars greeted Jake in the usual way. Matt spied Paul and Kai at a table and walked over to say hi. "Got room for two more?"

Paul motioned to the empty seat at the table, and said, "I'm afraid your partner is going to be busy with lunch behind the counter, but since nobody even said hi when you walked in, the least I can do is offer you a seat." As Matt sat down, Paul said, "Glad you came by. I was going to call you. We got the autopsy results back on Danny Goldman."

"Anything of note?" Matt inquired.

"Well, it sounds a lot like the results on Jason Trumble," Paul responded. "The pathologist said the kid was so banged up from the fall that it was difficult to tell, but he found a suspicious contusion on the side of his head that's inconsistent with the damage from the impact on the rocks. He said it the damage appeared to be more from an impact from a more malleable object on his temple. He speculated that it could have been from a human fist, but he wasn't willing to be all in on that conclusion."

"You're right. Sounds like we have similar outcomes," Matt agreed.

"Just as interesting," Kai chimed in. "We got a report back from forensics. The kid's prints are all over the contents. It's definitely his bag."

"Just out of curiosity," Matt responded, "any other prints?"

"No," Kai said, "just his."

"Matt, this brings up quite a lot of questions. We've talked to our district ranger, and he's put a call in to the Southwestern Region office to see if they will dispatch a special agent. In the meantime, he gave us permission to interview the professor and the student."

"You might have a few more questions when I tell you what I saw today. Maggie told me that the two had disappeared on Friday and she was worried about them. I was keeping an eye out on patrol this morning and came across them walking along the highway. They told me they had been camping at Fenton Lake for two nights, and their van broke down on the way back yesterday. After taking them to Nazar to see if he could help, I went looking for the van. I found it in a driveway off State Road 4 about a mile outside of Jemez Springs. I looked inside the van and there were a couple of shovels and picks in the back. The two had parked very close to a cabin. Someone had, coincidentally, I'm sure, broken into the cabin. They claim they spent the night in the van, but I have a wild guess that they may be the ones who broke into the cabin when their van broke down, and made themselves at home."

"Shovels and picks? I wonder what they might have needed them for," Paul said, giving a wry smile.

"Well, I'm not going to jump to any conclusions, but that's definitely on my list of questions," Matt rejoined. "Speaking of that, they should probably be back at Mineral Springs Lodge by now. I don't know if you have plans, but it might be efficient if we interviewed these two together."

Kai begged out, as he needed to make a drive to the Gillman Tunnels. The tunnels were old, abandoned railroad tunnels and a popular place for tourists to visit and, quite often, find trouble. The Forest Service regularly patrolled the Guadalupe Box and the tunnels, and usually found someone who was pushing their luck by attempting to scale the cliff. Kai mused at the variety of ways tourists could find themselves in a pickle or vandalize public property.

"On an entirely different subject, Matt," Paul said, "Benny called me this morning. He would like to visit your property on a scouting expedition to look for Sééeh-Wagi. Weh'ng Péh wasn't terrifically specific about the exact location, and given that it's probably four hundred years old, it might take a bit of doing to locate it. He would like to come out with Henry Romero, our sheriff and a respected elder of our tribe."

"That would be great," Matt responded. "I don't know if they can make it tomorrow, but I usually make Tuesdays a light day during the summer, as I'm working most weekends. I'm hoping they will allow me to help."

"I'll give Benny a call. And I'm sure you can. It's your land, Matt."

"Let's just say I'm a steward of that land, Paul."

"You sure you don't have any Jemez in you?" Paul replied, smiling.

"Maybe not the tribe, Paul, but definitely the place."

16

Predator or Prey?

Life is nothing but a competition to be the criminal rather than the victim.

(Bertrand Russell)

"Definitely the water pump," Nazar said to Sinclair in his thick Turkish accent.

"So, is that bad?" Sinclair replied, betraying his utter ignorance of auto mechanics.

"No, no, easy peasy," retorted Nazar. "Problem is, no auto parts stores here. I have friend who sells used parts in Cuba. I drive out there this afternoon, pick one up. Only take me maybe an hour to put on, then you good to go. Or we get new from Los Alamos or Bernalillo."

"If I put a new water pump on that crappy old van, it would be out of place," Sinclair said. "I appreciate you doing this. Of course, I'll gladly pay you for your time."

"Of course," Nazar said. "I take you to your hotel and you will have van back tomorrow at latest."

Sinclair and Naomi climbed into the cab of Nazar's pickup and the three headed north toward the lodge. A few minutes into the drive, Sinclair spotted the unmistakable visage of the Funk brothers' truck driving south toward them. As the truck passed, both Sinclair and Naomi attempted to shrink below the dashboard, hoping they would not be spotted.

As the Funk's truck passed Nazar's, Dory screamed and pointed, "Look, Dude, there they are!"

Chuchu gave a whoop, smacking his brother on the back. "It's total ruination, Dude!"

Dory, doing little to slow down, spun the wheel with all his might, putting the truck into a spin, barely recovering without flipping the truck, then jammed the gas pedal down in an effort to catch up to Nazar's truck. Unfortunately for Dory, he executed his Steve McQueen maneuver directly in front of Matt's Jimmy, forcing Matt to slam his brakes on. Just as the two sped up, they heard a siren and through the rear-view mirror Dory saw the deputy. "Shit, man," was all he could say.

The two sat in the cab of their truck, watching their prey drive away, waiting for the deputy to get out of his truck. Matt decided to let the two stew a bit before opening the door and walking toward their truck as slowly as possible. Paul pulled up behind Matt. He got out of his truck and walked up next to Matt. "Would you shut off your truck please sir, and pass me your driver's license and registration?" Matt said. He looked at Dory, one eye swollen shut and a gash in his forehead. "What the hell happened to you, Dory?" he exclaimed.

"I, uh, got hit by a door, man. And dude, deputy, you know us, man!" said Dory. "Besides, I think I left that shit at home, man," he said.

"Oh, come on, Dory," Matt said with incredulity. "We both know you are driving with a suspended license and your license plate tags are so out of date they say 'New Mexico Territory' on them. So, where were you two headed so fast?"

"Um, dude, we were, um, like—" Dory said.

Chuchu finished the sentence for him. "Fishing, man. We were going fishing."

"And your fishing equipment is where?"

Chuchu, believing he was the smart brother, said, "Exactly, man. We realized we forgot our fishing poles and were hurrying to get them, dude."

"And may I see your fishing licenses?" Matt said, enjoying the conversation immensely.

"Oh, man, we forgot those too," Dory exclaimed.

"So, one question before I write you up a couple of tickets for driving while suspended, an unlicensed vehicle, reckless driving, and a couple of other things I'll think of while I'm writing. You guys know anything about the break-ins at the Mineral Springs Lodge last Friday?"

It was Chuchu's turn again. "Wow, man, the lodge was broken into, man? That sucks, man. We didn't hear about it."

"That's just the answer I was expecting. Maybe we should drive together up to your cabin and take a look around."

"That's cool, man. We don't have anything to hide, dude. It was all stol—Um, I mean, we don't have anything we didn't buy fair and square."

"Well, maybe I'll make a 'surprise' visit here at some point. You boys just stay put while I write a couple of worthless pieces of paper that you'll shove into your glove box and not deal with."

As Matt walked back to his truck he looked into the bed of the Funks' truck, noting a sledgehammer in plain sight. Matt wrote the citations, considering it a waste of time. He estimated he had given the two at least thirty tickets since he started with SCSO a little less than a year before. The local magistrate had simply stopped dealing with them, and he was about to himself.

Sinclair looked behind the truck as they passed the Funks and gave a sigh of relief to see the deputy pulling them over. Nazar dropped them off at the lodge and Sinclair went into the front office to assuage Maggie. To his surprise, she seemed quite relieved to see him. "Oh, Sinclair, I was so worried about you. You are such an upright man. I knew you wouldn't have left without paying or saying goodbye. I'm so sorry about the break-in to your room. I want you to know that your stay is free."

"Thank you, my dear Maggie," Sinclair said, trying to put on professorial airs. "In fact, I don't suppose we could stay a few more nights? We are so rattled by all of this that we need a few moments to catch our breath."

"Of course, Sinclair. Perhaps we could finish the lovely evening we were having when we were interrupted the other night?"

"It would be a delight, Maggie. I, uh, don't suppose you have any more of that wonderful cognac we were sipping?"

"For you, Sinclair, I'll bring out my finest!"

Maggie gave Sinclair a new key for their cabin and he and Naomi walked to the cabin and went inside. The moment they were inside, Sinclair began melting down. "I don't know what we are going to do about those Funk brothers. They could turn us in and ruin our lives. Worse yet, they could, and will, if they get the chance, probably kill us. Oh, my, this is too terrible!"

"Oh, come on, Sinclair," Naomi retorted. "You be the victim if you want, Sinclair, but I choose to be the heroine of my fucking life, not the victim."

"Great, now you're quoting Nora Ephron. Well, a profane version, anyway. So, what do you propose, *heroine*?"

Just as Naomi was about to tell Sinclair in no uncertain terms how things needed to be resolved, there was a knock on the door. Sinclair answered, and Matt and Paul stood outside with Jake sitting in between the two. Sinclair could have sworn the dog had a rancorous look on his face. "Well, deputy, it's indeed good to see you," said Sinclair, endeavoring to camouflage any disingenuous expression he might have had on his face.

"Hi professor, may we come in for just a moment? You remember meeting Officer Toza the morning after Jason died? There are a few things we need to follow-up on regarding Jason's death," Matt said.

"Certainly, deputy. It's been quite a tough couple of days, however. I'm uncertain how much help we can be."

Matt and Paul asked the two academics questions regarding the timelines, when they had last seen Jason, when they went to bed, and Jason's level of inebriation that evening. "Unfortunately, deputy, I was the first one in bed that night. I think we were all imbibing a bit too much for our own good that evening, and I bid Jason and Naomi good night and went to bed."

Matt turned to Naomi. "So, you were the last one to see him?" he asked.

"I guess so. He was not making much sense, singing a stupid song, and he got so annoying that I finally went in. I tried to get him just to go to bed, but he insisted he wanted to soak. He was crying off and on about Danny."

"I appreciate your help. I know this is hard," Matt said.

Paul had been mostly listening, but he sensed it was time to test the mettle of the two. "There is something you need to know," Paul said, sounding unmistakably serious. "We took a hike up to Astialakwa. We found a backpack there. It was filled with artifacts from Astialakwa. Beautiful pottery, some still intact despite the tumble down the cliff, spearheads, arrowheads, and a portion of a breastplate from a Spaniard. Just today we got the forensics back on the backpack, and the autopsy results on Danny. The autopsy was inconclusive, but the forensics showed Danny's fingerprints all over the stolen items in the backpack.

"Oh, good god, man," Sinclair said. "How in the hell could that have happened?"

"That's my question for you two. Do you have any idea how he was able to acquire those items, and did you know your group was bringing artifacts back?"

Sinclair sputtered so Naomi jumped in. "Of course not, officer!" she said fervently. "The professor gave each of the boys a lecture about leaving any artifacts *in sitsu*. It's the law. And we know that Harvard and the Jemez Pueblo are beginning an extensive survey of the area in a month or two." Naomi intentionally paused, allowing an air of drama to permeate the room. "Now that I think about it, that's how we lost Danny. He lagged behind all of us, and it wasn't for a half hour or so that we realized he wasn't with us. That's when I went back to find him, and he was gone!"

Naomi took a deep breath, deciding the best course of action was to channel Claire Danes in *My So-Called Life*. She burst out with an "Ohmygod," and surged into a torrent of tears, gradually increasing to sobs. She fell onto Matt's chest, blubbing. "It's c-c-crazy! He stole artifacts that are incredibly important to the Jemez people, and now he's inexplicably dead and Jason is also puzzlingly dead. Oh crap! The spirits of the ancient people are taking vengeance on us because Danny took the treasures they have guarded for centuries! We're … we're screwed!"

Naomi put her arms around Matt, now unreservedly hysterical. Matt looked at Paul, who shook his head in wonder at the magnificently orchestrated histrionics they were witnessing. Both watched in amazed silence as the dramatic performance of the century, for the moment, bemused them.

"Now, just calm down, Naomi," Matt finally said, "Take some breaths. Now, I just don't think there is necessarily a supernatural explanation for this. I've been in the law enforcement business for a long time, and there is usually a very earthly explanation for what happens."

Naomi, in measured breaths, gradually brought down the intensity of her performance. Matt handed her his handkerchief, which she proceeded to fill with copious volumes of tears and snot.

"Before we go," Paul said, "I do have one more question. Deputy Bertram was looking through the rear window of your van and he spotted a couple of shovels and picks. Do you mind explaining what you were doing with them, and did you take them with you on your hike to Astialakwa?"

Sinclair stared for a moment at Paul as though he had just seen a ghost. Since Naomi was in the throes of an emotional seizure, he knew he couldn't rely on her proficient fabrications. "Oh, um, that. I, um, always bring a shovel or two and perhaps a pick when we go into the field. We don't disturb anything of importance, of course. Most ancient ruins have been covered with dirt and rock, and I often uncover, at least temporarily, what I identify as sites of archaeological significance. Without an experienced and trained eye, actual sites would go unnoticed. I've been on digs around the world for several dozen years. As a PhD archaeologist, I have the skills to spot such sites, which would probably be missed by most people. The shovel is there to illustrate for my students that what looks to the untrained eye like a pile of dirt can be unveiled as an incredible remnant of a past civilization. If we do uncover something with a shovel, we are always careful to restore it to the way it was before we dug."

"That's interesting, professor," Matt said. "Because when we were at Astialakwa, there were several places we saw that had been dug up and were simply left in the open."

Naomi spoke up, her chest still slightly heaving from her sobbing. "That would make sense, deputy," she said, swiftly regaining her calm. "If Danny went back to dig up artifacts, he would have had to do so quickly. He wouldn't have concerned himself with covering up any of his vandalism of the site."

Neither Matt nor Paul responded. Matt turned to Sinclair and said, "You know, professor, what you said about having a trained eye gave me a thought. There is a site of an ancient shrine on my property that we are going to be looking for tomorrow. Can you give us some tips about what to look for?"

Sinclair immediately perked up. "What kind of site? How did you discover it was there?" he said, looking like a wolf who had just spotted a rabbit.

"It's a long story about how we learned about it, but it is what the Jemez call Sééeh-Wagi, or Eagle's Altar. It is a site the Hemish Eagle Catching Society used for important ceremonies. Some of the tribe's elders, Paul and I, are going to look for it. We know the general area, but, if it is as you say, just a mound of rubble, we could easily miss it."

"Not only would I lend you my vast expertise, deputy, but I would be more than willing to accompany you on the search tomorrow. If it's there, I'll have the skills to find it."

Matt looked at Paul, whose expression betrayed the questionable judgment at bringing these two along, but finally shook his head. "Oh, it's set for tomorrow and it would probably be best that you didn't. There will be Jemez elders there, and they are pretty private about these things," he said, without displaying much enthusiasm.

Both Matt and Paul were eager to extricate themselves from this interview. "I tell you what," Matt said, "let's give Naomi a chance to recover a bit, and we can renew our conversation about Danny once the shock has worn off a bit."

"I understand, deputy," Sinclair said. "We were planning to be here a few more days anyway, just to recuperate a bit."

Matt and Paul said their goodbyes to Sinclair and Naomi and headed for their trucks. "Have you seen anything like that?" Matt said to Paul.

"It's times like this that I'm glad I come from more stoic stock,"

"I agree," said Matt. "With the evidence mounting, these two were not just on a field trip but more like a pilfering trip."

Matt got into his Jimmy. "And the Academy Award goes to ..." Randy said.

"Oh, come on, Randy, that young lady was obviously upset," Matt jokingly replied.

"Yeah, sure," Randy replied. "It's pretty obvious with that lady that appearances are just a bit deceptive. I find it hard to see that woman believing anything supernatural is going on. That's ridiculous. And pour one for me, Bertram. After that, we *both* need a good Jack Daniels."

Naomi peeked through the curtains to be certain the deputy and LEO were gone, then turned back toward Sinclair. "It would sure be interesting to see what they find at this shrine tomorrow. Too bad the deputy didn't want us there."

"Are you kidding, Naomi. We'll just show up tomorrow, and work our charm. I'll convince them of the value I can provide and they won't be able to say no. What if they find the holy grail of artifacts? We could add that to the pot and score plenty more. I sense an opportunity to take credit for a notable find heading my way!"

Naomi shook her head. "So we're going to just show up tomorrow? Leave it to you to capitalize on someone else's work," she said. "And speaking of that, we have some readjusting of our relationship to do."

"What do you mean?" asked Sinclair.

"Danny the toad is gone and Jason the drunk is, too. You were going to share the proceeds of the Black Heart with them. I've done a hell of a lot to help you in the last few days, so I think it's only fair for us to split the proceeds of the Black Heart fifty-fifty."

"Fifty-fifty, my ass!" shouted Sinclair. "It's been my hard and diligent research that discovered the treasure. You wanted a guaranteed pass into a PhD program, which is worth a boatload of cash. No possible way we are splitting things evenly!"

"Listen to me, you greedy third-rate archaeologist," Naomi spat, "It's going to be fifty-fifty or—"

"Or what, Naomi? What could you possibly do?"

"Don't tempt me to tell you, Sinclair. You would pee your pants and mess up your feet of clay!"

"What do you mean? What have you done that would give me any concern?" Sinclair said.

"I'm going to take a walk," Naomi responded, walking out of the cabin, slamming the door behind her.

Naomi was gone all of five minutes when she walked back in the door, exhibiting a much calmer demeanor. "You know, Sinclair, I was just thinking," she said, almost casually. "We have to take care of the Funk brothers. You and I both know you're a fucking coward, and we also both know that I'm a woman with resources. You don't successfully escape where I grew up without getting your hands dirty. I'm going to let you off the hook. I'll take care of the Funk brothers myself. You can stay out of it. In exchange, you give me half the proceeds of the Black Heart. If anything goes wrong, you'll have clean hands. What do you say?"

"I wouldn't have to do anything, and you'll just make them go away? How—"

"If you ask questions," Naomi interrupted, "your hands won't be clean."

Sinclair stared at Naomi for a moment. "OK, Naomi. You have yourself a deal."

Matt and Jake turned north on the highway, heading for home. As he was driving, Matt reviewed the events of the day in his mind. "Are you there, Randy?" he said.

"Of course, Bertram. I was just thinking about when we first met. You were such a goofy young guy, in way over your head, and I was, maybe, just a touch brash with you."

Matt smiled, thinking about their meeting at the Tokyo airport. He was a young sailor, and she was a new NIS special agent. When he was told he was meeting Randy Glasscock at the airport, he assumed he was meeting a man. The meeting did not go very well because of his sexist observations. "Well, once you forgave me, things improved," Matt said.

"Indeed, they did, Matthew," she said. "Indeed, they did."

Matt rounded the curve, heading east out of the village on his way home, daydreaming about Randy's face, realizing that her image was getting more difficult to picture in his mind. His attention was suddenly diverted to the road ahead as he saw a car swerve around something partially in the road. At first glance, he could swear it was a body, but he slowed down and lit up his Jimmy. He stopped in the middle of the road and jumped out of the truck and ran to the body. He kneeled down and realized he was seeing the face of Father O'Sullivan. He put his fingers on his carotid artery to check for a pulse and as he did, one of Amos's eyes opened. "I'm pretty sure I still have a pulse," Amos said smiling, casting a potent scent of alcohol on his breath.

"My God, Amos. What were you doing in the road?" Matt asked.

"Now that, my friend, is an excellent question," Amos replied with very slurred speech. "And I wish I had an excellent answer, other than I needed a wee bit of a nap."

Matt reached his hand down to Amos, saying, "Let me help you up, Coach. And how about I take you to my house? I can get some coffee down you and keep you safe from roadside naps."

"I'm afraid I'm not in a position to argue," Amos replied. Amos grabbed Matt's hand and pulled himself up, surprising Matt at how agile and strong the priest was, especially considering his level of inebriation.

Matt drove Amos back to his lodge, Amos napping most of the way. "Found yourself a stray dog, Bertram?" Randy said.

"Perhaps, Randy. But I think he's a good guy. I'm not sure how I can help, but I know his life at that mausoleum certainly isn't doing him much good. Maybe having a reason to live will help him decide not to kill himself with alcohol."

"Seems like you have yourself a plan, Matt," said Randy. "I like him, and maybe he'll be good for you, too."

17

The Eagle's Altar

We are not human beings having a spiritual experience. We are spiritual beings having a human experience.
(Pierre Teilhard de Chardin)

Matt was up the next morning before dawn. He enjoyed having coffee on his front porch in the summer just before daybreak, even though the altitude made the early morning temperatures cool, even for June. There was always something mysterious about the end of the night. The sky seemed to be at its darkest just before dawn, and Matt felt as though he was witnessing a miracle each morning as the horizon gradually turned from black to rust, then to crimson and finally, as fully inflamed by the sun. Jake was on his rug next to Matt's rocking chair, scanning the grounds for a chipmunk to torment.

The front door opened, and Father O'Sullivan walked out, holding a steaming mug of coffee. "I hope you don't mind if I helped myself," said Amos, taking a scalding sip.

"When you are in this house, Amos, please treat it as yours."

"In that case, boyo, I'll be sleeping in the master bedroom tonight," he said, patting Matt on the shoulder.

"Pull up a chair and enjoy the show," Matt said to Amos.

"That famous theologian Sissy Spacek once said, 'Nature is my church. The wind in the trees and the bugs and the frogs. All those things are comfort to me.' I would add the sunrise and sunset to that list," Amos said.

"If everyone thought that, it would put you religious guys out of business," Matt replied.

"Might not necessarily be a bad thing, my son."

"Amos," Matt said, "Benny, Paul, the Jemez Sheriff and those university people will be by in a little while. We're going to go up the hill to look for Sééeh-Wagi. If you're up for it, I'd love to have you along."

"Why, I'd be honored, Matthew."

"Amos, I was also wondering if, perhaps, you might be willing to lend me a hand here at the ranch for a few weeks. There are caretaker's quarters on the second floor of the barn, which would give you privacy and comfort. My work with SCSO is taking so much time, there's quite a lot that needs to be done to catch up. It might give you a breather from Saint Frumentius, and I could use a little company around here."

"And it also might distract me from alcohol, Matthew?"

"You never know. I think it's good for people to have a purpose, and I wonder if some time away from the church would help you gain something. I've always found that change helps you find your calling, or at least re-awakens what you might have once thought was a plan for your life. Hell, I'm giving advice to a priest. Sorry."

"Not at all, Matthew. Some of the best advice comes from people in your life who can see you in a way you don't see yourself. I'll certainly give your offer some thought. Yes, that I will."

The two sat for quite some time, not speaking, simply absorbing the exquisite sunrise. As the sun fully lit the morning, Matt went inside and cooked some eggs, bacon, and toast for them. Just as they were finishing, Jake gave the 'all-call' that visitors were arriving and the two went back out on the porch. Paul, Benny, and Henry Romero were walking up to the lodge. Matt offered them coffee, which all three gladly accepted.

Sinclair and Naomi were looking for Matt's place as they drove up the highway. "Maggie said his place is along this stretch of road somewhere. Keep on the lookout for a double-wide and his truck." The ranch came into view on their right, and Sinclair said, "No way. How in the hell does a Sandoval County Sheriff's deputy have the bucks to own a ranch like this?"

Naomi, never one for overreacting, said, "I don't know, but he just got a lot more interesting!"

Paul, watching the two turn into Matt's driveway, mumbled some Towan words Matt didn't understand, but assumed they were profane.

Sinclair and Naomi got out of the minivan. "I know you said it wasn't necessary to come, deputy," Sinclair said, "But my professionalism just wouldn't allow me to risk amateurs harming such a great treasure. We'll stay out of your way, but something this important demands a high degree of expertise."

"No way," Matt said.

Paul turned to Matt. "I'm not comfortable with this either, but he does make a good point. Benny? It should be up to you."

Benny thought for a moment, and then said, "I will allow it, but only if they keep their distance and leave if I tell them to."

Matt shrugged, took a deep breath, nonverbally and with great reservation indicated they could remain. He made introductions deferring to Benny's judgment that they could be of help. He leaned over to Paul and whispered in his ear, "I'm going to keep an eye on them and if I see so much as a flinch, they are out of here."

Matt had packed picks, shovels, and saws for the underbrush. Matt said to Benny, "You are the one who spoke with Weh'ng Péh, Benny. I think we should let you lead."

Sinclair gave Naomi a questioning look, which was returned in-kind. Matt felt no compulsion to fill them in on those details.

Matt's home, barn and outbuildings were on a level area of his ranch toward the bottom of a hill that rose into a steeper slope further above. To the front was a gentle slope down to the highway, and behind his home was a gradually inclining slope for about 500 feet, which then became much steeper above that. The far end of his property was almost 800 feet higher in elevation than his home. There was an open field near his home which became progressively more wooded on the land further from his home.

Benny pointed to a large stand of forest and said, "This is the area that Weh'ng Péh directed me to, but it could be anywhere in that forested area."

"I guess we have our work cut out for us," Matt said, grabbing the pack and a shovel, following Benny as he began the climb into the forest. He turned to Sinclair and said, "Professor, I'm hoping your archaeological skills will help Benny to narrow down what we're looking for. Maybe you could give us a quick lesson on what to look for."

"If it's up there, deputy, we'll find it," Sinclair offered. "And I'd be happy to share what I can. Observation is the most important. Look for piles of rock or dirt that look out of place. If you see rock, look for patterns. Humans tend to build things in geometric patterns that are usually less random than nature makes them. This will be more difficult because we don't know how large the shrine is."

"Pardon me, professor," Benny said, "but I have a very good idea what it will look like. Three or four feet high with three- or four-foot sides. We don't know if it has been demolished or if it's intact. Of course, intact would be much easier to spot. If something makes you curious, just call me and I can have a look."

They walked up the slope toward the area Benny directed. The forest on this part of the mountain was filled with a classic combination of native trees. Ponderosa pine was the most predominant tree, with some white fir scattered among the pine. The bottom brush was thick with Gambel oak, which made it difficult to see the ground in many places.

The group spread out to cover an area Matt guessed was about two acres in size. Without the Gambel oak, the job would have been much easier to accomplish. With it, each bush had to be pushed or cut back in order to see much of the ground, which made for very slow progress.

About a half an hour into their search, Amos called to Matt from a few hundred feet away, and he and Sinclair walked over to a large bush. Amos popped his head out. "Take a look here and see what you think," he said.

Sinclair pushed aside some branches and peered in. "Nope. It's just roots from the trees," he said.

Over the course of the day, several more possibilities were examined and disregarded. At lunchtime, Matt brought out a large bag of fried chicken which he made using his mother's neighborhood-famous recipe. Following a quick bite, they went back to work. It was after three o'clock that Matt started becoming concerned they would not find the shrine that day. He made his way to a stand of trees and shrubs further away and began poking around in the heavy underbrush. Jake was enjoying having the company on his property, and while the others were looking for a shrine, Jake was much more interested in chipmunks and squirrels. Matt was pawing through a bush when Jake jumped past him and under the bush, following a panicked chipmunk, trying to escape with his life. Jake's efforts created an opening in the bush, which allowed Matt to see further in. As he did, he glimpsed a structure that cause him to gasp. "Benny!" Matt shouted. "I don't think we need to be archaeologists to identify this!"

Benny and the rest of the group rushed to Matt's side. By the time they arrived, Matt had hacked enough of the bush back to have a clear view. Benny took one look and clapped Matt on the back. Sinclair pushed in on Matt's other side. "Wow," he said. "It looks like they built it last week."

As Matt used his machete to cut the scrub oak back, the others stood in awe. Before them was a completely intact structure, about six feet high, with four sides.

Sinclair could hardly contain himself. "They built the structure from stone that was carved from sharp tools and looks remarkably like stone ruins you see much further away, up on the Jicarilla Apache Reservation. It's absolutely amazing!"

Before them was an edifice that had been remarkably, almost unrealistically, preserved. It was simple, yet mesmerizing at the same time. Matt was silent in wonderment. In its silence, having been sitting there for hundreds of years, it demanded reverence and veneration.

Once they had cleared most of the brush away from it, Benny and Henry approached it. They said something in their language that Matt didn't understand, but he assumed it was a prayer of some sort. They both then got down on their knees in front of it. Matt thought it seemed odd that they would pray in a Catholic style when the spirituality which motivated its' builders was far from Rome. To Matt's surprise, Benny took out a knife and pushed it in between two of the stones in the very front. He slowly dug around the center brick until he had completely cleaned it out. Henry took his knife on one side, and Benny did the same on the other side and they eased the stone out of place. To Matt's eyes, it had looked like it was a solid construction, but as they pulled the center stone out, to his surprise, the inside was hollow. As they set the brick on the ground, Benny shined his flashlight into the hole it left behind. "Holy Mother of God," Amos said, "There's a treasure in there!"

Indeed, there was. Inside the shrine were dozens of beautiful pots, untouched and unspoiled and apparently undiscovered by four hundred years of weather, logging, hunters, campers, and others. There was turquoise jewelry, arrows and a bow, several blankets and much more. Henry turned to Matt. "This is something we thought was completely lost to our people. We have a ledger of our people from the past. It is yours, now, Matthew. It is no longer ours."

"Henry, I know legally it is mine, but it is not mine," said Matt. "It is your people's treasure. And it will remain that way."

"You are a good man, deputy. I thank you for that. I know I have no right to ask, but I will anyway. May our people come and bless the shrine and have a ceremony? We cannot remove any of the sacred objects without that."

"Of course, Henry. Any time you wish to do so," Matt replied.

The two men carefully replaced the stone, leaving everything inside the shrine intact. It had taken much of the day, but they found the shrine. As they rose to walk back to the lodge, Matt inquired, "Shouldn't we do something to protect this place?"

Henry smiled. "We already have," he said. "It will be protected until we return," Henry said with a strange and mysterious confidence.

They walked silently down the hill back to Matt's lodge. Sinclair and Naomi allowed themselves to lag behind until the others were far enough away that they couldn't be heard. Naomi looked at Sinclair and said, "Are you thinking what I'm thinking?"

"It won't be easy, but yes, I am. They didn't inventory the contents. Nobody will notice a few missing pieces which will be useful evidence of *my* discovery," Sinclair said, his brain already working on a 'strategy' to acquire a few pieces to prove the discovery to his peers. "When we come back, we need to take pictures. Any issues my department will have with the loss of two students just might be overshadowed by the 'glorious' discovery of The Eagle's Altar by Professor Sinclair Delano III!" Naomi stopped walking, staring at Sinclair with a look of absolute revulsion. *Fame is fleeting*, Naomi thought to herself.

As they reached the lodge, Matt invited everyone to stay for supper and an outdoor fire. "I've got smoked brisket and ribs that I can heat up for us, if you like," Matt announced. After an exhausting search, everyone agreed it would be a fitting end to the day. Matt fired up his smoker. Amos volunteered to get the fire going in Matt's fire pit behind his lodge, while Matt brought out the food and refreshments.

The mountains surrounding Matt's lodge meant the sun disappeared early each evening, even in the summer. As they feasted on Matt's food, Matt asked Sinclair, "So, how can the building style of the shrine look like the same style that has been found on the Jicarilla Apache Reservation? I didn't think the Apache were much into masonry. I imagined them more as raiders." The question obviously flummoxed Sinclair, and he was about to go into "professor" mode when Henry spoke up.

"It's really not strange at all, Matthew. The story that has been passed down from parents to children for centuries is that our people emerged from the underworld under the careful eye of the Creator, whom we call Hua-vu-na-tota. We emerged from a lake we call Hoa-sjela, what your people now call Boulder Lake. It is located on what is now the Jicarilla Apache reservation in Rio Arriba County. The professor can tell you that our people, meaning the ancestors of the pueblo peoples, have been in the southwest for at least twelve thousand years; maybe more. Our legends inform us that we lived for many centuries within fifty or sixty miles of Hoa-sjela. The archaeologists believe the Hemish came to these mountains, perhaps around 1300. We occupied nine or more pueblos from west of today's Cuba, west of La Ventana and to what we call Wachu-paa-wa, or what today is known as Rainbow Springs. Both have shrines which we maintain to this day. There is a complete ceremonial altar in the cliffs at Rainbow Springs.

"While we probably started our tribal existence in caves, we learned how to make homes and public buildings from mud and rock, and any ruins found on the Apache reservation are what our people left behind when we traveled here. It would make perfect sense that the shrine we found today appears much like similar structures near Boulder Lake, as our ancestors were the ones who made them. The shrine at Rainbow Springs is also on land owned by a non-Indian. There are minerals at this shrine we still use to paint our dance costumes. It can be difficult, as we must secure permission from the owner each time we need to acquire the needed mineral. This shrine, Séééh-Wagi, is most certainly not the only shrine remaining undiscovered and undisturbed. Now that the Valle Grande is a national refuge, we have started exploring, with the National Park Service, what was just a few years ago 100,000 acres of private ranch, and we expect there will be more discoveries of our sacred spots."

"That's truly amazing, Henry. I feel ashamed that I grew up so close to this place and spent so much time here, and yet I know nothing about your people or the fact that you occupied all of this land at one time," Matt said.

"It's not so amazing, Matt," Henry replied. "Out of a hard lesson learned during the Pueblo Revolt, we have been very private people for four hundred years. It is one reason we have survived so long, and have been displaced less, much less, than the plains Indians were."

"I appreciate you sharing this much, Henry. It has been an honor to get to know you, Benny and Paul, and I hope we can forge an even stronger friendship in the future."

Filled with brisket and ribs, a few beers and iced tea, the group lingered by the fire, Benny and Henry sharing other legends of the Jemez Indians. Matt thought to himself that he would never forget this day.

18

The Explorer's Code

Stealing, you'll go far in life. Actually, there is something funny about getting away with it.
(Mike Judge, Creator of Beavis and Butthead)

At nine o'clock the next morning, Matt had completed his morning ritual of dressing, putting on his hat and duty rig and grabbing the keys to the Jimmy. He left a note for Amos, who was still sleeping, that he would check in around noon, and he should walk over to the barn to see what the caretaker's quarters looked like. Matt called Jake, and the two headed down the driveway to the highway, turning left toward Jemez Springs.

A couple of hundred feet east of Matt's driveway, Sinclair and Naomi sat parked in the parking area for a popular rock climbing, called the "Cattle Wall." Sinclair had dozed off, being unused to being up and awake this early in the morning. Naomi jabbed Sinclair in the ribs with her elbow, causing Sinclair to jump in his seat, momentarily disoriented. "Wha—What?" he said, looking around, trying to remember why they were there.

"He just pulled out and is heading toward Jemez Springs," said Naomi.

"That means it's time to become a famous archaeologist!" Sinclair answered.

Sinclair started his minivan, working well now that Nazar had replaced the water pump, and pulled onto the highway for a few hundred feet, then turned into Matt's driveway. "You're sure there isn't anyone else there, right?" he said.

"He fucking lives alone, and takes that vicious, nasty dog of his everywhere he goes. We're good to fucking go," Naomi replied. Sinclair silently imagined Naomi giving a lecture to freshmen and using the "F" word in practically every sentence. He knew that academic freedom only went so far. Sinclair parked at the very bottom of the property so they could make an inconspicuous escape if needed. The two got out of the van and began walking up the long drive, past the lodge and up the side of the hill toward the grove where Sééeh-Wagi had been discovered. The grade was steep enough that the two needed to stop frequently to catch their breath. They entered the forest, and although they had been there just the day before, they were disoriented enough that it took some time to find the shrine.

After several minutes of near panicked searching, they finally found the shrine. Sinclair stopped and smiled. "You know, Naomi, this little discovery is going to be on the cover of the American Journal of Archaeology. I guarantee it. And Professor Sinclair Delano III will be a much sought-after speaker at conferences and gatherings. Hell, I might even get a Department Chair position out of this."

"Let me get this straight," Naomi said, a look of complete incredulity on her face, "You intend to take credit for finding the fucking shrine and you plan to steal artifacts from it, and you expect fame from it, when you did nothing to find it, you had never heard of it before, and you couldn't even successfully explain a basic piece of information about why the shrine looked like similar building projects further away? And you expect me to stand by and let you take all the credit?"

"Always two there are, no more, no less. A master and an apprentice."

"What the fuck?" Naomi said, a look on her face of complete and utter disgust.

"I'm saying you've got some learning to do, student."

"Oh my god. You are truly a sage and scholar, Sinclair."

Sinclair smiled. "Spare me your laconic sarcasm, Naomi. Of course, you'll get a mention in my upcoming article on the subject. Just as soon as I rope a certain grad student into writing it for me. Um, one who wants to get into a good PhD program, I suspect."

Naomi dared not say any more. She could feel her blood pressure setting new records. "OK, let's get a picture of me beside the shrine. You have a camera in your phone, right? Use your phone to take some pictures of me." Naomi took out her Samsung SCH-V200 and flipped it open to reveal a 1.5-inch screen. Her camera could take a maximum of 20 photos, and the camera had to be connected to a computer to retrieve the photos.

Naomi gave it some thought. "You know, Sinclair, I really want to get the shot you want, so why don't I pose by the shrine, and you can look at the picture you take to be sure it's what you want."

"Great idea, Naomi!" Sinclair said. "Show me what to do."

Naomi showed Sinclair, and then walked beside the shrine. Sinclair took a picture of Naomi with her hand touching the shrine, a look of pride on her face. "You better take a couple to be sure you have the angle you want," she said.

They looked at the pictures on the tiny screen on the phone. "Yes, yes, that will do nicely," Sinclair pronounced. He stood beside the shrine while Naomi took several pictures. Sinclair then took two long flat blades from his bag and, remembering how Benny and Henry had carefully extracted the stone, he began repeating what they had done the day before.

Before Sinclair removed the center stone, the two heard sounds in the shrubs just above them. "Shit," Sinclair said, "There's someone here!"

The two stood, scanning the bushes. They could hear the crack of branches and what sounded like someone pushing their way through the shrubs toward them. Suddenly, from under the bush burst a black bear. Naomi and Sinclair both screamed. Although, in actuality, the bear was small, it looked to Naomi and Sinclair the size of a grizzly. The bear stopped and looked at the two, then stood on his back legs, pawing the air with his mammoth claws and producing a very loud and angry sounding noise.

Sinclair didn't waste a moment. He turned and began running down the hill, screaming "Bear!" He did not stop for one second to look to see if Naomi was OK. He assumed the bear was probably tearing her limb from limb, which would buy him time to get to the van. Then, from just behind his peripheral vision, he detected movement coming at him. He grimaced, preparing for bear claws to puncture his back, perhaps even decapitating him. As he turned his head to the side, he saw it was not the bear at all, but Naomi, legs sprinting, boobs bouncing like Bo Derek's on the beach and moving her feet like she was putting the full-court press on Shaquille O'Neal. She passed Sinclair as though he was standing still. He took a quick glance back and saw that the bear was indeed still following the two and was about fifty feet behind them. He couldn't tell if the bear was gaining ground or not, and he really didn't care. Although it struck him as odd, there was an old joke which came to him about being chased by a bear. The joke's punchline was something like, "I don't have to be faster than the bear. I just have to be faster than you." He knew Naomi was faster than he was, which meant he would be the bear's lunch if he didn't put all he had into getting to the van. The two reached the van with thirty feet between them and the bear. They jumped in and slammed the doors shut. Sinclair fired up his van and drove out of the driveway as quickly as possible. He stole a quick look in the rear-view mirror. The bear was watching. Although he was certain it was his imagination, he could have sworn the bear was waving at them.

As the van pulled out of the driveway, Amos stood on the porch, a look of abundant amusement on his face. He watched the bear wander off into the stand of trees on the west side of Matt's property. He sat down on the rocking chair, memorizing the moment and sipping on his coffee. "Amazement awaits us at every corner," he said to himself.

Naomi was screaming a succession of profanities that would have made a sailor blush as they drove back toward the Mineral Springs Lodge. "You are an idiot. An imbecile. We trespassed on the property of a deputy sheriff, attempted to steal artifacts that he, in fact, owns, and were almost killed by a bear. We have nothing to show for this! Nothing!"

"I wouldn't say that," Sinclair retorted. "We have a wonderful photograph of me and my amazing discovery. Yes, the artifacts would have been nice as a keepsake of my career-changing discovery, but that photograph is what people will remember of the daring and handsome Professor Sinclair Delano III."

"You are a fucking clown, Sinclair. But you are going to make it up to me. Both of our names will be on that research paper, and you will share credit with me for the find. It's going to be a career-maker for me, too. Or, of course, I can share the truth and pollute your fabrications. And there is a deputy sheriff, a priest and three Jemez Indians who will back me up."

"We will see about that, Naomi. I have a lot of power to make or break you."

"I have a lot of power to break you, Sinclair. It's never wise to cross someone like me. Never."

19

Now This is a Whole New Thing

Searching is half the fun: life is much more manageable when thought of as a scavenger hunt as opposed to a surprise party.
(Jimmy Buffett)

Matt turned his Jimmy into his driveway and up to his lodge. He got out of the truck carrying a paper bag. As he approached his lodge, Amos came out on the porch to greet him. Jake sped around Matt and up the porch. Amos sat down on the top stair as Jake jumped into his arms. "Let me know if Jake is annoying you, and I'll settle him down," Matt said to Amos.

"Not at all, Matthew. It's been a while since I've had this kind of greeting!" Amos replied.

"I brought lunch for us, if you're hungry. Chavy brought these out of the kitchen freshly made, so I snapped some up for us." Matt pulled a couple of meat-filled empanadas out and handed them to Amos.

"Very kind of you, boyo," Amos said, as Matt sat on the step next to him. "You know, this morning is the first morning in quite some time that I haven't woken with a hangover. Gives one a bit of an appetite!" He took a huge bite and when he was done chewing, said, "I saw something this morning you're going to want to know about."

"What's that, Amos?" Matt inquired.

"You know those two from the university that were with us yesterday? Well, I saw the darndest thing. I was out on your porch, enjoying the sunshine, having a cup of coffee. I know what you're thinking, so stop. It was *just* coffee. At any rate, I heard screaming coming from behind your house and saw those two run from behind your house to the front. Here's the interesting part. They were being chased by a bear. They jumped into their vehicle and launched it out of your property like they were late to their own funerals."

"Wait," Matt said, "You're telling me those two were on my property behind my house?"

"Aye, it's the truth. And I must admit, I was ag gártha for the bear."

"Ag gártha?" Matt asked.

"Irish for cheering," Amos replied.

"What in the hell do you suppose they were doing on the prop—wait, they must have been at the shrine. Add another check mark in the suspect category. That makes this even more interesting. And you say a bear was chasing them?"

"Ay, a little guy with a white chest. I've never seen a white chest on a black bear. Should I be concerned about bears here?"

"Ah, OK. No, no concern at all. That was Yogi, one of the resident bears that pass through from time to time. I call him Yogi because the white around his neck looks a little like Yogi Bear's necktie. He's harmed no one that I'm aware of, and Jake and I see him quite often. One time Jake and I were camping out back at Los Griegos and Yogi came wandering by to see what we were doing. Jake walked up to him, and they touched noses. He knows I will not feed him on this place, and everything is as bear-proofed as I can make it. If he gets too close to the house, Jake barks him back. So far, Yogi is relatively intimidated by Jake. I'm guessing he was just having a good time freaking those two out. But I've got to admit, the two of them trespassing on this property is another fact in a growing pile of suspicion I have of those two."

"I had a feeling about that professor from the first moment," Amos said. "In Ireland, we called people like that 'melters.' I guess 'annoying idiot' would be a close translation."

"This adds a new wrinkle to things, Amos. I'm glad you were here, and I'm also glad that Yogi was on patrol up at the shrine. Those two have been involved in an artifact theft, two murders and now a trespass. I've been slow to take dramatic action, but that time is now."

Amos smiled. "One of my favorite quotes is from Ian Fleming: 'Once is happenstance. Twice is coincidence. Three times is enemy action.'"

Matt got up. “I’ll remember that one, and I think it’s time to start digging a bit more. I should be back around five or so. Did you have a chance to look at the caretaker’s quarters?”

“Aye, Matthew, I did. Pretty posh for an old priest, but I’ll be grateful for a couple of weeks of vacation from Saint Frumentius of Aksumite. And a little exercise and a wee bit less Jameson may just do me some good.”

“Excellent. I really can use your help. There is plenty that needs to be done around here. And just between the two of us, some company might also be good for me.”

Matt decided it would be a good idea to let Paul and Kai know the latest information on the UNM folks, so he headed toward their office. “That bear. Now, isn’t that amazing?”

“Not so amazing,” Randy replied. “Henry and Benny did say that they had left protection there, didn’t they?”

“No way. I’ve never been one to believe in the supernatural.”

“Matthew, you are talking to an invisible person. I’d say you’ve pretty much passed that notion by already.” Matt could imagine Randy’s amazing smile as he heard her words.

Matt turned off the highway into the Jemez Ranger District Headquarters and parked next to Paul’s truck. He and Jake walked into the office. Once Paul and Jake played their zombie greeting game, Paul waved Matt into his office. “I’m glad you showed up,” Paul said. “We got a little additional information from forensics, and I think you’ll be interested in it.”

“I’ve got a little news for you, too. Tell me, what did they find?”

Paul pulled out two sheets of paper. “Got it on the fax about a half hour ago. They found an additional set of prints on two of the artifacts.” Matt, while listening, was scanning the report.

“Naomi Canneloy. Well, I’ll be damned.”

“Yeah. And she has a criminal record. She was arrested for assaulting one of her teachers in high school and served six months in jail. We’ve got something bigger here than she let on. USFS has assigned a special agent to the case to investigate. He’ll be in town the day after tomorrow. So, what news did you bring, my friend?”

“Amos stayed at my place last night. This morning, after I left for work, we had visitors. The professor and Naomi snuck onto the property, and I imagine they went to the shrine. Amos saw them running past my lodge to their van, being chased by a black bear.”

Paul looked at Matt as though he was expecting a punch line. “A bear. Now that we suspect Naomi of assisting in the theft of the artifacts, that bit of information is even more interesting than it would have been otherwise. And—a bear? It sounds like Benny and Henry may have posted a guard.”

“That’s what someone else told me, but I didn’t believe them.”

“I would agree with whoever it was, Matt.”

Now Matt looked at Paul unaware his mouth was hanging open. Paul had said it so matter-of-factly that Matt was struggling to say anything cogent. “The older I get, the less I understand things,” was all Matt could say.

“I think, Matt,” Paul said, “We’re in another one of those inter-agency investigations. You’ve got Jason’s death to look into, and we have an artifact theft and possible murder of Danny. We have two university academics who have a growing layer of muck on their hands. I don't know about you, but this feels like it's getting serious."

"I'm going to give a call to Sergeant Bobby Hanson. He's the Investigations Division Sergeant. I feel like I've been behind this investigation, and it's time to get ahead of it. I want to get search warrants for the professor's cabin and car, and get it buttoned up."

Matt used Paul's phone to call Sergeant Hanson. Matt explained the situation, leaving out the parts about Weh'ng Péh and Yogi the bear. "I agree, Matt, we probably have enough to get a search warrant of the professor's cabin and vehicle. I'll call the forest service and see how they want to progress, but I would suggest that you make a trip into Bernalillo tomorrow and we'll work together on applying for a warrant. You haven't visited the District Court here yet, other than a couple of times testifying in Jemez cases. It will be an excellent opportunity to meet our judge in this district, secure a warrant, and at least poke around in their stuff. But I'll see first if the USFS wants to take charge. I'll give you a call when I get their take on it."

It was no more than a half hour later that Sergeant Hanson called Matt. "Looks like we have an inter-agency task force now," he said. "The USFS wants you and the local USFS law enforcement officer to secure a warrant tomorrow. I understand that a special agent from the USFS will be there on Thursday. The three of you can do the search and I want you and the special agent to interview the two. Of course, he will focus on the artifact thefts, but I want to be prepared in case we uncover any additional evidence regarding the student's death. That's our concern. Why don't you see if the LEO is available at ten tomorrow morning, and we'll meet, do the paperwork for the warrants, and visit with the judge."

"Sounds good, Sergeant," Matt replied. "We'll see you tomorrow at ten a.m."

20

Play that Funky Music

There are three kinds of men. The one that learns by reading. The few who learn by observation. The rest of them have to pee on the electric fence for themselves.
(Will Rogers)

The next morning, Sinclair was enjoying scones at a table in the courtyard of Mineral Springs Lodge, sipping a coffee that Maggie had brought him. While he would have preferred a heartier breakfast, fear of the Funk brothers suggested scones and coffee had a better chance of keeping him out of sight and unscathed. As Sinclair was preparing to bite into the second delicious scone, Naomi came out of the cabin with a force that Sinclair imagined would bend trees as she passed them. She put on the brakes and managed to stop the Naomi train, just shy of plowing through his table.

"Good morning, Naomi," Sinclair said quietly. "Coffee?"

"No time for that, Sinclair. I have to go unfuck the clusterfuck you've created."

"I created no such a thing. It simply happened by coincidence. It just so happens that you've got the abject integrity needed to eliminate the current threat to a successful field trip."

"Coupled," Naomi replied, "with the fact that you're a fucking coward. If you were a knight, your name would be *Sir Ender.*"

"Cute," Sinclair said as he sipped on his coffee.

"Let me have the keys to your van, Sinclair, and I'll get going."

Naomi headed out east, toward Soda Dam. Because Sinclair was driving the night they visited the Funk's camp, she had paid little attention to where they turned. She remembered it was a dirt road and was not easily spotted from the highway. She saw what she thought might be the dirt road, slowed, and peered as far down the road as possible, realizing it was not the right one. Twice more she did the same thing, only to decide they were not either. "Fuck, there are a lot of dirt roads in this place!" she yelled to herself. The next road seemed to be closer to what she remembered, and she turned in, looking for something she recognized. She continued down the road for a couple of hundred yards. The road curved to the left, and she continued, beginning to feel she had once again, chosen an incorrect road, when, in the distance the Funks' truck came into view. She pumped her fist in the air. "Yes!" she said and shut off the van.

Exiting the van, Naomi grabbed the revolver she had taken from the Funks and put it in her back pocket. She quietly shut the van's door and began the walk up to the camp. She slowed as she got within sight of the Funk bivouac, squatting low. Remembering the brothers' booby traps and trip wires, she was careful to look for strands of fishing line. When she was within about twenty feet of the camper, she stopped to plan her attack. One brother, Chuchu, was sleeping on one of the pink chaise lounges in front, but she couldn't see Dory. She stood up to try to see if she could spot Dory. As she did, from directly behind her, she heard a pump-action shotgun being cocked, about three inches behind her head. "Fuck," was all Naomi could say.

"Well, man, if the rolling stone hasn't come home to roost?" Dory said, the barrel of the shotgun pointed at her head. "You get those hands up high, little girl. And I don't want no funny business, dude." He shouted out, "Chuchu, look what I hunted up for supper, man!"

Chuchu, rousing out of a sleep, sat up, yawned, farted, then looked toward Dory. "Woh, dude, where did she come from? He said through a lion-sized yawn."

"I don't know, man, but I think we just got a gift horse in our hand, man!" Dory said, metaphor mixing with great proficiency.

Dory reclaimed his pistol from Naomi's back pocket and walked her up to the camp. Naomi decided she would stay quiet until an opportune moment. The two sat her down on a chair and tied her hands and feet with insulated wire they had stolen from a construction site, then sat back and looked at their prize. Chuchu slapped his brother on the back. "I knew we'd catch her, man. We're like, the best bloodhounds!" He then looked quizzically at his brother. "What do we do with her, man?"

"Hmmm," said Dory. "There's lots we could do. We could stake her over an anthill like the Indians did to the pioneers, and let her get eaten up by ants, man."

"Or we could keep her here as our slave, dude," Chuchu said.

"Dude, you are really thinking. But we could also hold her hostage. Her family or UNM probably has big bucks they would pay us."

"Oh, dude, I know," Chuchu said. "Remember that awesome movie we watched, man? It was called *Emmanuel and the White Slave Trade*. We could sell her into slavery to some rich dudes!"

"I think she ought to be *our* slave for a while, dude," Dory said, looking a bit bereft at the prospect of a rich 'dude' getting the prize.

Naomi had had just about enough of these two, both of whom were a bunch of french fries short of a happy meal. She looked up at the two criminals and stared at them with a steely confidence, unafraid of their foolishness. "OK, boys, let's get this right. First, you didn't catch me. I walked into your camp unescorted. Second, you don't have the skills necessary to stake me to an anthill. Third, I'm a grad student living on student loans, so I doubt the government would pay up. Fourth, any man who bought me into slavery would ask for his money back in about two hours after I annoyed his brains out of his ears. Fifth, it's the 'chicken has come home to roost,' and 'you don't look a gift horse in the mouth.' And finally, I came here to propose that I make you two, who are about as sharp as fucking bowling balls, very wealthy. That is, if you are smart enough to come to work for me."

Chuchu looked at Dory for a moment. "Dude, I don't know about you, but I need a beer and a doob, man."

"Oh, exactamentee, my favorite brother. That will most definitely clear our heads."

Naomi lowered her head to her chest and shook her head as the two took a beer and pot break. *They have the attention spans of three-year-olds*, she thought to herself.

Dory downed a beer and cracked two more. He was about to hand Naomi one when he realized they had tied her hands behind her back. "So, Naomi, right? Naomi, I'm pretty pissed off at you, man. You stole our shit and you beat the shit out of me. That's just not right, man."

"You were trying to rape me, you fucking Neanderthal."

"Good point, dude," Dory grudgingly admitted.

"And the shit we stole, you had stolen from us earlier in the day. We were staying at the Mineral Springs Lodge, and you stole our backpacks. Inside them were valuable artifacts and a tremendous prize. Something called the Black Heart of God. We had to have it back as it's worth a lot of money—a shitload, to be exact."

Chuchu started laughing, partly because the pot was kicking in, and partly because, despite his limited intellectual bandwidth, he saw the irony. "Whoa, whoa, man. So, you stole some shit, then we stole that shit from you, then you stole it back. What's stopping us from just stealing it back again, man?"

"Because, you stoned moron, you don't have the first idea of how to sell it. Let me guess, you two would have taken it to a pawnshop, am I right?"

"Well, um, like yeah, man. Isn't that how you sell shit?" Dory asked.

"You do if you want to get about twenty bucks for it. This is not shit. This is valuable stuff. And to the right buyer, it could be worth hundreds of thousands of dollars. Sinclair has introduced me to his connection, a rare collectibles guy, who has a list of buyers for this kind of thing. He'll get top dollar for it."

Chuchu tried to whistle, but the pot had given him cotton mouth, so all he managed to do was to make a small whooshing noise.

While Chuchu remained diligent in trying to form a whistle, Dory asked, "So why don't you just sell the shit, man? Why did you come back to us?"

"Because the professor is going to sell it, take all the credit for himself, and leave me with nothing. I'm just as capable as he is of putting these artifacts on the market. Sinclair has become a complete asshole, and I'm sick of him. He'll never give me the credit I deserve if I stick with him. And he'll control the sale of the artifacts, which means he'll get a boatload of money. I don't like him. And I've done too much to allow that twit to prosper from this. That's where you come in. I want you to kill him for me, then we will share the money 50/50."

"No way, dude," Chuchu said. "We want half. And we ain't never killed nobody, man."

"Yeah," Dory chimed in, "and I hear it's expensive to hire a hitman, so we need to be paid for our work. That is, if we do it, man. Half or nothing. None of that 50/50 shit."

Naomi stared at Chuchu like he was a worm on the wall. "Alright. You drive a hard bargain, but I'll let you have half."

The two brothers high-fived at their adroit negotiation skills. Each took another slurp of beer. Dory finally said to Chuchu, "Dude, we really never killed nobody before."

Chuchu sat and thought for a moment. "Man, you're right," he said. "We'll have to be totally baked to do that, dude."

"I think I like the slave idea better, man," Dory said woefully.

"But it won't put a hundred thousand dollars in your pocket, boys," Naomi said. "Now let's get me untied and I'll explain to you exactly what we're going to do. And let me have one of those fucking beers."

Once they untied Naomi, Dory kept his distance from her, remembering the thrashing he had received at her hand. "OK, boys, now in order for this to work, and in order to get away with this, you have to do exactly what I say. I'm a *very* smart person, and let's just say you're fatuous. This has to be done just right."

Chuchu turned to Dory. "I've never been called fatuous before, man. I'm, like, seriously buff."

"Pay attention, boys," Naomi said, sounding like a schoolteacher lecturing naughty students. "Tomorrow morning, I'll get Sinclair in the van and out on the road. I want you guys to park your truck at the parking lot at Battleship Rock. I'll get Sinclair to pull in, and you jump into action. Now, here's the important part. I'm going to tell him we have made peace with you and we are going to share a stash of Coronado's gold we found so that you will help us carry it out. You have to *act* like you are working with both of us. Don't let on that you and I are working together, got it? And don't tell him you are going to kill him, OK?"

"Dude, why would we do that? We're totally partners now, man," Dory posited.

"Because we have to have Sinclair's cooperation. He can't have a meltdown until we are at the place that you are going to kill him."

"But, like, we're not killing you, too, man, are we?" Chuchu asked.

Naomi sat speechless for a moment. "Um. No. You can't kill me, because I'm the one who is going to share all the money with you when I sell the Black Heart. Understand?"

"Dude, yeah. Good plan," Chuchu said, looking at Dory, sending his best body language, *you understand this, right dude*?

"So, where are we going to kill him? And how?" Dory asked.

"I'm pretty sure that Jemez Falls is the best choice. I'm going to go over there when I'm done here to walk the trail to be sure it will work. If it does, we're going to take a little hike out to the cliff above the falls. When we get there, you are going to shoot him in the back of the head and push him over the cliff into the falls. You guys have guns, right?"

Chuchu smiled, "Oh hell to the yeah, dude. We got a great stash from one of the cabins we broke into."

"Good," said Naomi. "So, can you be there at eight a.m.? We can be at the falls before the tourists arrive."

The two looked at each other as though they had been asked to run a marathon. Dory shook his head. "Oh, wow, man, that's kinda early, don't you think?" Dory looked at Chuchu who was nodding his head. "Well, I guess for the big bucks, we can handle it, man," Dory reluctantly approved. "I still like the slave idea better, man."

21

Suspicion

The moment there is suspicion about a person's motives, everything he does becomes tainted.

(Mahatma Gandhi)

Paul and Matt were going to spend the day driving to Bernalillo, securing a search warrant for the professor's cabin and minivan. Matt's patrol lieutenant, under pressure from his boss and Matt's old navy buddy Hector Vigil, allowed Matt to dress like a cowboy when he was on duty in the Jemez. That exception did not apply when Matt was at the Sheriff's Office in Bernalillo. When Matt had pulled into Paul's parking lot to pick Paul up, Paul almost fell over with a laugh, then mockingly gave Matt an inspection. "Hmm, let's see. Pressed green trousers instead of jeans, black tactical boots instead of your Lucchese cowboy boots, a starched khaki shirt with a shined badge, and—Matt, what in the hell is that on your head? A black duty cap with a badge on it instead of your signature cowboy hat? I didn't know that your cowboy hat was even removable. I imagined you wore it to bed at night! Wow, SCSO is committed to its 1950's uniforms, isn't it?"

"You enjoy yourself, Paul. I'm always happy to be the butt of someone's humor," Matt said, smiling. "Although I do feel like I should be walking along the street swinging a billy club!"

"And there's something else, Matt," Paul said. Matt raised his eyebrows, waiting for another round of teasing. "I'm sure this is the first time I've ever seen you without Jake. It's sad!"

"Don't talk to me about sad. You should have seen how bereft he was to find out he was going to be spending the day helping Amos with chores at the Circle R. He'll be punishing me for a week about this!"

Matt's experience in acquiring warrants had been limited. Although he had spent twenty-four years with the NCIS, his cases primarily focused on dealing with sailors or navy employees, and the fourth amendment didn't have much application to active-duty military personnel. NCIS special agents had not received the authority to make arrests or undertake searches until the year 2000, so when they encountered such a situation, they had been required to bring in the FBI or local law enforcement officers to execute a warrant or make an arrest.

Matt enjoyed the ride with Paul. He was beginning to feel very close to the man, who was both the consummate law enforcement officer and exemplary Jemez tribal member. Their working relationship was relaxed, and because Matt essentially worked alone, being able to talk to another law enforcement officer was important to him.

As they were driving to Bernalillo, the county seat of Sandoval County, Paul's cellphone rang. From the conversation, Matt could tell that Paul was talking to the USFS special agent. The agent did most of the talking, and Paul finished the call, saying, "Got it, sir. I'm sure we can handle this ourselves."

"Let me guess. We will not have a special agent with us tomorrow to serve the warrants, will we?" Matt inquired.

"No, some big deal in the Sandia Mountains came up, so he's got to be in Tijeras tomorrow. He says for us to execute the warrants tomorrow ourselves, and if we find what we both think we are going to find, just keep the two under surveillance, and he'll be out on Friday. Frankly, that's just fine with me. How about you?"

"I'm feeling a sense that we need to proceed with a little more haste on this one, Paul," Matt replied. "I hate to give them more time to pack up and go back to Albuquerque."

"I'm feeling the same way, Matt, but USFS has its way of doing things, and I would appreciate it if you would wait for the special agent to be here."

"It's pretty clear the Canneloy lady was assisting, or, more likely, directing the theft of artifacts in Astialakwa, which not only makes her a thief but a pretty good liar, Paul. And now that we know she has a criminal record it makes the deaths of the two young men even more suspicious to me. I was pretty underwhelmed by her descriptions of what they did, and her suggestion that the two boys died from evil spirits seeking revenge on them for stealing the artifacts. Even more disconcerting is the fact that Danny died falling off the mesa in a place that there appears to have been a scuffle, and that both autopsies resulted in the pathologists intimating there was a possibility of foul play. I think our day tomorrow may be less of a cake walk than we think.

"Just one more thing to think about, Matt," Paul said. "There's another strange coincidence in the break-in at Mineral Springs Lodge. Don't you think it's odd that Sinclair's cabin was one of the cabins that were broken into?"

"I do, and, frankly, their claim that nothing was stolen is absurd," Matt added.

Sergeant Bobby Hansen met the two at the SCSO headquarters, and they sat down to complete affidavits and warrant applications. As they worked under the direction of Sergeant Hansen, another man came into the room. "Hey, deputy, you look pretty sharp in that uniform," said the man.

Matt turned around to see Hector Vigil behind them. "You never had wonderful taste in clothes, Hector," Matt said, standing and putting out his hand. "I guess it's just a navy OS thing."

Matt could see that Hector was about to meet Matt's comment with an insult of his own, so Matt said, "Hector, I want you to meet a great USFS law enforcement officer, Paul Toza. Paul, this is former OS3, and currently elected sheriff of Sandoval County, Hector Vigil.

Paul held out his hand and said, "Pleased to meet you, sir."

Hector gave a chuckle. "This is a very small and very relaxed office, Paul. No 'sirs' needed here."

Matt explained to Paul his past life with Hector in the navy. "Hector was an Operations Specialist, or 'OS' in navy acronym world. We radiomen and the OS's had a friendly rivalry onboard. I would tease Hector that 'OS' stood for 'occasionally sober.' Hector and I had more than a few wild rides on liberty."

They chatted for a few more minutes until Sergeant Hansen said, "We better get this paperwork in before the judge goes home for the night." Hector bowed out. As he was leaving, he said, "I hear you're going to be here for roll call once a week. I'm going to enjoy seeing you in uniform for a few minutes, Deputy Bertram."

Matt and Paul secured their warrants from the judge and were walking to Matt's Jimmy to head back to Jemez Springs. "Paul, would you mind if we made a quick detour into Albuquerque? I need to pick up some papers at my lawyer's office."

"You're not getting sued, are you?" Paul replied, half joking.

"No, just some BS regarding the ranch," Matt replied. When they reached the lawyer's office, Matt went in and was back out in just a couple of minutes carrying a large manilla envelope. On the way back to Jemez Springs, they agreed they would meet at Mineral Springs Lodge a little before eight a.m. the next morning to execute the warrant. When they reached the ranger district headquarters, Matt let Paul out. Matt said, "Tell Miranda hello for me, and I'll see you here in the morning."

"I'll do that, my friend. Now go home and kiss your dog," Paul responded.

Amos and Jake were sitting on the front porch of Matt's lodge, enjoying watching the sun disappear over the mountain peaks. Jake had taken a liking to the big Irish priest and was lying next to Amos as Amos was enjoying a cup of hot tea. Suddenly, Jake's ears went to full mast, his attention on the road below. From around the corner came Matt's Jimmy. Jake sprang to his feet, ran down the porch, wagging his long, foxlike tail to beat the band. Jake sat at the base of the porch wagging his tail. Matt pulled into his driveway, drove up to the front of the house, and got out of the truck. While Jake was trembling with anticipation, he didn't move a muscle, other than the extraordinary wags of his tail. Matt stood for a few seconds, knowingly torturing the poor dog when, finally, he said, "Come Jake," and Jake launched toward Matt. Matt held out his hands, which was Jake's signal that he had permission to go airborne, which he did, right into Matt's awaiting arms, giving Matt a fat, cattle dog kiss. Matt put Jake down and Jake raced around Matt to walk alongside on Matt's right side.

Amos stood up, smiling, and said, "Jake and I have become fast friends today, Matthew. He may just decide to go home with me."

"I believe he would. Jake is always available to the highest affection-giver. But I'm afraid you'll have competition from other people."

"You know, Matthew, I was thinking today as Jake and I worked together, that I haven't had a dog since I left Ireland. I was thirteen when I left home to come to the US. It seems to me the Catholic church would do well to let the priests they require to be celibate have dogs for company. Might be a good mental health move."

Matt laughed. "How was your day, Amos?"

"It was simply marvelous, Matthew. Jake and I repaired that place in your corral that had broken, we straightened up the caretaker's quarters, which I have to say I'm already fond of, and I hope you don't mind, but I built a fire in the fire pit, and found a couple of ribeyes to grill in your freezer. They've been thawing for some time now, and there are potatoes in the oven, baking as we speak."

"You're hired," Matt said, smiling.

Amos went inside and came back out with a beer. Matt looked at Amos suspiciously but said nothing. Amos opened the beer and handed it to Matt. "Good summer day deserves something cold, eh Matthew?"

"What about you, Amos?" Matt inquired.

"I'm not saying it's going to be forever, but at least for today, I think I'll keep my drinks alcohol free," Amos replied.

"I'm happy to hear that, Amos, but I want you to know that this is not alcohol rehab, so I will not be judging what you decide to do about your drinking. I am happy to support you if you choose to at least let your blood alcohol content time to recover."

"As I said before, I'm *not* saying I'm never having another drink, boyo," Amos replied, "but I am enjoying the world I see through sober eyes."

The two enjoyed the fire, the steaks and baked potatoes, and the conversation until well after dark. Amos told stories about growing up in Ireland and his parents' decision to send him to an uncle and an aunt in the US to go to high school and seminary, with four years of the US Marine Corps in between. The priesthood was a choice his parents made for him. He was the designated priest among the brothers in the family. "It's odd, you know, they spend a lot of time in the Catholic church talking about hearing God 'call' you to the priesthood. If being kicked out of your house and told not to come back until you're ordained is a 'call,' then I wasn't just called, I was *sentenced*. I responded by drinking as a means of rebellion, and before I knew it, I was a full-fledged alcoholic. While it's a little late, I've decided to put my parental grievances on the shelf for the time-being and give a shot at living a more sober life."

"Anything I can do to support you, Amos, I'm there for you," Matt said.

"You've been doing it since we met, my friend," said Amos, his eyes misting. "By the way, would it be possible for me to get a lift into the village tomorrow so that I can pack a few things for my little sabbatical?"

"Of course, Amos," said Matt. "We are going to be executing a search warrant early in the morning, but I can drop you off before we do that. And, by the way, as far as I'm concerned, you can stay as long as you care to, Amos. I enjoy having a friend here. We'll need to be out of here by 7:30 at the latest."

The two said their goodnights. Amos headed toward the barn, and Matt toward the lodge. Jake sat in between the two, looking one way, then the other. "I had a feeling I'd be punished for today, Jake. But your bed in the bedroom is pretty comfy," Matt told the dog.

Jake stood and wagged his tail at Matt. When Matt started walking, he followed Matt up the porch and into the lodge, his abandonment for the day forgotten and forgiven.

As Matt climbed into bed, Randy said, "I'm worried about tomorrow, Matt."

"What's there to worry about, Randy?" Matt replied.

"I'm not sure. I just feel like something is going to go wrong. I need you to be careful, my darling deputy."

Matt smiled. "Even now, you worry about me. I promise I'll be on guard for unexpected happenings."

Suddenly, Randy began speaking with surprise in her voice. "Matt? Matt? Where are you?" she called.

"I'm right here, Randy. What's wrong?"

"Matt! Something is happening to me. I, I'm awake," Randy said.

"What do you mean, awake?" Matt implored. But there was no response. "Randy? Randy!" Matt roared, which was met with silence. He called Randy's name several more times, each time with no reply. "Randy. Don't go away! I need you! You can't leave me again!" A few minutes of silence from Randy turned into hours. Although Randy had come and gone from his head before, he was certain this was different. Matt, although he could not rationally understand why, deep in his soul really felt Randy was *gone* this time Matt hung his head, sobbing. *I can't lose her a second time,* he thought.

It was just after nine p.m. when Naomi returned to the Mineral Springs Lodge. Sinclair and Maggie were sitting at a table in the courtyard. Sinclair was swilling down Maggie's best cognac. He was regaling her with exaggerated stories of his stunning exploits finding the world's treasures as an archaeologist and Maggie was eating it up like an eighth-grade schoolgirl with a mad crush on her teacher.

As Naomi walked up to the table, she could hear Sinclair's swaggering storytelling in full-adventure film mode. "And that was the point," Sinclair was boasting, "that I found the idol hidden in the cavern, despite the booby traps the ancient Aboriginals had laid to thwart grave robbers from pilfering the tomb."

"Oh my, Sinclair," Maggie swooned, "you have certainly led a fascinating and exciting life!"

"Oh yeah," Naomi said, with all the sarcasm she could muster, "Professor Delano makes Indiana Jones look like a slapdash amateur, alright."

"You are very fortunate to be studying under him, Naomi," Maggie replied.

"Oh, I don't know about that," Sinclair said. "I'm just a simple archaeologist."

"Well, Professor Simple," Naomi said. "I'm sorry to interrupt, but I need to chat with you for a few minutes about our next adventure. Maggie, I'm sorry to take Harrison Ford away from you, but I'll return him quickly."

"No, no, Naomi. I have a few tasks to do before I close up the office for the night," Maggie said. "Sinclair, it has been a wonderful evening. I do so hope that we can do it again."

"I'm certain of it, my dear Maggie. But for now, duty calls. Adieu, Maggie," Sinclair said.

As Maggie went inside the office, Naomi scowled at Sinclair. "I'm going to have to take a bath just to get your fucking smarm off of me."

"Never mind that," Sinclair said, unscathed by Naomi's acidic commentary. "Did you take care of our problem?"

"Yes and no," Naomi answered, to which Sinclair simply returned a questioning look. "I went to their camp today and convinced them to make an alliance with us."

"I thought you'd just kill them and be done with that," Sinclair said. "I thought you said you would handle it!"

"Oh, I did. But you have to help me finish it," Naomi replied. "Two dead dumb fucks would have caused a stir, which I fear would have come back to haunt us. No, they have to plausibly die, and I have a plan. I told them we had found an ancient stash of gold coins, hidden by Coronado, that we will share if they help us carry them out of the hiding place. They told me they would, but if I was lying, they would kill us."

"That's getting the problem fixed?" Sinclair shrieked. "How is that fixing it? We don't have a stash of Coronado's gold. Hell, even Coronado didn't have a stash of Coronado's gold, and when they find out, they'll still shoot us."

"Calm yourself down, Sinclair," Naomi said. "It's all a ruse to get them to the top of Jemez Falls. When we get there, I'll give them a push over the falls, and that will be that."

"Why couldn't you just kill them at their camp, like I thought you were going to?" whined Sinclair.

"Two reasons, Sinclair, and try to pay attention to what I just told you," Naomi said, looking into Sinclair's eyes with a ferocity Sinclair had not seen in Naomi; and Sinclair had seen some intense looks on her face. "First, their deaths can't look like murder, and getting shot in their camp might look just a tiny little bit suspicious. Second, I need you to be as culpable as I am, Sinclair. There's no way I'm going to let you pin this on me if something goes wrong. I'll do the fucking dirty work, but you are going to be with me when it happens."

"That's really selfish, Naomi. I thought my prize grad student would have a little more respect for a noted archaeology professor," Sinclair replied.

"Really? Really Sinclair? You started at the bottom, and it's been fucking downhill for you ever since. I have *no* respect for you. None. At all. I'd explain it to you, but I don't have any crayons with me. But we are bound now, and in order for me to take care of *your* business, you have to be as culpable as me."

Sinclair stared for a minute, then shock his head. "OK, I get it. But I don't have to actually kill anybody, right?"

"I'll take care of that, but you have to be there to help. We're going to go for a little walk with the Funks, and when the timing is right, they'll have a little accident at the falls."

"I guess I don't have any choice, do I?" Sinclair conceded.

"Not unless you want the Funks to be the ones doing the killing."

22

An Unexpected Hike

A zombie film is not fun without a bunch of stupid people running around and observing how they fail to handle the situation.

(George A. Romero)

The sun was just poking over Cerro Pelado peak as Matt, Amos, and Jake loaded into Matt's Jimmy. It was another incredible New Mexico summer day with a bright blue, cloudless sky and a warmer than usual morning. Although Matt appreciated his usual, less than adrenaline-filled work as a sheriff's deputy, it had become fulfilling to be doing something that was enlivening. His renewed sense of commitment to life had aroused a feeling of adventure that had been lost. When Matt had awoken that morning he tried, once again, to gain a response from Randy, but he was met with only silence, which greatly worried him. He had become used to having her "along" with him the past weeks and couldn't understand where she had gone. Matt hoped it was temporary, but he feared their conversations had, for some unexplained reason, come to an end.

Matt drove the Jimmy south on Highway 4 toward Jemez Springs. They passed signs to many of the places Matt had spent much of his childhood backpacking and fishing, which always brought back countless memories of times both alone and with friends enjoying the mountains. He had brought Randy to the Jemez on brief vacations several times, and each time they passed a sign for a particular spot, he thought of Randy or an experience in that area. As they drove toward Jemez Springs, they first passed the sign for the East Fork trailhead, then Slot Canyon, then Jemez Falls trailhead.

As they pulled into the parking lot at the USFS Ranger Station, Paul was putting equipment in the back of his truck. As they got out of the truck, Paul greeted Matt and Amos and said, "Kai won't be with us today. There was yet another incident up at the Gillman Tunnels, so he's gone to help out. Father O'Sullivan coming along?" Being a devout Catholic, Paul was unable to address Amos as anything other than "Father," an act of respect that was deeply rooted in his upbringing.

"We're just going to drop Amos off at Saint Frumentius to gather some of his stuff. He's going to be staying with me at the Circle R for a few weeks, helping me to tend the ranch," Matt said.

"Well, it'll be a tight squeeze, but I think we can manage it," Paul replied. It was indeed a tight squeeze. Paul drove a Ford Ranger pickup with a supercab, which meant Amos, at well over 200 pounds, and Jake, were relegated to the rear benches in the cab. Amos was happy to have Jake on his lap as they pulled out of the lot toward Jemez Springs, which was less than a mile down the highway.

As they entered the village and approached Saint Frumentius, they passed the professor's minivan traveling in the opposite direction. "Que Mierda!" Paul said as they passed the van. "What do we do now?"

"We could just go ahead and execute the warrant on the cabin without them there," Paul replied, "But I'm very curious where those two are going this time of day. I think we should turn around and follow them."

"I'm with you," said Matt. "OK if we delay taking you back to Saint Frumentius, Father?"

"This sounds rather like fun, Paul," Amos replied.

"OK," said Paul. "Let's give them some room and hope they don't spot us," he said, making a U-turn on the highway once the van was around the bend. They maintained enough distance to keep from being seen as they followed the van toward the north.

"Was that a ranger truck we just passed?" Sinclair said to Naomi.

Naomi was turned, looking out the dirty rear window of the minivan, trying to spot the truck. "Well, if it was, they didn't see us," she said. "And besides, it could have just been a crew going to clean bathrooms or empty trash."

Sinclair took a long draw of air, unsuccessfully attempting to clear his anxiety. "We are meeting up with the Funks at the parking lot at Battleship Rock," Naomi said.

"Are you sure there isn't another way to handle this, Naomi?" Sinclair said, his voice breaking slightly.

Naomi shook her head. "Anybody who told you to just be yourself couldn't have given you worse fucking advice, Sinclair," was all she said.

The two continued traveling north toward Battleship Rock. Naomi regularly checked out the rear windows for any sign of rangers. After ten minutes, she gradually relaxed and began focusing on what was ahead. She worried about the ability of the Funks to carry out their end of the bargain. She imagined the billions of brain cells the two had smoked and drank away during their lives, and was certain, because of inbreeding, they probably did not have a full complement of brain cells to begin with. Because of this, she tried to assuage her fears with the fact that their role in her plan was very simple. Her part was much more complex. She needed to herd everyone up to the cliff at the falls, have the brothers shoot Sinclair in the back of the head and push his body over the edge. Then she would kill the brothers and call for help, claiming they had kidnapped her and Sinclair in order to kill them. Her story would be that her only choice was to defend herself, and, fortunately, she was a black belt in Taekwondo as well as an excellent liar. She would leave the *liar* part out when she told the story. The law enforcement rangers were, in her estimation, a couple of Barney

Fifes, and that sheriff's deputy was a burned out and washed-up NCIS agent. *He must have fucked up badly to end up here*, she thought. She smiled, thinking of her plan and how awesome she would play the part of the victim when the time came.

The van approached Battleship Rock from the south, gradually revealing the cliffs of the rock. The huge, pointed edge of the rock appeared, which, applying a bit of pareidolia, somewhat resembled the bow of an enormous ship. It was a popular place for tourist picnics. At the bottom of the rock outcropping, there was a trail that wound its way up to the top of the plateau and was attractive for day hikes among the visitors. Most importantly, there was an easily accessed parking lot, which was the reason Naomi chose to meet the Funks here.

Sinclair turned into the parking lot and seeing the Funks sitting on the tailgate of their truck, started hyperventilating. "Easy, boy," Naomi said, as though she was talking to a horse. "Just breathe through your nose and it will all be over soon. I promise."

Sinclair parked next to the truck. Naomi told Sinclair to stay in the van and she would talk to the Funks. "Hey lady dude," Chuchu said as though they were passing each other on the street. "Dory and me were wondering if you had just, like, made that shit up just to get us to let you go."

"Wow, you two are regular sleuths, aren't you?" Naomi said, the sarcasm lost on them. "I want you two to ride with us. Now, do we need to go over things again?"

"I'm not totally sure about the middle part," Dory said.

"Middle part? What the fuck, Clem?" Naomi snarled. "Let's go over this quickly. We go to Jemez Falls, and when we get there, you shoot Sinclair in the head and push him over the edge. I don't know what the fuck the middle part is, but that's how it goes down. Until we get there, you just be relaxed and friendly, and don't let Sinclair know you plan to shoot him. Can I make it any simpler for you?"

"Oh shit, man, we got to get our guns out of the truck. Almost forgot, dude," Chuchu said. "That would have been totally funny, man!" Chuchu slapped Dory on the back as they opened the door of the truck, and each stashed a pistol in his respective back pocket.

Naomi stared at the two brothers with disdain. "Calling you two idiots would be an insult to all the stupid people," she said under her breath.

Naomi opened the sliding door of the van, and Dory and Chuchu climbed in. Naomi got back in the front seat next to Sinclair. As the brothers entered the van, Sinclair couldn't help but notice the noxious scent of two men who only occasionally bathed, and when they did, used Fenton Lake as their spa. Dory, looking at Sinclair, said, "Man, you don't look so hot, doc, man."

Sinclair managed half a smile, saying, "I didn't get a lot of sleep last night." Indeed, Sinclair looked as tense as a five-year-old on a haunted house carnival ride. His normally ruddy complexion had become a pasty white. He had beads of sweat on his forehead and upper lip, and his lower lip was trembling. He realized he must look terrible if two stoners who can't focus their eyes noticed his physical and emotional condition.

While Naomi was orchestrating the logistics of stuffing the Funks into the van, Matt, Paul and Amos watched from the truck with deep fascination. "What in the hell are those two doing with the Funks?" Paul mused.

"Everything seems to be converging, Paul," Matt replied. "My brain says the academics have somehow enlisted the Funks in their shenanigans, and that can't be good." Paul had found a spot on the side of the road where they could watch Sinclair and Naomi and not be seen. They observed the minivan back out of the parking spot and exit the lot, turning right on the highway. Once the van was a safe distance, Paul pulled his truck back on the highway, following the minivan. The van stayed on the highway, passing La Cueva and continuing on toward the Valles Caldera.

Matt was grateful that Paul was driving, as he rarely had the luxury of being a passenger in the Jemez Mountains. The portion of the highway they were driving on Matt considered to be the most attractive scenery in the Jemez Mountains, with tall Ponderosa and Jack Pine trees and lush, (for New Mexico), vegetation. He was forever aware that they were living on top of the remnants of the world's largest extinct volcano, the Valle Grande. Twelve thousand centuries before, long before the first humans appeared in what would someday be northern New Mexico, a series of explosions dwarfing anything ever witnessed by modern man besieged this area. A giant chamber filled with molten rock had long been growing deep underground, and when the lava finally exploded to the surface, the results were catastrophic. For miles in all directions, volcanic ash and gas covered the ground in an incandescent mixture. Finer ash was deposited up to 300 miles downwind, dimming the sun for months and disrupting the Earth's climate for decades. The roof of the emptied chamber collapsed to produce a volcanic crater, 12 miles across and 3500 feet deep. Los Alamos, the town Matt grew up in, sits atop the Pajarito Plateau on the eastern skirt of the Jemez Mountains, where remnants of the thick layers of volcanic ash deposited by the eruption formed the characteristic finger mesas which surround Los Alamos.

Matt watched as the minivan ahead continued north on the highway. He could not help but speculate the meaning of the convergence of these four people, and that he was seeing it only fueled his intense suspicions regarding the archeologist and his student. It was certainly not wholesome. As they followed the minivan, Matt struggled to find connections that might make sense. The only connection he was aware of was that the Funks had broken into the professor's cabin. Although he claimed nothing had been taken, it had become clear that Naomi had taken part in the pilfering of the artifacts at Astialakwa.

Paul was on the same track. "I'm trying to figure out how these four unlikely characters got together," Paul remarked. "All I can know for certain is that it must have had something to do with the break-in of the professor's cabin at Mineral Springs Lodge. I don't want to jump to conclusions, but I wonder if the Funks didn't find something in that cabin the professor didn't disclose, and somehow it has brought them together."

"I was thinking the same thing," Matt replied. He watched as the minivan slowed and signaled a right turn. "We may not have to wait too long to find out," Matt said, seeing the van turn ahead. "That's Jemez Falls Road they are turning onto, and I kinda doubt they are going to have a picnic." Paul slowed his truck and crept up to the turnoff, trying to remain unseen. The road they had turned onto was compact dirt and gravel, which made the job of tailing them easier as they could follow the trail of dust in front of them. The van passed the Jemez Falls campground and continued down the road, then pulled into a parking area at the picnic site and parked. Paul kept his truck out of sight as they watched the Funks and Naomi exit the van. It appeared they were trying to persuade the professor to exist also, but, for the moment, he was still seated behind the wheel.

"Sinclair," Naomi said, "What's the problem?"

"I'm, um, coming. I just need a minute," Sinclair replied.

Naomi felt in her back pocket to be certain the Funks' pistol she had "acquired," was still secure. Dory looked at Naomi. "What's up with the professor dude, man?" he inquired.

"He'll be OK. He just needs a second."

Chuchu decided to be helpful. "Hey, professor, dude, you want to share a doob, man?" he said.

Sinclair thought for a second and said, "No thanks. I've just got a little arthritis, is all."

"Weed is good for that shit, man," Dory said, taking out a joint and lighting it. He took a long, slow toke and handed it to Chuchu, who repeated the ritual. "I don't have arthritis, man, but it's also good for relaxing, dude."

"What the hell," Sinclair said, taking the joint and inhaling, which caused a convulsion of coughing. "It's been a few years," he said between coughs, "since I've had any of that."

Naomi turned to the Funks. "We have to take the trail to Jemez Falls. They stashed the gold in a cave on the side of the cliff."

"So, I've been down this trail to the falls a bunch of times, and I don't remember seeing anyplace you could stash a fortune in gold, man," Dory said. "How did you find this gold, anyway?"

Sinclair was already feeling the effects of the marijuana and, coupled with his intense enjoyment of making up stories of his remarkable exploits as an adventurer and archeologist, launched into storytelling mode. "It's a little-known fact," Sinclair began, "that the great conquistador Francisco Vázquez de Coronado y Luján undertook a major search for what was known as the 'seven cities of gold.' Although he didn't find the seven cities, he did find a stash of gold at the Zuni River as he was crossing what is now New Mexico. People commonly think he didn't find anything and nearly starved, but he found something amazing. He found a mountain of gold, which he took for the good of Spain. He happened to be crossing the Jemez Mountains and found a cave near what is now Jemez Falls where he stashed the gold. After years of searching for the stash, I found evidence that it existed, and I made over a dozen trips to the Jemez looking for it. Finally, one day when I was exploring the Jemez Falls area, I found it. It's amazing and worth a vast fortune. We are here today to take it back and become fabulously wealthy."

"Dude, fabulously wealthy sounds awesome, man," Chuchu said, smiling at his brother.

Dory, a look of confusion on his face, stopped and turned to Sinclair. "I don't understand why Coronado would have stashed gold around here."

"Why is that, uh," Sinclair realized he didn't remember either of their names, "Funk number one?"

"Isn't Coronado, like a mall in Albuquerque, man? Why don't they just keep their stuff in a bank?"

Sinclair and Naomi stood, staring at Dory without the ability to muster even a simple answer.

"Let's get cracking, folks," Naomi suggested. "We don't have all day."

Paul was watching the four with binoculars from the truck. "They are on the move. Looks like they are heading for the Jemez Falls trailhead."

Matt turned to Amos. "I want you to stay here in the truck with Jake, OK?"

"Matthew, I could be a wee bit helpful, boyo," Amos responded.

"Amos, this is a law enforcement matter. I don't want anything unexpected happening, and even though I don't want to relegate you to dog-sitter, we can't bring Jake with us. We've got to be stealthy and the last thing I need is Jake bolting after a chipmunk or squirrel, or, even worse, the Funk brothers."

Amos reluctantly agreed, and folded his arms across his chest, resigned to missing the "fun." Paul went to the rear of his truck and unlocked his rifle, a SIG Sauer MCX Virtus Patrol rifle. Matt looked at the rifle and whistled. "We're not issued anything as cool as that! I'll never call you forest service guys wimps again!"

"We're badasses, deputy. Just kind of quiet ones," Paul replied.

Paul and Matt could see that their four suspects had begun to walk down the Jemez Falls trail. If they were going to the falls, they didn't have a long hike. From the parking lot to the overlook was less than a mile. Unusual for a summer weekday, there seemed to be no one else on the trail. Paul kept an eye out for other hikers, but hoped that the trail would remain empty, just in case problems presented themselves. Judging from where they were, who they were following, and the early morning hours, his law enforcement experience suggested that nothing good was going to happen.

The two began tailing their suspects, staying off the trail and far enough back that they would not be seen. From their vantage point, it appeared as though the four were chatting, calm and unaggressive toward one another. Matt thought it ironic that two highly educated academics and two ignorant stoners would ever have the slightest reason to be together, most especially, on a friendly hike in the Jemez Mountains.

The Jemez Falls trail was a beautiful footpath that skirted the East Fork of the Jemez River. At this point in the mountains, the river was several hundred feet below the trail in the bottom of a rocky canyon. The trail paralleled the river at the top of the canyon. It was the perfect morning for a hike through the pines. Naomi led the way, followed by Sinclair, then the Funks.

Sinclair was still in full-professor mode, attempting to assuage his increasing anxiety over the upcoming murders by talking incessantly and mostly inventing an alternative history of the Coronado expedition, which had no basis in actual historical fact. Naomi felt herself fortunate that she was in the lead so that Sinclair could not see her mouthing the words, "What the fuck?" and pretending to vomit when yet another complete falsehood escaped from Sinclair's mouth. Like the two law enforcement officers who were following them, Naomi was watching closely for other hikers. She hoped that because it was mid-week and early, they could avoid other hikers until the time came to execute on her plan. She hoped that the sound of gunshots and her manufactured histrionics would bring other hikers to them after the fact, so that she could have witnesses to her immense distress when the time came.

Almost as though they had been summoned, two hikers appeared in the distance ahead of Naomi, walking in their direction, returning from the falls. As they approached, Naomi gave them a big smile. "How were the falls today?" she asked with a friendliness unseen before by the other three.

The woman in the lead smiled back. "Absolutely beautiful," she said, looking suspiciously at the four odd people coming their direction. Had it not been for Naomi's presence, coupled with her award-worthy portrayal of a friendly hiker, the sight of the four strange bedfellows on the trail could have easily aroused suspicion and concern.

As the hikers disappeared down the trail, Naomi saw they were closer to the overlook than she had realized. There was one especially large boulder at the top of the falls. That rock was her goal, and in order to reach it, it would force them to leave the trail. "Follow me this way," she said as she left the path in the boulder's direction. Soon she could see they were almost at her intended destination. She reached the boulder and peered down at the river below as she waited for the others to join her. On any other day, she would have admired the incredible view. The canyon was spectacular, with immense boulders piled one upon the other from earthquakes and other cataclysms millions of years ago, narrowing the canyon at the bottom 75 feet below. While the falls were not particularly large, they were dramatic and stunning, and she estimated that a fall from this height into the rocks below would nearly guarantee mortality for anyone. Even with that thought, Naomi would make sure Sinclair was dead before he "fell" off the cliff. She would take no chances on his survival.

"What in the hell are they doing here?" Paul rhetorically questioned.

"Let's get as close as we can without being seen," Matt replied, as he moved closer, crouching in the shrubs to provide camouflage in order to observe the four.

Sinclair walked to the edge of the boulder and looked back, waiting for the Funks to arrive. Despite his ceaseless chatter during the hike, he was visibly worried and was sweating far beyond what the gentle hike would have produced. He took out a handkerchief and wiped his forehead. His heart was pumping like he had just broken the world's record in sprinting and felt like it would propel itself out of his chest. In soft tones, he whispered to Naomi, "This is a bad idea. We can't do this."

The Funks arrived and looked to Naomi for guidance. Naomi and Sinclair faced the Funks. Paul and Matt struggled to see what was going on as the Funks' backs were facing them. "Let's see if we can get a little closer now," Paul said, and the two edged up as close to the four as they dared. They were still too far away to hear their conversation, so they struggled to discern what was going on from their body language.

Naomi finally smiled at Sinclair. "Oh, we're doing this, Sinclair. It's just not what you think," she spat, her voice becoming a vicious snarl; far from the friendly hiker she had impersonated a few minutes before.

"What do you mean, Naomi?" Sinclair said, failing to comprehend what was coming next.

"Sinclair, you're a loser," Naomi began. "I've despised you since the first time I heard you lecturing at UNM. In fact, not only are you a loser, but you're also a fraud. If stupidity was painful, you'd be in agony. You could have avoided all this by playing fair with me, but now I have to return your treatment with a little of my own."

"What are you talking about?" Sinclair whimpered. "I've been nothing but good to you. You're the one who is the fraud. You never would have gotten into grad school if I hadn't laid down a gilded path for you. And besides that, you're a true and honest bitch, Naomi."

"I refuse to have a battle of wits with an unarmed person, Sinclair. If you have something to say, raise your hand—and put it over your mouth. Now, because you are who you are, I am going to be who you think I am. I'm taking my exquisite, treasured Black Heart, financing both my education and my retirement, and I'm going to milk the 'tragic' events of today for all the sympathy the academic community can provide," she expelled.

"Um, dude, you're not forgetting about us, right, man?" Chuchu said with a bit of worry in his voice.

"Of course not, Chuchu," Naomi said. "You're going to get everything you deserve, and perhaps a little bit more."

The interaction between Sinclair and Naomi had reached a feverish pitch, and their shouts suggested an escalation of emotions to Paul and Matt. Paul cocked his rifle and Matt withdrew his pistol and chambered a round. There was nothing physical happening, so they remained in their hiding spot, ready to move in at any time.

"I don't understand, Naomi. Wha—what are you going to do?" Sinclair whined.

"I'm not going to do much of anything, Sinclair. My good buddies are going to do it." With that she motioned to the Funks, who looked at her with questioning looks on their faces. Naomi looked back, incredulous that these two stoners were missing the point of the conversation. "Shoot him like I told you to do," she said.

The Funks looked at each other, smiled and pulled their weapons. Chuchu turned to Dory, showing a change of heart. "Dory, man, we've never killed anybody. We're like, thieves, man, not killers!"

Ignoring Chuchu, Dory walked closer to Sinclair. "Sorry, dude," Dory said, as he pointed his pistol at Sinclair, who reflexively emptied his bladder.

"Shit, they're going to shoot them!" Paul cried. In the same instant, Matt and Paul stood, weapons drawn, Dory pulled the trigger on his gun. The bullet hit Sinclair in the middle of his forehead, snapping his head backward. The momentum carried the rest of his body over the cliff, completing two full backflips before landing on the rocks below. Naomi watched with the same fascination that a spectator at the Olympics would have watching a diver plunge into a pool.

Naomi was snatched from her momentary reverie as she looked behind the Funks to see Matt and Paul walking toward them, Paul's rifle to his shoulder, ready to fire. "Freeze!" Paul shouted as the two advanced on them.

Naomi turned to Dory. "Grab me around my neck and put the gun to my head," she said.

"What dude?" Dory responded.

"It's the only way we get saved, asshole!" she sputtered. Dory did as Naomi commanded and turned to see the two cops for the first time.

"Please! Stop!" Naomi shouted to Matt and Paul. "He's going to kill me if you come any closer." She elbowed Dory at the same time, hoping that Dory would understand.

Somewhere in the marijuana infused brain cells of Dory Funk, a light came on, and he got the message. "Put your guns down, man," Dory shouted, "Or I kill the girl right in front of you, dudes!"

Matt glanced at Paul, hesitating to do anything. "Dory, you're not a killer. If you give yourself up now, things will be easy on you." Dory simply smiled, pulling the hammer back on the revolver in his hand, and giving them a steely eyed and uncharacteristically frightening stare. Matt raised his hand and set his pistol on the ground. Paul looked at Matt, an incredulous look on his face, did the same. "Trust me," Matt whispered.

"Get on your knees, and put your hands on your heads," Dory said, suddenly channeling all the bad guys he had seen in the movies. As Paul and Matt went to their knees and interlocked their hands on their heads, Dory told Chuchu to collect their weapons. Chuchu put Matt's pistol in his waistband and picked up Paul's rifle. "Woh, dude," Chuchu said, "This rifle is like too cool, man!"

Paul stared at his own rifle being pointed at his head. "Careful, Chuchu," he said. "It's ready to fire. Look, man, you don't want to do this. You're already in trouble enough. You put your weapons down and let the girl go, and we'll be sure you're treated fair and square."

"I wouldn't say you're in the strongest fucking bargaining position," Naomi said, drawing her weapon from her back pocket.

"What the hell?" was all Paul could say.

"Yeah, uh huh," Naomi replied. "You picked the wrong day to be diligent cops, because you just put me in a really shitty position. You two law enforcement fuckers witnessed the murder of good old Professor Delano by these two low-life potheads. And, unfortunately, now you have to die too. They did it because I told them to."

"I don't understand, Naomi. Why kill him?" Matt asked.

Naomi paused for a minute, weighing her options. It didn't take long for her to realize that her plan needed a bit of amending. Perhaps overestimating her ability to carry it off, she imagined explaining the scenario to arriving law enforcement. The Funk brothers killed Sinclair, the cops came to the rescue, and they killed them too. Poor Naomi, somehow by the grace of God, managed to wrestle a gun from one of the Funks and she shot them both, in self-defense of course. She would be lauded as having acted heroically in the situation. "Oh, what the hell. I guess there's no risk in letting you know why you're going to die today, and I'll tell you right now. This is going to be fun. Sinclair, the two dweebs and I weren't on a field trip at all. We were here on a very specific mission to raid Astialakwa, and our goal was to find El Corazón Negro de Dios. The Black Heart of God. Have you heard of it?"

"What, you found it?" Paul said, stunned. "Our people have spoken about and searched for El Corazón Negro de Dios for many generations. We have never found it."

"Good thing you're not an archeologist," Naomi replied. "Because we found it. Along with four backpacks full of artifacts. Sinclair promised to share the proceeds with Danny, Jason, and me in exchange for helping him. That was pretty fucking stupid, if you ask me. I took care of Danny on the mesa, pushing him over. Those years of Taekwondo my parents paid for came in handy. *More for me*. I took care of Jason in the springs. *More for me*. I took care of Sinclair just now. Even *more* for me."

"And, dudes, they found Coronado's gold stash up here, man," Dory added. "She's going to share it with us, and we are going to buy, like an island in Arizona, man."

"Coronado's gold?" Paul said with a wry smile. "Now I know you're hallucinating."

"Never mind that, right now, Dory," Naomi said. "That's just between us. But now we have another issue. These two. They saw you kill Sinclair, and they know what we've been up to. I just fucking confessed to two murders and a felony. Seems to me we only have one choice in how we resolve this little dilemma."

"Wait, Naomi, that's just crazy," Matt said. "Yeah, you're looking at some trouble in your future, but nothing like the trouble you'll find if you kill us. We're talking death penalty trouble, and you don't want that, now, do you?"

"We're only talking trouble if we don't kill you. See, this is a perfect scenario for my future fame and fortune. The Funk brothers kidnapped Sinclair and me. You tried to stop them, but they got the best of you and killed you, and then, in self-defense, I dispatch them with prejudice. I'll be on every talk show in the country!"

"Dude, what about us?" Chuchu asked.

"Chuchu, you and Dory will be living high off the hog on your own island in Arizona, I'm sure," Naomi replied.

"Is that what you mean by getting our gazpacho, man?" asked Dory.

"Exactly, you fatuous, injudicious brothers!"

Chuchu looked at Dory, hoping he would know what she was talking about. Dory decided she must be complimenting them. "Thanks, man," he said. "We try our best."

"Well," Naomi said, "Much as I'm enjoying this get-together, it's time to put an end to this merrymaking." She pointed her gun at Matt and Paul and said, "Stand up. Keep your hands on your heads and walk this way," she said, pointing to the boulder Sinclair had just vacated. When they hesitated, she said, "OK, fuck you. We'll do this the hard way. Dory, Chuchu, shoot them!"

"Whoa, wait a minute, lady dude," Chuchu said. "Killing that slimy little professor guy is one thing, but killing cops is a major downer, man."

"If you don't kill them, they will arrest you and you will spend the rest of your lives in prison, *dudes*," Naomi hissed.

"Dory, man, what should we do?" Chuchu implored.

"I guess it can't get much worse, dude," Dory confessed, raising his pistol. Chuchu followed suit, putting Paul's rifle to his shoulder. "OK, dude, on three." Dory started counting. At the count of two, from the other side of the trail and out of the bushes charged a hulking Irish freight train, sprinting full speed towards Dory, Chuchu and Naomi. By his side was Jake, teeth bared and in full-attack posture.

The three were so dumbfounded by the sight of Amos in full gallop, they pointed their weapons at Amos and Jake. Matt reached back to the concealed holster in the small of his back, drew a weapon and fired, hitting Dory in the shoulder. Dory fell into Chuchu and Chuchu's weapon went flying in the air. Amos continued his sprint and dove for Naomi who was now the only one standing. She fired her pistol, grazing Amos as he was about to tackle her. His momentum continued as he slammed into Naomi, sending her to the ground. Matt and Paul launched after the three, grabbing weapons and ordering them onto their stomachs. They rapidly placed handcuffs on their wrists.

Naomi began alternately sobbing and swearing at the two officers, neither of whom responded with anything close to resembling empathy. Matt helped Amos to his feet. "Are you OK, Amos?" Matt asked.

"Fit as a fiddle, boyo. Just got a little scratch," Amos replied through gasps of air. "That was more fun than I've had since I was in the marine corps!" he added.

"I'm very grateful that you didn't care to heed my instructions, Father," Paul said. "I'll jog back to the truck and call this in. Matt, if you would do the honors reading these people their rights, we'll just hang out and sing Kumbaya until reinforcements arrive. I have a feeling the falls are going to be bustling for some time."

Matt read the three their rights. Chuchu and Dory immediately asked for their "doobs," a request that was denied, while Naomi continued her rants and swearing. Finally, in exasperation, Matt said to Naomi, "You know that part of the *Miranda* warning about the right to remain silent? I would be deeply grateful if you would exercise it."

A helicopter was overhead within fifteen minutes, but it took little time for them to determine there was no place to land for several miles, so they all waited for an investigation team to arrive, which took over two hours. When they did, five trucks containing a shooting investigation team, forensics, search and rescue descended upon Jemez Falls. A forest service special agent took over the scene, and the search and rescue team recovered Sinclair's body from the river at the bottom of the cliffs. It was almost dark by the time the special agents were satisfied they had sufficient preliminary statements from Matt, Paul and Amos and let them go home. As they reached the parking lot, Naomi and the Funk brothers were sitting in the back seats of the trucks. Chuchu said out the window, "What are you going to do with Coronado's gold, man?"

"Really, Chuchu?" Matt replied with wonder at the depths of the Funk brothers' senselessness.

As he passed the truck with Naomi in the back seat, she, too, felt compelled to offer some parting words. "A lawyer will have me out by midnight, you fucker," she said.

"Not my monkey, not my circus," Matt replied, giving her a backward wave as he walked away from her toward Paul's truck.

Matt let Jake in the pickup and then fell on the seat next to Paul, sighing with relief. "So you had a backup gun, huh?" Paul said.

"I've been carrying what we called at the NCIS a BUG since I started there," Matt said. "But this is no ordinary backup gun, my friend. It's Randy's service pistol. I've carried it since I lost her. And it saved our lives today."

23

Another Visit to the Eagle's Altar

By having a reverence for life, we enter into a spiritual relation with the world. By practicing reverence for life, we become good, deep, and alive.

(Albert Schweitzer)

Matt and Amos were finishing their morning coffee on the front porch of the lodge, enjoying the warm, sunny morning while they were waiting for their guests to arrive. From the west, Matt spotted Paul's USFS truck in the distance, followed by two other pickups. As all three trucks pulled into Matt's drive, Matt and Amos stood and walked down to the parking area, accompanied by Jake, who stayed by Matt's side, suspiciously eyeing the men in the trucks. Paul got out of his truck first. In the passenger side of the truck was Benny. All the men, including Paul, were dressed in traditional Jemez ceremonial attire, which was striking and beautiful. They each wore bright white linen pants and shirts. The shirts were ornamented with hand-sewn embroidery with a variety of patterns. Some had eagle feathers embroidered on their chests, and some had intricate geometric patterns. Each of the men wore red moccasins that extended to their knees. They wore concha belts with large silver ovals and turquoise stones in the center. Each man had an array of turquoise necklaces, heishi and pendants around their necks. They each also wore thick cloth headbands and around their shoulders were brilliantly colored woven blankets with stripes of yellow, orange and purple. Each man had three eagle's feathers in his hair. The bold and vivid colors that adorned the group were dazzling and gave each man an extraordinarily commanding presence.

Paul gave Matt a hug and held out his hand to greet Amos. Benny and the other men gathered around Paul and Matt. Paul made introductions of each of the men. "I'm sorry we cannot invite you to attend the ceremony, Matt," Paul said apologetically, "but you know that we carefully guard our ceremonies and the nature of our roles in the ceremony."

"I can't say I'm not disappointed, Paul, but I understand. I didn't realize you would take part today," Matt said.

"Well, just between you and me, I am a member of the Men's Eagle Society and am also a War Captain this year. Our society has existed for as long as anyone can remember. Although we no longer have to protect our tribe from the Apache, Navajo, Comanche and Ute, we still serve an important job protecting our tribe. The men here today are also members of the Eagle Catching Society, which we rarely talk about outside our pueblo. Sééh-wagi, the Eagles Altar, here on your property was the shrine of the Eagle Catching

Society, and today we have the honor of blessing it and returning it, at least in spirit, to our tribe. It is, of course, your land, so we will be at your mercy in accessing the shrine for ceremonies."

"No, Paul, you won't be at my mercy," Matt replied. He held up a manila envelope and handed it to Paul. "I've had my attorney draw up papers to subdivide the perimeter of the shrine into a square that is a hundred feet on each side. The land is now in a trust which your tribe will manage. My attorney created a perpetual easement from the highway to the shrine, which allows your people to visit any time they choose. The shrine is, once again, pueblo land."

Paul's eyes teared, and he shook Matt's hand. "Matt, this is above and beyond anything any landowner has done for us. We are truly grateful. We also have custody of the Black Heart of God. It has been returned to our people, after four hundred years. Although it will be needed as evidence in Naomi's trial, our council has decided that it was intended to be buried and it should remain buried. We can't take it back to Astialakwa. We would ask if we can place it in the bóveda in this shrine, as we know the public won't have access to it. Benny suggests that in the right spot, it will provide protection and good fortune, and we would like to bless you with its spirit here."

Matt had few words to use to respond so he grabbed Paul and gave him a hug. "It's my turn to thank you, my friend," was the most he could coax out.

The men walked up the hill behind Matt's home toward the shrine, while Matt and Amos began their chores for the day. The men were too far away for Matt and Amos to see anything, but they could hear an occasional voice and drumming. About a half hour from their start, Matt noticed the breeze had disappeared completely and an eerie silence ensued. A moment later, they heard the screams of golden eagles and looked in the sky to see three eagles circling the location of the shrine, then disappearing up the mountain. Matt looked at Amos, who returned the look and smiled. He turned to Matt and said, "But those who hope in the Lord will renew their strength. They will soar on wings like eagles; they will run and not grow weary; they will walk and not be faint."

Matt returned the smile. "I'm not very well educated on religion, but I'm guessing that's from the Bible?"

"It certainly is, Matthew. One of my favorite passages."

Amos and Matt went into the lodge and brought out iced tea and water for the men and waited for them to return from their ceremony at the shrine. As they were waiting, Matt said to Amos, "Randy isn't talking to me anymore."

"She just stopped?" Amos asked.

"She said something strange. She said, 'I'm awake,' and then there was just silence."

"Maybe her job was done with you," Amos suggested.

"I don't know. It bothered me when she came back into my head, but I got to where I depended on her. When she stopped talking, it was as though I had lost her for the second time."

"I do think that's an odd way to end your, um, relationship, Matthew, but I'm afraid I don't have any experience with this sort of thing. I am sorry for that sense of loss for the second time, however. Perhaps it's just temporary."

They spotted the men returning from the shrine and offered them refreshments, which they gladly accepted. Matt turned to Paul and said, "We saw the eagles afterward."

"So, you got to see part of the ceremony after all!" Paul replied. "Eagles are a rare sight here in these mountains. I have a feeling you may see more eagles around than you have before."

Benny and Hector approached Matt. Benny held out his hand. "We have much to be grateful for, deputy. You have given us a gift that, to my knowledge, our tribe has never received before. There are shrines in many places in these mountains. Most are on forest service property, like Daha-enu, which you call Battleship Rock, or Guisewa, what you call Jemez Springs, and more. Several are on private property and the landowners have been quite inflexible in sharing 'their' property with us. You and Paul are responsible for the recovery of precious artifacts, including El Corazón Negro de Dios. I know they are evidence right now, but they have assured me they will return the artifacts to the tribe when the justice system completes its job. You, Matt, are very special to our tribe. I have written to the Sandoval County Sheriff informing them of our gratefulness for your help. It is much kindness and will be remembered in the stories we tell our young."

Matt wasn't sure how to respond, other than to give Benny a hug and let him know he was honored to have been able to help. As they sat down to enjoy iced tea and conversation, Matt looked up at the hill where the shrine was. Above the trees the three golden eagles were riding the air currents, singing the song of the séésh.

Afterward

Being deeply loved by someone gives you strength, while loving someone deeply gives you courage.
(Lao Tzu)

The following Saturday, Matt was sitting in his rocking chair on the front porch, drinking his coffee and basking in the early morning sunshine. Jake was lying next to Matt's rocking chair, also enjoying the warm sun. Matt looked down the hill toward the highway, remembering Weh'ng Péh, standing in the fog, motioning to the mountain. The mother of the Eagle Catching Society had accomplished her goal and was now just a memory; one that Matt would forever hold in his mind. He had seen eagles on the mountain practically every day since the ceremony, which had been a rare occurrence before. As he enjoyed his coffee and the memories of his encounter, he spotted a car on the road. The car slowed as it approached the entrance to his ranch, then turned into the driveway. It was obviously a rental car, and Matt assumed it was a tourist who was either lost or inappropriately curious. Jake gave a low growl as the car stopped and shut off. "Wait," Matt said to Jake, and both stood to see who this was. The car door opened, and a tall man got out and stood, stretching his back. The man was in his sixties. He was in excellent physical condition with a full head of gray hair and looked as though he had just come off a movie set where he played the leading man. Matt said softly, "Jake?" The dog looked up at Matt, waiting for a command. Matt burst into a huge smile and turned to the dog and said, "friend!"

The man raised his hand to block the sun out of his eyes. "Pardon me, cowboy, but I'm looking for a friend of mine. I like to call him Sherlock!"

Matt ran down the porch and walked up to the man, both arms held out to give the man a warm embrace. "Jake Packer," Matt said, "you are a sight for sore eyes!"

"And you are not easy to find, *Supervising* Special Agent Bertram!" Jake replied, "Even for a former CIA officer!"

"That's because it's *Deputy* Bertram, now, Captain America."

"I know. I've been keeping tabs on you. You come to a quiet place in the middle of nowhere, where nothing happens, ever, go to work for a small sheriff's department, spend your days writing tickets and busting teenage shoplifters, and you, in typical Bertram fashion I might add, embroil yourself in a triple homicide right out of the chute. I really need to keep a closer eye on you, Sherlock." He kneeled down to meet Jake and gave him a neck scratch, which seemed to win the dog over. "So, what's the dog's name?" Jake inquired.

"There was only one appropriate name for this dog. Jake, meet Jake."

"I've never had a dog named after me," Jake the person said. "I guess I'll take that as a compliment."

Matt invited Jake up to the lodge, showed him around the place, and poured him a mug of hot coffee. They sat down on the front porch. "I'm sure you were just in the neighborhood, Jake," Matt said, smiling, "but I can't help but think you made a trip all the way from Washington, DC for a purpose other than to check up on me."

Jake's winsome smile disappeared and was replaced by the most serious look Matt had ever seen on Jake's face. "Something important happened, and I just couldn't bring myself to tell you on the phone. You may have heard that I scored a great job with the state department."

"What could be that important that you would come this distance?" Matt asked, his stomach rising into his throat.

Jake stared at Matt for a moment, then smiled. "Randy's alive," he said.

"What? Alive? How? Why am I just hearing this?" Matt exclaimed.

"You're hearing it because we just found out a few days ago. The Russians lied to us, Matt. They told us the church had caved in and they were abandoning it, but the truth was they recovered her. She's been in a coma since the accident. A few days ago, she woke up, out of the blue. The Russians say they are putting her on trial for espionage. It makes for some great publicity and an opportunity for some bartering or at least public relations for their cause."

"What's being done?" Matt asked.

"The state department is working around the clock to get her back. The president has intervened. It could be a very long diplomatic chess game, Matt."

"Unless we go and get her," Matt replied.

"I had a feeling you would say that," Jake said with a smile.

About the Author

Mark David Albertson was born and grew up in Los Alamos, New Mexico. Los Alamos, known as "The Atomic City," was the birthplace of the atomic bomb. Tucked in the Jemez Mountains of northern New Mexico, Mark grew up in a secured city with gates, armed guards, and mountain patrols in the surrounding mountains.

Although Los Alamos was a wonderful place to grow up, Mark longed for adventure. After graduating from High School, he joined the navy and set off for the adventure only a sailor could have. During his time in the US Navy, he became a radioman and visited 19 countries. Mark left the navy with an idea for a novel based in part upon his experiences and those of his shipmates. Little did he know that it would take forty-two years to accomplish this goal.

Following his discharge from the navy, Mark moved to San Antonio, Texas, where he went to college and served in the Texas Air

National Guard as a military police staff sergeant. Upon graduating from college, Mark attended law school at St. Mary's University. Following his law school graduation, he moved to Washington State, where he lived and practiced law for the next thirty-four years.

Mark's career and the raising of three children took precedence over novels but not his writing. During his law career, Mark wrote dozens of articles, two law books, and collaborated on several more over his career, and on the side built a successful private investigation practice and became a well-known and much sought-after speaker. Over the course of his career, Mark spoke to many dozens of organizations and gave over a thousand seminars and speeches.

When the 2000s came, Mark suffered a series of painful events. His 24-year marriage ended in 2005, he was diagnosed with a rare cancer with little hope of surviving and became involved in a twelve-year relationship that was far from functional. In 2017 he decided to leave his career, extract himself from the dysfunctional relationship and learn to live a life he had chosen, which he did. It turned out to be the best choice of his life as he met a wonderful, kind, and loving life partner and wife, who encouraged him to finish the book that had been in his head for all those years.

Mark's first book, *Steaming*, was the completion of a 42-year goal, followed closely by his second book, *Spying* in 2021. His third book, *Stalking*, was the final book in what he calls his "Sea Story" series. This book, *Jemez*, is his fourth novel, and he is hard at work on his fifth novel, due for publication in 2024.

To learn more and keep up to date on Mark's writing, you can find his website at www.mdalbertson.com or you can follow him on Facebook, Instagram, Goodreads and Amazon Author

www.ingramcontent.com/pod-product-compliance
Lightning Source LLC
LaVergne TN
LVHW041151150826
845673LV00001B/127

9798218188788